BRYANT

SLAP SHOT

USA TODAY *BESTSELLING AUTHOR* ALICIA HUNTER PACE

Nashville Sound, Book 2

Crimson Romance
New York London Toronto Sydney New Delhi

CRIMSON
ROMANCE

Crimson Romance
An Imprint of Simon & Schuster, Inc.
1230 Avenue of the Americas
New York, NY 10020

First Crimson Romance ebook edition OCTOBER 2017

CRIMSON ROMANCE and colophon are trademarks of Simon and Schuster.

For information about special discounts for bulk purchases, please contact Simon & Schuster Special Sales at 1-866-506-1949 or business@simonandschuster.com.

The Simon & Schuster Speakers Bureau can bring authors to your live event. For more information or to book an event contact the Simon & Schuster Speakers Bureau at 1-866-248-3049 or visit our website at www.simonspeakers.com.

Manufactured in the United States of America

ISBN 978-1-5072-0802-1
ISBN 978-1-5072-0586-0 (ebook)

DEDICATION

In memory of John Wesley Baxter

CHAPTER ONE

"Have you ever noticed how big Krystal Voleck's feet are? Do you think she's a clown?"

Gabriella Charbonnet almost knew that voice, but only almost. She turned from the Eat Cake pastry shop work counter to look into eyes every bit as blue as the crystallized pansies she had used to decorate the white chocolate and Swiss meringue buttercream cake she was working on.

Bryant Taylor had a big head, but you didn't notice it so much because of those cobalt eyes and that choppy, chin-length hair that was at least twenty shades of blond, from French vanilla to honey caramel.

But what was he doing in Beauford? She doubted if he'd driven from Nashville for a cookie, though Eat Cake was the finest bakery in the state. *Garden & Gun Magazine* said so.

Bryant was a defenseman for the Nashville Sound and Gabriella's brother's teammate and best friend. As a goalie, Emile valued a good D-man above most things in life, and he said Bryant was one of the best in the NHL. Bryant had been on *Hot Nashville's* most eligible singles list last year, probably in part because—big head, or not—he was absolutely walking physical perfection. It had been said that he was the best looking player on the team, maybe in all of professional hockey. Gabriella might have even said it herself. She particularly liked the little scar above his right eye that made it seem like the eyebrow was perpetually raised just a hair higher than the left one.

If Gabriella had a talent beyond turning sugar, butter, and flour into an edible masterpiece, it was the ability to get a date without having to do the asking. And she dated steadily but no one steady, hardly ever anyone more than twice—at least not since the pastry chef from Nashville she'd been involved with for about six months moved to New York. That had been almost two years ago.

Since then, it had been coffee with tourists, dinner with bakery supply reps, late night drinks with semi-somebody musicians— but no physical relationship. She wasn't one for casual sex, but casual dating was easy. She smiled, they asked, and she said either yes or no. She might have worked her magic on Bryant if he were anything other than a hockey player.

She didn't date hockey players, ever. For one thing, it would send Emile into big-brother-hell-no orbit. He didn't ask much of her, but he did ask that, claiming that interfamily dating made for bad team dynamics.

That wasn't the main reason she steered clear of hockey players, though. For all that Gabriella was a people pleaser and wanted to please Emile above all others, she would not let him dictate who she dated if she didn't agree. But she did agree—emphatically.

Gabriella's father had been a hockey player, though not a very good one even in the dead-end minor league he'd last played for. If watching him beat the hell out of Emile on a regular basis hadn't been enough to make Gabriella's mind up about getting involved with a hockey player, clutching a broken arm at the top of the stairs while her mother lay dead at the bottom would have certainly sealed the deal.

Intellectually, she knew that most hockey players left the violence and aggression on the ice, but she wasn't taking any chances. She was never going to be at the bottom of those stairs, never going to have to be the shield between her child and a fist. She unconsciously rubbed her arm.

Bryant Taylor—Swifty, his teammates called him—smiled and winked, charm oozing from every inch of his being like it was his job to make the whole universe fall at his feet. But just because she wouldn't touch him with a ten-foot whisk didn't mean she couldn't enjoy the view.

And what a view.

He dropped his long-lashed eyelids at half-mast and spoke again. "And if Krystal *is* a clown, do you think she's a freelance clown or actually works for a circus?"

"I have no reason to think she's a clown." Gabriella thought the team was a little too hard on their teammate Jan Voleck's wife. So what if she had been a notorious puck bunny and was seven years older than Jan? If they were happy, who cared? Sometimes Gabriella thought those hell-raising, woman-chasing, beer-swilling men were worse than a bunch of Regency era Almack's patronesses who just sat around looking for reasons to deny debutantes permission to waltz.

Bryant cocked his head to the side. "No? I wouldn't have taken you for Alice in Wonderland, but there you are." He gestured to her blue dress and white pinafore.

"It's my Halloween costume."

He looked around and let his eyes light on the jack-o'-lanterns and Halloween cupcakes and cookies in the front window. "Is today Halloween?" He didn't look happy about it. What was that about? What was to dislike about Halloween?

"Yes. And tonight is the Beauford Harvest Festival."

Located about forty minutes from Nashville, Beauford was a small artisan boutique town with some of the best master craftsmen in the country. People came from all over to buy handmade one-of-a-kind goods. Gabriella had been lucky to land a four-year master baker/pastry arts apprenticeship with June Champion, who owned Eat Cake. After two years of junior college, Gabriella had gone to work at Eat Cake and begun her apprenticeship a year later. Now, at twenty-five, she was due to finish her apprenticeship in the spring.

"Harvest Festival?" Bryant looked around. "Just where did you harvest all these cakes from? A Candy Land game?"

Gabriella laughed. Bryant did have a way about him. Her father had been an incredibly good-looking man, and there had been a time when Gabriella had steered clear of men with Bryant's kind of looks, but she'd gotten past that. Too bad Bryant wasn't an accountant or a lawyer. But if she'd learned nothing else in life, she'd learned that hockey players would always be hockey players—even when their bodies failed them. It was a mentality.

"You have your sweets mixed up. You can't harvest pastry from a Candy Land game."

He grinned. "Candy corn? Can you harvest that?"

"Absolutely. All you need is a candy corn picking basket and a ladder. The best candy corn grows in the tops of the trees, you know."

"I would have thought it grew on stalks."

"That's regular corn. Candy corn is different."

"Will there be any candy corn trees at this festival?

"Absolutely. You should stay around and check it out. It starts in about an hour. All the shops stay open late. Everyone serves refreshments and has candy for the trick-or-treaters. There'll be games, and Jackson Beauford is going to perform a little later. He's big country star and Beauford's most famous resident. He owns Beauford Bend plantation."

Bryant cocked his head to the side and grinned. "I know who Jackson Beauford is. You know—since I don't live under a rock."

"Oh, right," Gabriella said. "I forget that all hockey players aren't like Emile. He knows not one thing about pop culture."

"Emile is unique for sure. Too bad I didn't know about this festival. I would have worn my vampire suit. You can't show up at a harvest festival without your vampire suit." He gave her a smile that, if sold, would buy and sell Bill Gates. "I hate to miss a cornhole game. I'm good at it."

"Not to mention all that candy corn. If not the Harvest Festival, what brings you all the way to us from Sound Town?" Sound Town was the area of downtown Nashville informally called so because of the location of the Sound practice rink and the number of players and team-connected people—including Emile—who lived there.

"No practice today. I came to watch some game film with Glaz." Nickolai Glazov was the Sound team captain and was married to Beauford artisan quilt maker, Noel, who owned Piece by Piece. "Your brother was supposed to join us, but I gather he's somewhere in Georgia chasing Amy."

"Hmm." It was true, in a sense. After a huge mess, most of it of Emile's own making, he'd almost lost Amy. But happily, he'd called last night to report that she had accepted his engagement ring and that Amy would call her later. But Gabriella wasn't telling. That was Emile's news to deliver. Besides, it gave her a warm feeling that she knew what others didn't, and she wanted to hang on to the secret a little longer. "He's coming back tonight."

"Coming here? Or back to Nashville?"

Good question. "I assume back to Nashville." Though it was possible he would stop off to see her. Emile liked Halloween and would, no doubt, want to share more of his news in person.

"Is Amy coming with him?" Bryant asked.

"That remains to be seen." That was technically the truth too. Emile had morning skate tomorrow before leaving for a road trip, so he had to hurry back, but Gabriella didn't know if Amy would be with him or if she would spend some more time with her family.

"Maybe I can catch him at home tonight. I wanted to hear about him beating the hell out of Cameron Snow Saturday night."

Ah, yes—the very public, televised fight Emile had had two nights ago with Amy's former boyfriend. Cameron Snow had stolen everything she owned—including several million dollars—and abandoned her. What had made the fight especially remarkable, other than that Emile never fought, was that his opponent wasn't a hockey player and the brawl had occurred in the tunnel *after* the game.

"You probably know more than I do," she said. "I've talked to him once briefly since then. You were there, and didn't you help pull Emile off him?"

Bryant nodded. "Thor, Jarrett, and me. I'll tell you a secret." He smiled and leaned on the counter. His teeth were very white. "We let it go on a couple of minutes longer than we had to. The son-of-a-bitch had it coming. Thor wanted to join in."

"Figures." Did anyone ever have a beating coming? Gabriella supposed if anyone did, it was Cameron Snow. And Snow had thrown the first blows. Emile had already been bleeding before he retaliated. But Gabriella had never liked the fighting in hockey. Bryant wasn't in the same class with the Sound's big, old-school enforcer, Lars "Thor" Eastrom, but he tangled with his opponents on a regular basis. Gabriella always looked away when a fight broke out.

"Can I get you something?" Gabriella gestured to the pastry case.

Bryant nodded. "I'd like an ice cream cone."

"You're kidding, right?"

"Why would I? Ice cream is serious business."

"Bryant, you've got your sweets mixed up again. Are you aware you are in a pastry shop?"

He nodded. "Said so right there on the sign. But I figured a place with cake was bound to have ice cream."

"No. We don't. I'm sorry. How about an éclair? Or some *tarte tatin*? And this is the last day for our October limited edition cake—apple cider cinnamon. It's really good."

"No. I *need* an ice cream cone."

She sighed. Why did she always feel like such a failure when she had to tell someone *no?* Even if it was out of her control?

"Then you *need* to go around the corner to Scoops and Sprinkles. It's in the middle of the block on Lee Street. It's all organic and made in-house. Of course there's also the Dairy Barn out by the high school, and The Apothecary next to Noel's quilt shop has a soda fountain."

He shook his head and leaned on the counter. "You mean to tell me that in this entire emporium dedicated to decadence and tooth decay, there's not even one small spoonful of ice cream? No pint of Ben & Jerry's or Häagen-Dazs that you have squirreled away for your own use?"

She hesitated just long enough that he read the struggle in her eyes.

"Ah ha!" He fist pumped. "What is it? Chunky Monkey? Coffee Toffee Bar Crunch?"

"Neither. I don't have any ice cream squirreled away for my own use. And neither does anyone else who works here."

"There's ice cream here. I smell it. I smell it from the look on your face."

"There isn't any ice cream here," she said firmly. There was, however, the candied chestnut gelato she'd made this morning, but that was for a special order—a chocolate caramel chestnut cheesecake that was to be picked up tomorrow at noon.

He shook his head. "I don't believe you, Gabriella."

"Even if there were, there are no cones." And that was the gospel truth.

He pointed to the pastry case. "What's that?"

"Puff pastry cornucopias with pumpkin chiffon." She brightened. "Would you like one of those?"

He grimaced. "No! I rate pumpkin slightly above stinky cheese and below liver. But you can put the ice cream in one of those cone things. I know you've got some in the back."

"We don't have ice cream."

His eyes bored into hers—blue pansy eyes. The last light of day shone through the window, bouncing off his blond hair and creating the illusion of an aura. He looked like an angel.

"We only have a bit of gelato, intended for another use. And you wouldn't like it. It's chestnut flavored."

"What's gelato?" he asked.

Damn, damn, damn. Why did she always do this? Try so hard to please everyone that she told more than she should?

"Gelato is … is *like* ice cream. Only not. More milk than cream. And it's churned slower …"

"Is it cold? Sweet? Sign me up. That's what I'll have. In one of those cornucopia things." He smiled and she was lost—and not because of his smile, his eyes, or any part of his angel looks. She was lost because she was weak and a pleaser.

She merely nodded and went to the kitchen. She should have saved herself the time and given it to him to begin with. Maybe if she only gave him a small scoop there would still be enough for the chestnut layer of the cheesecake.

Her reward was that he was pleased when she handed it over.

He reached for his wallet.

"Never mind. It's on the house," she said, even though Eat Cake wasn't her house. But she wouldn't even have known what to charge.

"Thanks, Gabriella! I owe you one." And he left, licking his prize as he walked away. She watched him go. God had not made him choose between high cheekbones and outstanding glutes, and the world was a better place for it.

Unfortunately, June, back from setting up the refreshments at the stained glass shop, passed Bryant as she entered Eat Cake.

"Gabriella, was that my chestnut gelato going out the door?"

"Yes, but don't worry. I'll make some more after we close tonight."

"Tonight? After the Harvest Festival is over? And we've broken down the refreshment table at Spectrum, cleaned up here, and gotten ready for the morning?"

It would be midnight, at the earliest, before she could even start the gelato. So much for her plan to finish reading *Invitation From the Duke*.

"Yes. I promise. I won't leave until it's perfect."

June shook head. "You never do. But, Gabriella, it *was* perfect. What am I going to do with you?"

That was the trouble with being a pleaser. Every time you pleased one person, you disappointed another.

CHAPTER TWO

Bryant licked his ice cream and thought about Emile's sister. The ice cream—*gelato,* Gabriella had called it—was different and certainly no Blue Bell mint chocolate chip, but good. It was kind of buttery, salty, and sweet—same as Gabriella, come to think of it. At least, that's what he suspected. He'd never been close enough to verify that and he never would.

The last time he'd gotten involved with a friend and teammate's sister, he'd found himself like a butterfly trapped in its cocoon. It had been a good safe place for a long time. And then it wasn't. Not that he thought of himself as a butterfly.

However, it wasn't too much of a stretch to think of Gabriella as a butterfly—a knockout, gorgeous butterfly more suited to a magazine cover than a bakery. She was tall and graceful, with waist length blond hair and all those curls that went this way and that. A man could get lost in that hair. Not this man though.

In view of all of that, he didn't know why he'd gone into Eat Cake. Having just come from a late lunch/early dinner with Glaz, he certainly hadn't been hungry. But on the way back to his car, he'd caught sight of Gabriella through the window and had gone in to say hello. Hello had turned into a huge surprise. It had struck him that, though he'd spent countless hours with Gabriella over the past few years, it had always been in a group—which usually included Emile. One-on-one, she was so clever, so funny—something that either didn't come out in a group setting or he hadn't bothered to notice before. He supposed that was why he hadn't been able to let the ice cream issue go. He'd been enjoying the banter too much—not to mention that he'd needed the diversion after he'd realized it was Halloween.

It was still daylight, but there were a couple of gangs of little costumed goblins, witches, and Disney characters stirring around. A little Superman caught Bryant's eye, but he turned away quickly, as he always did when a saw a boy of a certain age—a boy who would have been the age of his son.

His phone rang. Glad for the distraction, he eagerly reached for it. Then he saw who was calling and eager morphed into dread. He would have been glad for any distraction except this one.

"Hello, Ma." He loved his mother, even admired that she was a force of nature—when her high winds and lightning were directed at someone else. But, no doubt about it, today it was his turn.

"Bry?" She always said it like a question, as if she were calling a 1970s landline shared by 175 people.

"Yes. The one and only." He sat down on a park bench. Might as well. This was probably going to take a while. Storms always did, though she would start out slow. "How are you?"

"Good. I went to the obstetrician with your sister this morning. Everything looks good."

"Which sister?"

"The one who's *pregnant,* Bry. Mary Catherine. Did you not hear me say *obstetrician?*"

"You never know. It could have been any of the other three."

"It had better *not* be Michelle, for sure." Michelle was the baby, just seventeen, and his only unmarried sister. "Though I wouldn't be surprised to get some news from Patricia soon as far as that goes. Michael is two now—just the age Molly was when we found out you were on the way. That was just about perfect. You were barely one when I got pregnant with Luke. Anyway. Things are fine with Mary Catherine. Ryan would have gone with her, but he had the chance to double-out, and a man has to work."

Yes, a man did. And in Bryant's small Minnesota hometown, for most that meant the St. Sebastian Paper Mill. They all viewed a chance at a back-to-back double shift as a gift from God unless it caused them to miss a hockey game. His dad, both his brothers, and all his brothers-in-law worked there, as would—no doubt—Michelle's eventual husband.

As would have Bryant himself had he not been able to skate a little faster, check a little harder, and shoot a little straighter than the other boys on the pond. Life in St. Sebastian wasn't a bad one—Mass on Sunday at St. Joseph's, school and work when required, and hockey watching, if not playing, the rest of the time for all four thousand inhabitants. St. Sebastian might have limited shopping choices, some rundown storefronts, and no Latin taught at the high school, but there was a state-of-the-art rink, and they could fill it any night of the week.

Lots of people in other small towns thought of their homes as Hockeytown, USA, and maybe they were right. But Bryant didn't know about those other towns. He only knew about St. Sebastian and how hockey pulsed through the veins of every single member of the population, from the two-year-olds wearing their first pair of skates to the old men who still played pickup at ten o'clock on Saturday nights when the high school team, youth leagues, and juniors were done. Hell, the town was named for the patron saint of hockey.

"Anyway," his mother went on, "I don't know where it came from, this idea that the father is supposed to go to all the doctor's appointments." Couples prenatal appointments might be a nice idea, but they couldn't always work for blue-collar workers—or hockey players. "But that's not why I gave you a jingle."

No kidding. He knew why she was calling.

"Mary Philomena's birthday is in three days." There it was.

Believe me, Ma, I am well aware of that. True, it had kind of gotten away from me until today when I realized it was Halloween.

"So we—our family and Mary Philomena's—thought we would have a Mass said for her."

Like that was new this year. And there was that thing with her name. She'd been Philie all her life. Now, she was *Mary Philomena,* whispered in reverent tones like she was some kind of especially chosen celestial handmaiden to the Holy Mother herself.

"So I was wondering about your coming home."

"I can't, Ma. I have a game the Sunday after Philie's birthday. We play Ottawa."

"I've known your schedule better than you since you were a mite. Don't you know that then?" Bryant smiled at his mother's Minnesota vernacular. He'd all but lost his own, though it sometimes popped out. She went on, "Who drove you to that rink before daybreak for practice all those years? It was always below zero, and half the time I was pregnant with your brothers and sisters." *Come on, Ma. It wasn't* always *below zero.* But he wouldn't say that. That would be construed as sassing, and sassing called for a lecture—not that he wasn't already getting one. "And sat in that cold rink so I could bring you home, feed you, and get you to school on time? Not that I minded. We knew you had promise even back then. That's true for sure."

That again. Other mothers played the martyr over the hours they'd spent in labor or the sleep they'd lost over colic. But not Margaret Murphy Taylor. Uh uh. It was always the early morning sojourns to before school practice. Good thing they'd only lived eight minutes from the rink, or he'd never live long enough to pay her back. That Cadillac Escalade and house expansion and remodel hadn't begun to scratch the surface.

Maggie went on, "We don't have to do the Mass that Sunday. You have a Sunday off the next weekend. I thought maybe you could fly directly here the night after you play St. Louis at home. Then you could go back to Nashville Sunday afternoon in plenty of time for you to fly out with the team for the Pittsburgh game on Tuesday."

"I don't think I can do that, Ma." He would be physically exhausted, not to mention emotionally tortured.

"No? We could do it at Christmas since you have five days off then."

"Is it really five days?" He couldn't remember when they'd had more than four days at Christmas.

"You betcha." She really did know his schedule better than he did. "But think about what I suggested. Beverly and I would really like to do it in Mary Philomena's birthday month."

"Then you and Philie's mom should just go ahead and do that. In fact, why don't you call Father Martin and plan on doing it the Sunday after her birthday? Just plan on it without me."

"Without you? That's impossible. We'll just have to do it when you can come. If it's Christmas, it's Christmas."

Now for the hard part. "Actually, Ma, I thought I would take a pass on Philie's memorial Mass this year. I will pay for it, of course."

Silence—aggressive silence. Anybody who doubted such a thing existed did not know Margaret Murphy Taylor.

But it didn't last long; it never did. She liked to have her say too well. "I don't understand. I can't believe you wouldn't want to be there for your wife's memorial Mass."

Wife. If he had a wife, why was he sleeping alone and coming home to a dark house every night? Why didn't he feel married? But he never had. He'd been so young and Philie had been his wife such a short time that he hadn't had time to get used to it.

"Ma, we have done this every birthday for five years now—and on the anniversaries of her death. Having memorial Masses isn't going to bring her back. Philie is dead."

"Do you think I don't know that then? That girl was like a daughter to me. She was in and out of this house like one of my own all her life, but especially after she was fifteen and you turned up sweet on her. Even if you aren't, I'm well aware every single day that she's gone and that sweet, unborn baby boy with her. *Your son.*"

"I'm aware." His face felt hot despite the October dusk cool that was settling in.

"I just don't know what to say, Bry, to you or to Beverly and Alan. You know they think of you as their son. And Patrick—what will he say if you don't come home to honor his sister?"

Maybe he would also say, "Enough. When will it ever end?" But Bryant didn't know. Even though they'd been friends since the cradle, he and Patrick had never discussed it.

"All right, Ma. I'll come. The Sunday after St. Louis. I'll work it out."

"Good. You won't be sorry, don't you know."

He was already sorry. And he did know.

CHAPTER THREE

Gabriella put the finishing touches on Eat Cake's refreshment table and peered out the front window at the costumed children gathering on the street. She hoped they had made enough food.

In addition to the spider cupcakes, pumpkin cheesecake bars, and jack-o'-lantern-shaped apple hand pies that she had just put out for shoppers, they had made several hundred festive cellophane wrapped cookies to give out for trick-or-treat. June had also bought little orange and black bottles of bubbles, witch whistles, and pumpkin erasers to give the children.

"The table looks wonderful!" June came out of the kitchen and poured a tub of ice over bottles of water in the large black cauldron. "I hope people won't be disappointed that we aren't having the hot spiced cider that we had last year."

The chestnut gelato incident had been forgotten—or at least forgotten by June. Gabriella couldn't forget it until she'd made more.

"I think the water is a better idea. The weather is cool enough for a warm drink, but with all the activity, people will want something cold."

"Are you going to be warm enough outside?" June asked. Eat Cake wasn't selling anything outside, but people could register to win a free cake per month for a year, and of course there were the trick-or-treaters. Gabriella had volunteered to man the table.

"I'll be fine. Remember, I'm North Dakotan." And before that a Canadian, but it had been a long time since she'd felt that particular chill.

"If you get cold, let me know. Haddie or I can switch off with you—I don't think we want Quincy giving out cookies to the children." June, Haddie, and Quincy were to work the inside, serving food and selling cakes and pastries to those who wanted to buy.

Gabriella laughed. "True. But we wouldn't have to worry about running out of treats, because he'd scare them all off."

"I guess I should have specified no bloody zombie costumes."

"If you don't need me here, I'll go finish up out front." Trick-or-treating was scheduled to start in fifteen minutes, but Miss Sticky and Miss Julia were already handing out candy in front of their knitting shop, String. Like always, Miss Sticky was wearing her ham costume identical to the one Scout wore in *To Kill a Mockingbird.* Miss Julia was Wonder Woman.

"Go ahead," June said. "Haddie and Quincy are putting the things for trick-or-treat in baskets. I'll send them out when they're finished."

Gabriella retrieved the box of salt dough Halloween cookies from behind the counter. It had been her idea to have a gnarly, faux wooden oak Halloween tree decorated with fake cookies that were replicas of the ones she'd be giving out to the children. The salt dough cookies would last for years, and they wouldn't have to reinvent the wheel next year.

Once outside, Gabriella straightened the candy corn tablecloth that Quincy had put in place earlier, opened the box of pens and prize registration slips, and moved the tree away from the front table edge. If someone tried to eat one of those fake cookies, Eat Cake might have to go out of business.

The street had been blocked off and a stage set up at the end where Jackson Beauford would perform. She was just finishing hanging the cookie ornaments when something—or rather someone—down the street caught her eye.

Now that was odd. Hadn't Bryant said he was headed back to Nashville, that he'd catch Emile at home? He'd left the shop at least an hour ago, but he was sitting on a bench in front of The Café Down On The Corner. He wasn't doing anything, just sitting there staring into space. Maybe he was waiting for someone to join him there for dinner. Probably not Nickolai. He'd be with Noel at Piece By Piece, giving out candy and autographed hockey pucks to trick-or-treaters.

Maybe Emile. Gabriella brightened at the thought. He ought to be back from Georgia soon. And hadn't Bryant said Emile had been supposed to meet him and Nickolai to watch film? Since he'd stood them up for that, maybe he had arranged to meet Bryant here for dinner. Then she could see for herself if Amy had come back with him, and maybe get some information about their plans—if they knew themselves. But no. Now Bryant was on his feet and walking away—walking with his head down and slumped like an old man walking into strong, frigid wind—of which there was none. What was wrong with him?

"Here you go." Quincy came out and set two baskets on the table—one with cookies, the other with the small toys. "June said to remind you not to give little children the erasers, because they might choke on them. The bubbles and whistles are okay. But I guess little kids don't have anything to erase anyway."

"I wish I could erase your costume," Gabriella said. "Go be bloody inside before you scare the kids."

"Might scare them more if you erased it."

"Might scare *me* more."

They laughed together as he turned to go. "Just knock on the window when you get low on treats.

Gabriella lit the jack-o'-lantern to signal that they were open for business.

"Baa! Trick or treat!" It was Amelia Beauford, Jackson and Emory Beauford's two-and- a-half-year-old, dressed as an adorable wooly lamb.

"Sh. Not yet, Amelia." Emory swung her daughter to her hip. "I told you. Five more minutes until trick-or-treat time. I need to talk to Miss Gabriella for a minute."

Though she didn't seem to know it, Emory Beauford, who was dressed as Little Bo Peep, was the reigning queen of Beauford and not just because she was married to town's most famous citizen. When she needed services and goods for her party planning business, Around the Bend, Emory never went outside Beauford for caterers, limos, florists, or anything else that was available locally. When she had married Jackson, lots of the townspeople were afraid that she would close the Beauford family plantation business, which would have had a serious adverse effect on the town's economy, but it had never missed a beat and neither had she. She could have walked down the street and gotten anything she wanted at any time, but she would not even allow her child to trick-or-treat one minute before the appointed time.

"I think you're right on time." Gabriella held out a cookie to Amelia. "How about a jack-o'-lantern?"

"Hold your bag open, Amelia," Emory said. "And say thank you to Miss Gabriella."

Amelia shook her head vigorously and her lamb ears flopped. "Thank you! But I eat it *now!*"

Emory took the cookie and removed the cellophane. "All right. But you get to have this before dinner only because this is a special night." She handed the cookie to her daughter as Gabriella put some of the small toys into Amelia's bag. "I'm a terrible mother."

No. A terrible mother lets her husband abuse her children and allows them to eat cereal for meals because she can't get up from bed to shop or cook. You're doing just fine, Emory.

"You're doing just fine, Emory."

Emory laughed. "Some days I do better than others. But I wanted to talk to you. I'm so happy about Emile."

Gabriella felt her eyes go wide. She had to be talking about the engagement. How in the thunder did this woman know about that? Did Jackson Beauford have some kind to pipeline to all information?

"I don't know him well," Emory said, "but you know we were all in Nickolai and Noel's wedding, and then I saw him again at the baby's christening. I have always liked him, and I was so pleased when he called today."

Emile had called Emory Beauford? To tell her he was engaged? None of this made sense.

"I admit there are not a lot of people I would be willing to do a wedding of this size for with this kind of notice and *especially* with the timing, but he was so excited. And he can be charming."

Gabriella was having trouble finding any charm in him right now.

This was as surreal as the steampunk teenagers across the street with gears and watch parts hanging all over them. Just how big was this wedding going to be? And more important, when? Emory Beauford knew more about Emile's wedding plans than she did— apparently including the date. How could this be? Emile was her brother, her best friend, the one person on earth who had always, always put her first.

Certainly, Johanna and Paul loved them and were there for them without question, but there had been a time when Emile was all Gabriella had. And then there was that dark, brief time when she'd had no one. Johanna and Paul Lindell had become Emile's billet parents when, at sixteen, he had gone to North Dakota to play junior hockey, leaving Gabriella in Quebec with her monster father and her beaten down mother. After Andre Charbonnet had broken Gabriella's arm and knocked her mother down the stairs when she'd tried to intervene, the Lindells had brought Emile to Quebec for the funeral. They had taken Gabriella from the neighbor's house where she had been staying to be with them at the hotel, and Johanna had taken her shopping for a dress for the funeral. When they'd learned she had no one, they'd taken her home with them and loved her, too.

Gabriella loved them completely and knew how incredibly lucky she'd been that they had rescued her. But there had always been Emile, and now things—big things—were happening that she didn't know about. She had to find something to say to Emory that didn't give away that Emile had not bothered to tell her when he was getting married.

"The timing is … is … really something, isn't it?"

Emory set Amelia on her feet. "Hold my hand, Amelia." She turned back to Gabriella. "I know! I asked if he was absolutely sure they wanted to get married on December 22, and he said no, that he wanted to get married today, but Amy needs some time to get everything together. Like six weeks is time enough. I had six months and that was barely enough time."

Six weeks. December 22. Gabriella couldn't begin to process that the wedding train—and Emile's new life—had left the station and she wasn't on it.

"It will be a busy time for sure," Gabriella managed to get out. But what about Christmas? For the first time in three years, Emile had enough off days that they could spend Christmas in North Dakota. June had given Gabriella the time off, and they had been planning it since the Sound schedule came out early last summer.

But that was before Amy. Not that Gabriella didn't like Amy. To the contrary, she adored her and they had become friends. Amy was perfect for Emile. But everything was moving too fast. No matter where she and Emile had been born, North Dakota with Paul and Johanna was home, and Gabriella had hoped Amy would go home with them for Christmas —but as Emile's girlfriend or fiancée, not his wife. Now, it looked like no one would be going to North Dakota, because Johanna and Paul would certainly come for the wedding, which apparently was going to be at Beauford Bend Plantation.

"Of course, we don't know what kind of cake they want, yet, or even exactly how many it will need to feed, though Emile said they want a large celebration." Finally, something Emory didn't know. "But I wanted to go ahead and get penciled in. Should I go inside and tell June?"

"I can take care of it," Gabriella said. "Though there are some nice refreshments inside."

"I'll come back by," Emory said. "Abby is saving us a table at The Café Down On The Corner. We're going to feed the kids before sugar takes complete charge of the night."

Apparently, Emory didn't even know that her sister-in-law didn't have to save her a table. Robin and Billy Joe Reynolds always had room for Emory Beauford.

"Mama!" Amelia cried out. "Want another cookie!"

Emory picked her up. "Not yet, baby. We're going to see your cousins and have a grilled cheese."

"Want to tell my daddy *baa* and give him a kiss."

"Good idea. We'll do that. After grilled cheese." She smiled as she walked away. "Bye, Gabriella. We'll have such fun with the wedding!"

Yeah, buddy. Fun aplenty. On some level, she knew she was overreacting. After all, he'd told her he was engaged. But now it sounded like the whole wedding was planned, and he hadn't bothered to tell her. Why had he not wanted to share this with her, at least before the event planner? Or maybe he'd tried. She'd been so busy; it was possible he'd tried to call. She pulled her phone from her apron pocket. No. Nothing.

Fear shot through her gut—fear of being alone. She hadn't felt that in a long time. Nonetheless, she recognized the feeling. It wasn't rational, but there it was anyway.

"Trick or treat!" The chorus brought Gabriella back from her musing.

She gave out treats to a few dozen kids and posed for pictures with several before there was a lull. She found her bottle of water under the table, drank deeply, and commanded herself to change her attitude. So what if he'd reserved the venue?

"Gabriella!" Hélène-Louise, Gabriella's good friend and the owner of the Gossamer Web, was hurrying down the street. Hélène-Louise had gone out with Emile a few times. She had been fond of him, but not romantically. She had recently married Bennett Watkins, whom she'd been in love with since she was eighteen.

"Hi. Where are you going in such a hurry? Aren't you supposed to be giving out candy and selling lace?"

Hélène-Louise stopped in front of her. "Olivia and Whitney are covering for a few minutes, though I have to get back. But I had to come down here and tell you how excited I am for Emile! Isn't it wonderful?"

"I guess you've been talking to Emory."

Hélène-Louise looked puzzled. "Emory? No, I haven't seen her. Why?"

"Nothing. I assume you're talking about my brother's wedding plans."

"A Christmas wedding!" Hélène-Louise's eyes shone. It looked like Emile was calling old girlfriends now. No wonder it was taking him so long to get to his sister. "You know Bennett and I reconciled on Christmas Eve."

"Yes." Hélène-Louise had been so hurt and miserable without Bennett, and Gabriella had been so happy to stand up with her at their wedding six months later. "So my brother called you?"

She nodded. "He wanted me to make Amy a veil."

"What is he, the wedding planner? Did you tell him you can't make a whole wedding veil in six weeks?" She'd meant for her tone to express humor she didn't feel. No. She just sounded mad.

Hélène-Louise looked taken aback. "I did tell him that I can't make a whole veil. But I can make enough to edge it. He was on his way back to Nashville when I talked to him. Since he's going on the road tomorrow and won't be back until Thursday, Amy isn't coming back for a few days. Then she's going to come in and we'll talk about exactly what she wants."

At least she knew now what Amy's plans were. "Well, that's nice that she's having some input. Is he planning to make her dress himself? Grow the flowers?"

Hélène-Louise laid a hand on her arm. "What's wrong, Gabriella? I thought you liked Amy."

"I do. It's just that he's told me nothing, except that she took the ring. But he called Emory and now you."

"He's just making arrangements, Gabriella, and he's not thinking. You know how he is."

"I do. And I don't mean to sound like I think this is about me."

"It's a little about you. And you don't want feel left out." That was it exactly. She didn't want to feel alone. "But, honey, they won't leave you out. You will be part of things. They both thought all was lost. Then they reconciled and they're riding high and making plans. That's all. They'll calm down."

Apparently, he'd told her the whole story. No surprise there. He told everybody everything.

"I'm sure you're right. Thank you for letting me vent."

"You won't feel this way tomorrow." Hélène-Louise looked down the street. "It looks like you've got a gang headed this way. And I'd better get back and help the girls. We'll talk tomorrow. But I promise—you'll probably be laughing about this in an hour."

But she didn't feel better in an hour, or two. In fact, she felt worse. In between giving out hundreds of treats and registering almost as many people for free cake, she received visits from all the people Emile had found time to call to share his news—Nickolai Glazov, Sheriff Brad Stanton, who Gabriella had dated a few times, Abby Beauford, who Emile had been interested in before she married Rafe Beauford. Then came Miss Sticky, Heath Becket, and Coach Conrad MacKenzie—none of whom Gabriella was aware even knew Emile. Apparently, he got around town quite a bit and he wanted them all to save the date. Hell, this wasn't even the Harvest Festival anymore. It was Let's Celebrate Emile Giroux's Engagement Day.

Thank God it was nearly over. She was almost out of cookies and patience. All the children had full bags and sleepy eyes, and Gabriella could hear Jackson Beauford's band tuning up.

"The candle's nearly out in your pumpkin." She looked up and then relaxed. It was the one person who would not know more about Emile's future plans than she did.

Jimmy Simpson was the high school janitor and one of the most beloved people in Beauford. The story went that he had left town an eighteen-year-old golden boy and returned from Vietnam broken in ways that would never be fixed. He was wise and kind, but he was known for disrobing in public from time to time. Gabriella was glad to see that he was wearing a space suit and a cowboy hat.

"Hi, Jimpson. My candle *is* nearly out. I guess that means Halloween is almost over." She handed him a Frankenstein's monster head. "Have a cookie."

"Did you make it?"

"I did."

He put it in a pocket of his space suit. "Thank you. I'll save it until tomorrow. You're too young to know what my costume is."

"I'm not. Maurice. You're a space cowboy."

He laughed. "I guess everybody knows that song, but not everyone remembers when it was new." He touched the brim of his hat. "Rafe Beauford gave me this hat. He wore it when he won a rodeo championship."

"It's very fetching."

"You're very fetching in your Alice in Wonderland costume. I can't wait to see you all fixed up for Emile's wedding. I guess you'll be a bridesmaid?"

Angels above and demons below! Now Jimpson.

But she was pretty sure she didn't look surprised. She'd gotten over that about eight people ago. And would she be a bridesmaid? Would she even be invited?

"So you heard Emile's news?"

He nodded and laughed. "I was over at Firefly Hall helping Christian with a few things when he called to reserve the place for the wedding." Christian was yet another Beauford wife, married to the youngest brother, Beau. She had turned her family plantation home into a successful bed and breakfast.

"The whole inn?"

Jimpson nodded. "The whole thing—from three days before the wedding until Christmas Eve."

"Wait." Hadn't Emory said the wedding was the twenty-second? "Christian always closes Firefly Hall from the twenty-third until the twenty-seventh."

Jimpson nodded. "Usually. But her mother is coming here for Christmas this year, and Christian said why not? That it would be fun." Not only was Emile convincing everyone to do what he wanted, he was making them like it. "When Emile found out I was there buffing the floors, he asked to speak to me and invited me to the wedding."

"I'm so glad he did." And she was. She just wished he would invite her.

The instruments down the way were sounding more like music and less like tuning up now.

"Jackson is about to sing. Are you going?"

"I'm afraid not." She had miles to go and gelato to make before she slept. "But I'll be able to hear. You enjoy."

He nodded. "I always try to."

Gabriella left the cookie and toy baskets out on the table, but picked up the bucket with the prize registration slips and went inside.

"I was about to tell you to come in," June said. "I think it's over."

"I put the few treats we have left on the table in case stragglers come by."

"Good idea." June picked up a tray of cupcakes.

"It just happened and I haven't had time to mention it, but Emile is getting married at Beauford Bend on December 22. Can we put the wedding cake on the schedule?"

June smiled. "Lori Shelton told me he was getting married, but she didn't say when." Why wouldn't the middle school football coach's wife have been informed? "Put a note on my desk, will you? I'll put it on the schedule. I might let Haddie help me with it since you won't have time. But I promise you this will be a very special cake."

"I'll do that. Then I need a few minutes to make a phone call, if that's okay," Gabriella said. "I'll be out to help clean up soon."

"Of course," June said. "I sent Quincy to break down the table at Spectrum. Take your time."

Gabriella went through the kitchen where Haddie was loading the dishwasher, into June's office, closed the door, and made the note about the cake.

Then she took out her phone. She wasn't surprised when Emile's phone went straight to voicemail. Since Amy had stayed in Georgia, they were probably talking. Or maybe not. Maybe he was informing the rest of the world. Maybe this was going to be the biggest wedding since William and Kate. Hell, probably William and Kate were coming and bringing the little royal kids. Queen Grandma, too.

Anyway, that wasn't the call she'd intended to make.

Johanna kept up with hockey news and followed all social media that remotely had anything to do with the Sound or Emile.

Gabriella didn't want her to find out that way. The only reason Emile wouldn't have tweeted it by now was he didn't know how. Or maybe he did now. A lot had happened in twenty-four hours so why not that?

"Darling!" Johanna answered on the first ring. Her voice was balm for Gabriella's bruised feelings.

"Hi. How are you?"

"Good. Same as yesterday morning when we talked." That was before the engagement. They had mostly talked about Emile's fight and speculated how Amy would react when he showed up at her family home. "But isn't it wonderful how everything turned out?"

"So you've talked to him?" Apparently, it should have been Johanna who made a call to keep Gabriella from hearing everything through the vine. Of course, Johanna would not have imagined that Gabriella would ever have to hear anything about Emile secondhand. Gabriella wouldn't have imagined it herself before tonight.

"Of course. And I have to say, Gabriella, I know I was concerned that this was happening too fast, but after talking to Amy, I know this is the right thing. She's wonderful."

"She is." There was no denying it. So they'd called Johanna and Paul, together, like couples do when they get engaged. First they kiss. Then they call the people important to them. Gabriella knew this for a fact. She'd read it in books and seen it on TV. They would have done it in Regency romances if they'd had phones.

"Really, all it would have taken to convince me was seeing that ring. She has to love him to be willing to wear that thing."

So they'd texted her a picture of the ring, too. "Was it bad?"

Johanna laughed. "You haven't seen it? Let's just say it's a little flamboyant."

"You mean vulgar and tasteless."

"I would never say my boy was vulgar and tasteless. Of course, this will change Christmas for us." Indeed. "We don't have to decide right now. Emile thought that since you already have the time off and he and Amy are only going to go up to North Carolina to stay at the Biltmore Estate for two nights, that you, Paul, and I should stay at his condo and get things ready for when they get back on Christmas Eve. Then Paul and I could stay for his game on the twenty-seventh and go home the next day."

So, really, it sounded like there was nothing to decide later. Emile had figured all that out, too.

"That sounds fine." If anyone would understand how Gabriella felt, it was Johanna. She opened her mouth to confide how mean-spirited and immature she was feeling and why.

But just then, Johanna began to cry. "Gabriella, do you know what that sweet boy said to me? To be sure to wear shoes I could dance in because we had a mother/son dance to do. It never crossed my mind … I never dreamed …"

Gabriella would not take this moment from Johanna with her petty, immature thoughts.

"Of course, Johanna. Who else? Are you not our mother in every way that counts?" That made Johanna cry harder, and Gabriella joined in, but the emotion behind her tears was as mixed up as a box of spare buttons.

CHAPTER FOUR

Bryant was Colorado bound, then after that, Arizona.

The first hour of the flight had been rowdy with lots of good-natured ribbing directed at Emile about his engagement, but now—with two hours left before touch down—everyone was settling down for naps or plugging into noise-canceling headphones.

Emile rose from where he'd been sitting beside Bryant. "I must go up front. Coach Colton has summoned me. But you will be my best man?"

Bryant had not thought of that, but he was pleased. "Of course. But I thought you would have asked Paul. Are you sure it won't upset him?" Bryant knew the feelings were deep between Emile and Paul Linden. The man was more father than billet dad to Emile.

Emile slung his backpack over his shoulder. "I will have two best men—my billet dad and my best friend. Paul said I need all the help I can get."

"I don't know how much help I'll be, but I'm honored to try." He'd been in a few weddings and attended more than he could count, but that didn't mean he knew much about what was supposed to happen. His own wedding had been put together in three days with no participation from him beyond *stand here* and *say this*.

"'Keep me in line,' was Paul's exact quote," Emile said.

"I know I can't do that, but I can come up with a decent bachelor party."

Emile shook his head. *"Non.* No bachelor party. Perhaps just you, Paul, Glaz, Jarrett, Mikhail, Thor, and me for a beer. No dancing girls and wildness."

Bryant should have been relieved not to have to plan a big blowout, but he felt a little sad. "That might sound like the lamest bachelor party ever. Who are you and what have you done with Emile?"

A voice from the front of the plane bellowed, "Giroux! Get your ass up here!"

Emile said over his shoulder as he started up the aisle, "You'll see, my friend. Someday you will see."

Unlikely.

With the team camaraderie, comfortable private plane, nice hotels, and good food that he didn't have to make happen for himself, Bryant usually liked a road trip—but not this time and not this destination.

As far as the destination, he had nothing against Denver. It was nice. So maybe it wasn't the place so much as the *who* he was dreading—that asshole Scott Alvin, the Avalanche's top D-man.

Alvin hated Bryant, had since their junior years when they'd played in the same league and for two years in a row Bryant had been named Defenseman of the Year. Alvin had a big mouth and had never minded telling the world that the only reason he had come up short was because Bryant was an American and played not only in his home league, but also in his hometown, while he—Alvin—was Canadian. Never mind that they'd both gone on to land big, fat NHL contracts. Alvin had never gotten over it, and he baited Bryant every time they met on the ice. More often than not, Bryant took the bait and ended up in the penalty box.

As for the time—tomorrow was Philie's birthday, bad enough in and of itself, but worse because it was also game day. Every member of his family and Philie's would feel compelled to commiserate with him. The calls would start early and go late.

His mother had probably handed out a schedule so they could be sure at least two people would talk to him every hour. For hockey people who ordinarily understood the importance of game day, none of his family nor former in-laws seemed to remember that—birthday or not—he needed to be left alone to rest and get his head right.

And these marathon, high drama calls couldn't happen only once a year. Oh, no. They'd all have to go through it again in February on the anniversary of Philie's death. Once, three years ago, he'd been in Boston on that day, and he'd turned off his phone for his pregame nap. Next thing he knew, the hotel manager was pounding on his door, telling him to call his mother, who was afraid he'd committed suicide.

At least he wouldn't have to hear it from his teammates. None of them—even Emile—knew he'd ever had a wife, let alone a dead one.

Guilt stepped up and slapped him in the face. He had it coming. What kind of monster was he to begrudge mourning Philie and their baby in favor of getting ready for a hockey game? The family had their priorities in order.

Didn't they? Sure they did. It was a tale for a tearjerker movie for sure—high school sweethearts expecting a baby and married—in that order—before they were twenty. The child groom, a promising professional athlete; the child bride, dead of preeclampsia at eighteen.

That was surely something meant to be mourned forever, and the family knew that.

Only sometimes, it seemed like all this perpetual mourning was less about remembering Philie and their lost baby and more about reminding Bryant that he was forever and irrevocably cemented to the place and people he came from—not that he could forget, not that he wanted to forget. They seemed to think if he moved on emotionally, he would be lost to them and St.

Sebastian, Minnesota. But wasn't there room in life for the future and the past?

Still, he ought to feel something more than annoyance and conflict. He closed his eyes and tried to conjure up Philie's face. He wasn't surprised when he couldn't—but what did surprise him, what jarred the very core of his being, was the face that *did* flash before him.

Gabriella Charbonnet. What kind of sense did that make? It was probably because she was the last woman he'd had a face-to-face conversation with.

Thinking about all that hurt his head. Maybe he'd take a nap and pray for dreamless sleep.

Bryant reached into his bag for his headphones, but when he looked up again, the head equipment manager and resident sage, Oliver Klepacki, had materialized in the seat beside him—materialized was the only word for it. Glaz and Emile swore the man could appear out of nowhere, but Bryant had never witnessed it until now. He'd been too preoccupied. He'd have to work on that.

"Packi. Where did you come from?"

"Nashville. Before that, Wisconsin." He reached into a bag at his feet and handed Bryant a pint of mint chocolate chip ice cream and a spoon. "Here you go. This is for you."

Bryant looked skeptical. "How did you keep that from melting? Is that bag magic?" He was only half kidding.

Packi nodded solemnly. "Yes. It is. It lets me transport a number of items all at one time. But it was the magic freezer in the plane galley that kept the ice cream frozen until a minute ago when I put it in my magic bag."

Feeling foolish, Bryant shrugged, opened the carton, and took a bite. Glaz swore Packi had magical powers, but Glaz believed a lot of things that Bryant didn't. "I ate the salmon salad and prime rib that chef served when we first boarded, but I'm still hungry.

I'm surprised you brought me ice cream. Emile says you don't approve of eating sugar during the season."

"No. I don't approve of Emile eating sugar during the season. It affects his game. It doesn't affect yours. You need to stay away from white bread and white rice."

"Why is that?"

Packi shook his head. "No clue. I know the ways of my boys, but not a lot of whys."

"Mint chocolate chip is my favorite."

"I know that, too. I don't know why."

Bryant laughed quietly. "Neither do I." He took another bite of ice cream. "If you're looking for Emile, he's up front with Coach."

Packi supervised the other equipment managers and locker room attendants, ordered equipment, and made repairs on the bench during games. But from time to time, he took a player under his wing and gave him special attention—usually in times of stress, whether it was for a good reason like an impending wedding or birth or a bad one such as a death in the family or divorce. Lately, he'd been watching after Emile.

"I'm not looking for Emile." Bryant locked eyes with Packi and saw that the wisdom there surpassed his years—which Bryant figured to be somewhere in the neighborhood of sixty. Packi had played minor league professional hockey in the days before helmets and state-of-the-art sticks. He wore his scars and age well. "Emile's troubles are over."

"Because he got engaged? I'd think that would just be the beginning of his trouble."

"How do you feel about that?"

"Emile getting engaged? It seems a little soon, but if he's happy, I'm happy. Though it looks like I'm going to be out of carousing buddies. First, Glaz. Now Emile."

"There's always Jarrett." Packi named Bryant's other close, single friend. "Don't forget him."

The two men laughed together quietly.

"For sure," Bryant said. "Jarrett's always on the make." Jarrett MacPherson was a good friend, but a more straitlaced guy you would never find. He had earned his nickname—The Saint.

Packi reached into the bag at his feet again and removed a helmet, new visor, and screwdriver. "You could always stop carousing."

"Not likely."

"I didn't think so." Packi set about removing the half visor for the helmet.

"Hey! Is that my helmet?"

Packi nodded without looking up. "Your visor has some scratches, so I'm replacing it. You need a clear field of vision, especially with Alvin on the ice."

"And you're doing it yourself?"

"I'm going to be looking after you for a while. I sharpened your skates and packed your equipment bag myself. I called ahead to the hotel and had them put wheat bread, peanut butter, oranges, and almonds in your room."

"The hell you say." Bryant was taken aback. "Thank you, Packi, but I'm not having any trouble." At least no more than usual. "Unless you count going up against Alvin."

"Uh huh." Packi nodded, but there was something in his tone that said he didn't believe it for a second. "Is that right?"

Bryant's gut bottomed out. Could he know about Philie? And that it was her birthday? No. Impossible. What had happened five years ago when he was nineteen had never made the news. He hadn't been important enough. Not like now. These days, if he bought a pack of light bulbs, a picture would show up somewhere. And he'd never told anyone. He knew what it was like to be viewed as the tragic man-child widower. Once you were that, that's *all* you were.

"I'll take all this helmet-fixing, ice cream, almonds, and stuff—and be glad about it. But I'm okay. Really."

"You *have* been." The inflection of his words indicated that Packi didn't think he was okay anymore.

"I am now."

"Uh huh. Good." Packi might as well have said, "Yeah, right."

Why did everybody think he wasn't all right? Why was he not allowed to be all right?

Packi pointed with his screwdriver. "Your ice cream is melting."

"Yeah." He shoveled the rest of it in his mouth. Tasteless, but at least he wasn't hungry anymore.

Packi took the empty carton and the spoon. "Why don't you get some sleep? I'll wake you before we touch down." He reached into his bag again, pulled out a Sound blanket, and held it to Bryant.

"Are you sure that bag isn't magic? Do you have everything in it?"

Packi laughed a little. "The only magic I've got is planning ahead."

Bryant took the blanket. "Thank you." He wanted this conversation to end more than he wanted to sleep, but he put on his headphones, leaned his head back, and closed his eyes.

With the darkness and silence for company, logic told him that Packi couldn't know about Philie—though his gut disagreed. But if Packi knew, who else? And how? There was always talk among coaches and front office brass from different teams, so it was possible they knew, but no one had ever said anything.

Every once in a while, he Googled himself to see if anything about that time of his life had surfaced. But it had been a long time and he should do it again. He wouldn't put it past his mother to put the entire tragic tale on Wikipedia, except she probably didn't know how.

But he knew how. He could have put the whole mess out for the world to see, if he'd wanted. God knows he hadn't forgotten a bit of it.

After the Red Wings had drafted Bryant when he was eighteen, no one—not his family, not his friends, and certainly not Philie who, as his girlfriend of two years, was accustomed to being ice rink royalty—had understood when Bryant wanted to delay signing the NHL contract and accept the full ride hockey scholarship that Boston College had offered. Sure, it happened all the time. If a drafted player elected to play college hockey, he had thirty days after graduating or leaving school to sign the pro contract. But, according to everyone in Bryant's life, why would he want to do that when the Red Wings held the keys to the kingdom?

Heck, don't you know Detroit is only ten hours driving distance from St. Sebastian, as far as that goes? Not as good as if you'd gotten on with the Wild, but it could be worse. Darn tootin'. For sure.

Shame washed over him. Who was he to make fun of the back home vernacular, even in his head? He came from those people. He *was* those people, even if they hadn't understood why he'd wanted to go to college.

But he'd stood firm and gone off to Boston. Sure, he'd wanted to play in the NHL—intended to play in the NHL—but he needed something to fall back on if his hockey career went bad. And it could go bad so fast—a wrong fall, a bad hit, and it was all over. He hadn't known what that fallback plan would be exactly, but his counselor had said the freshman year was basic academics anyway, so he could take some time before deciding on a major.

But he'd never gotten that far. Philie had gotten pregnant that fall and they'd gotten married over Thanksgiving. He'd left school, signed with the Red Wings, and Philie had died in February of preeclampsia—something Bryant had never even heard of.

After the funeral, Bryant had gone back to Detroit and finished out the season. As a late-to-the-party rookie, he hadn't gotten a lot of ice time, but he'd made a decent enough showing when he had played.

When he'd asked his agent to get him traded as far from Minnesota, Michigan, and Massachusetts as possible, he had hoped for the West Coast. He had gotten Nashville. And that was fine. The owner, Pickens Davenport, had been willing to pay plenty. It wasn't as physically far away as California, but culturally it was light years from anything he'd ever known. To say that his family had been less than pleased was like saying water was wet, but they'd been somewhat appeased after he'd hoisted the Stanley Cup for the first time.

And it was just that simple.

Ah, yeah, keep telling yourself that, Swifty, a voice inside him said. *Have you forgotten that you were going to break up with Philie when you went home for Thanksgiving but found yourself standing in front of Father Martin instead? Or how mad you were when you quit school, signed with the Red Wings, and did what everyone had wanted you to do all along?*

He'd been mad all right—but mostly with himself. He'd never blamed Philie. It was all on him.

Though he hadn't left for Boston with any notion that he'd ever break up with Philie, by early October he'd known he needed to do just that. He'd found out there was life outside of St. Sebastian and he'd changed already. Yet, when Philie had come with his family to Madison for the University of Wisconsin/Boston College game series, he'd slept with her anyway, telling himself he needed to wait until the Thanksgiving holidays to end the relationship. It had never occurred to him at the time that the two weren't mutually exclusive. He'd only thought that the worst kind of asshole would break up with his girlfriend when she was on a road trip with his parents. Turns out there was an even worse kind of asshole—the kind who would sleep with her knowing he was going to break it off.

So they'd gotten married. He'd told himself it would be all right. Before going to college, he'd thought he'd play in the NHL, marry Philie, and have children. He just needed to rewind and be happy about it.

But Philie hated Detroit and everything about it—the size, the traffic, the church, the distance from home, and, maybe most of all, that her guy wasn't the hotshot on the ice that he'd been in the youth leagues and as a junior.

Her *guy.* Just because he'd never felt like a husband didn't mean he hadn't been one—though he hadn't been much of one.

She'd told him she wasn't feeling well the day before that road trip to DC for the Caps series. She'd wanted him to drive her to St. Sebastian before he left, something that was logistically impossible. He'd tried to explain that even if he drove there, put her out, and immediately headed back to Detroit, he wouldn't be able to make it in time to fly out with the team. But she'd been in one of her irrational moods, and there had been no reasoning with her.

And he'd tried. He'd offered to put her on a plane (no—she'd never flown and was afraid); ask his fellow rookie teammate's girlfriend if she would stay with Philie while the team was gone (no—that woman thought she was better than everyone else); fly his mother or hers in (no—she wanted to go home), hire a nurse (just no, no, no). So, in his frustration, he'd quit trying and convinced himself she wasn't sick at all, that she was once again—though he'd never given her any reason to doubt his fidelity—obsessing that he would sleep with four women in every city.

So he'd left mad and had marked it up to Philie's belligerence when he couldn't reach her by phone—and in truth, he hadn't tried many times.

Then, he'd come home to find out that he never should have left.

Finding a body wasn't pretty. Philie hadn't died serenely in bed or sitting in her favorite club chair wearing her pink robe with her little ankles crossed and propped on the ottoman. No. Apparently she'd been about to take a shower, because it was still running and she was naked. The pink robe was hanging on the back of the bathroom door. She'd been sick when the seizure began, but she had only half hit the toilet, so she'd died lying in her vomit on the cold tile floor, the little bump that was their son just beginning to show.

He had not known what to do. It was too late for an ambulance. It had briefly crossed his mind to call the police, but it wasn't as if she'd been murdered. In the end, he hadn't handled it at all. He'd called his dad. To this day, he couldn't remember what he'd said, but things began to happen quickly—the ambulance, coroner, the arrival of his parents and Philie's. It had been one big, blurry nightmare, and he'd known almost immediately that he had to get to another part of the country, somewhere he'd never been.

The doctor had said that preeclampsia didn't usually happen until later in pregnancy, but teenagers were one of the high-risk groups. Philie had been eighteen.

It was months later, when he was packing up to move to Nashville, that he'd found the confession Philie had written out and placed in her prayer book. He'd been gathering some things to give to Philie's mother when the paper fell out of the book. It took a few minutes for him to recognize it for what it was. It was an oddity, for sure. Despite the years he'd spent as an altar boy and on bended knee at St. Joseph's, Bryant had never known anyone to write down a confession. But after reading it twice, the reality of why she'd done it hit him. It would have been a hard confession to make. It read:

Bless me, Father, for I have sinned. It has been two weeks since my last confession. These are my sins:

I took God's name in vain in anger when my husband was late coming home from hockey practice.

> Because I didn't feel like company, I lied and said I had a doctor's appointment when the girlfriend of one of my husband's teammates asked to come over to visit.
>
> I gossiped with my sister about our cousin in a mean-spirited way.
>
> I have taken Holy Communion with an unconfessed sin in my heart. Though I tried to convince myself that I had done the right thing, I know now I was deceiving myself as well as my spouse. I knowingly and deliberately conceived a child with my husband, before he was my husband. Things were changing and I was afraid of losing him, so I told him it was a safe time, when I knew I was most fertile.

Bryant had stared at the paper for a long time. It had all come back to him. That weekend, she had whispered in his ear that there was no need for a condom because she'd just had her period. He hadn't questioned, hadn't hesitated. It wasn't a question of safe sex for health's sake. They'd lost their virginity to each other and had been faithful, so why not?

Why not, indeed. The end result answered that.

He'd read the confession again. And what penance would she have been asked to perform? Two Hail Marys? Three? An Our Father? Perhaps a whole rosary? Whatever it had been, he deserved that multiplied many times.

Then he'd torn the confession into tiny pieces and flushed it down the toilet. He owed her that much.

There had been no women since Philie, unless you counted the puck bunnies who drifted through his bed—and he didn't. Those encounters were honest and open—he was looking for sex, and they were looking for sex with a hockey player. Everybody got what they wanted and didn't ask for anything else.

It was an empty life, but it was the one he had and he didn't see that changing. He made it sound like a joke when he said he was emotionally unavailable—but that didn't make it any less true. He had been emotionally unavailable to Philie. Maybe that hadn't killed her, but it sure felt like it. He had gone into one relationship he wasn't ready for, and he'd failed her—and his baby. He would never do that again.

Besides, he owed Philie. He couldn't rewind and make himself love her, but he could at least refuse to give another woman what he hadn't been able to give her. Not that it had been a problem. Hell, he couldn't even choose a sacrifice that cost him anything.

Bryant hadn't expected to go to sleep on the plane, but the next thing he knew, there was a hand on his shoulder shaking him awake. He sat up and removed his headphones.

"Thanks, Packi. Are we there?"

"Not yet. But you were talking in your sleep. I thought I'd better quiet you down before the whole team finds out your secret."

Fuck.

He knew he sometimes talked in his sleep, always had according to his brother Luke and, later, Philie. But it had been a long time since he'd actually slept with anyone, so he'd forgotten. What had he said? He couldn't even remember dreaming, but that would teach him to fall asleep with the past on his mind. "I'm sure whatever I was saying didn't mean anything."

"Yeah?" Packi said. "Maybe not, but I'd be careful about going to sleep in front of Emile if I were you."

"Why?"

"Do you know more than one woman named Gabriella?"

Now he remembered the dream.

Double fuck. Literally—at least in dreamland.

CHAPTER FIVE

Gabriella's doorbell rang, signaling that someone was downstairs at the rear entrance of Eat Cake. That would be Amy. She had finally called, though they had not discussed the wedding. She was on her way back from Georgia and thought it would be fun to watch the game together. Gabriella had offered to join her in Nashville at Emile's condo, but Amy had said that made no sense when she would be passing by Beauford. Besides, she had never seen Gabriella's apartment.

This made her feel better, more normal, though she still hadn't talked to Emile. But she seldom talked to him on travel and game days, which yesterday and today had been.

"I am so happy to see you!" Amy rushed through the door toward Gabriella with her arms wide open. Gabriella hesitated but hugged her future sister-in-law. Despite the friendship they'd struck up, they had never hugged before. Gabriella's hesitancy came from her reserved nature and had nothing to do with her feelings for Amy. She wouldn't have pegged Amy for a hugger either, and maybe she hadn't been before. Apparently that had changed now that she was going to be a bride.

Gabriella untangled herself and reached for Amy's hand. "Let me see this ring. Johanna told me about it."

Amy held out her hand and frowned. "I didn't text you a picture of it?"

"No." Admitting that felt a little awkward. Thankfully, Amy didn't notice.

"I'm sorry. I meant to, but for a while I didn't have a phone, and then everything has been so crazy!" And she laughed liked crazy was the best thing in the world. "Anyway, now you get to see it in person."

Gabriella thought she'd been prepared, until she saw it. "Oh, my." It wasn't as big as a Dixie cup, but it wasn't far off. The central diamond was the size of a nickel and that was just the beginning. It looked like a mini Niagara Falls on crack. "Do you like it?" She fought to keep her tone neutral.

Amy withdrew her hand from Gabriella's and looked at the ring. "I do. Is it what I would have chosen? No. But I like it because I love your brother and choosing a ring like this is part of who he is."

Amy's words warmed Gabriella. She'd known almost from the moment she met Amy that she was right for Emile, and Emile deserved to be loved so much. She felt guilty about pouting because their relationship hadn't progressed on her own timeframe.

"You can always set up a gypsy wagon on Broadway and use it to tell fortunes."

They laughed together, and any awkwardness that Gabriella might have felt dissipated.

"Let's go up." Gabriella led Amy up the stairs to the apartment over Eat Cake. "My television isn't as big as Emile's, but it's a decent size for watching hockey, and I have soup in the Crock-Pot, bread in the oven, and black forest brownies for dessert."

"You shouldn't have gone to so much trouble."

"Cooking is therapeutic for me."

"I hope you haven't really been in need of therapy!"

You have no idea, Amy. But that's over. I will be a good girl. No one will be unhappy because of me.

They entered the apartment.

Amy took a deep breath. "There is nothing better than the smell of baking bread."

"Nothing?" Gabriella teased.

"Well ..." Amy blushed. *No, Amy! Don't blush. Because if you blush, that leads me to think you are thinking about sex with my brother, and I can't be in the same room with that train of thought!*

"Let me show you around," Gabriella said quickly.

Amy looked around the little living room. Gabriella was proud of it. She'd done it in moss green and gray with splashes of apricot.

"Oh, Gabriella! This is lovely. I wouldn't have thought about putting these colors together, but it's so warm and happy. And the furniture." She stepped over to the small drop front secretary desk and ran her hand over the smooth oak. "Such lovely wood." She looked around at the other pieces in the room. "Complementary, but not too matchy, matchy. What style is the furniture?"

"All mission style."

"It's beautiful."

"You sound surprised."

"Not really. Or I shouldn't be. You have such style and dress so beautifully that it would naturally transfer to your décor. It's just that ..." Her voice trailed off.

Gabriella felt an amused little laugh bloom inside her. It felt good. "You thought that because my brother has whole catalog pages from Pottery Barn that I would too?" After Emile had bought a seven-bedroom condo in the most upscale building in Nashville, he'd gone to Pottery Barn and literally pointed to pages in the catalog.

Amy blushed. "Well, no. Yes. I mean I shouldn't have."

Gabriella let the laugh out and Amy joined in. "Are you saying you might want to rethink the Pottery Barn look?"

Amy nodded. "I can put things in order." That was an understatement. Amy had sold her professional organizing business, Apple Pie Order, to a large New York firm for six million dollars—which her former boyfriend had stolen. "But I'm not so good at putting together décor. Maybe you can help me when we get the house."

Gabriella stopped short. "House?"

Amy nodded happily. "Yes. We want to sell the condo and buy a house—with a porch and a fence so Emile can get a dog. He's always wanted a dog, but then you would know that."

Gabriella, in fact, did not know that. Emile had never said a word about a dog. That insecure, left out feeling began to creep in again.

"I'm hoping for a historic house, though I'm not sure what period, but something with character. We want to stay in Sound Town, of course."

"Makes sense." More news, more changes. And that was fine. She just wasn't used to hearing Emile's news from a third party.

Amy gestured to the room. "Tell me more about this beautiful furniture. I love the simplicity and the clean lines." She ran her hands over the bookcase front. "And the leaded glass." She stopped abruptly. "Not that I would copy your style. I just want to hear about it."

Excellent idea. It would be a relief to talk about something she knew about.

"As I said, it's mission style. It originated at the end of the nineteenth century. It's plain—made up of flat panels and vertical lines. Most of it is made of quartersawn oak. These pieces are not usually embellished very much—just a bit of leaded glass, substantial metal hardware, or simple wooden inlays like the dragonflies on the secretary or the small geometric shapes on the bookcase."

Amy walked over to the bookcase. "Lovely." She turned her head so that she could read the titles of the books stored there. *The Earl's Lady. Diamond of the First Water. Deceiving the Ton. Permission to Waltz.* Amy smiled. "I like a Regency romance from time to time, too, but I mostly read mysteries. I like the surprise."

"I am not fond of a surprise." *Like this pop-up marriage.* "Not that there aren't surprises in Regencies. But there's structure. There are the rules of society. Everyone knows how things are supposed to be, even if the characters don't follow the rules."

"If you'd been a Regency debutante, you would have certainly been a diamond of the first water."

"Unlikely that I would have been a debutante at all. More likely some kind of under-cook."

"Maybe," Amy said, "but one who sweeps the duke's heir off his feet and one day becomes duchess."

Right. Probably she'd get pregnant and the housekeeper and the old duchess would turn her out into the snow during the Christmas Eve ball, just as the duke was announcing her lover's—the marquess—betrothal to The Lady Octavia Got Money and Breeding. Insufferable snobs would eat her jam tarts and Banbury cakes, though. And they'd better enjoy them, because they wouldn't be getting any more. It was over for the mean old cook passing off the sweets Gabriella made as her own. That would show them all.

"Gabriella?" Amy said. "Are you all right?"

"Oh." She hadn't gotten pregnant by a marquess who looked like Bryant after all. "I spaced for a second."

"Probably all the cooking you've done today." Amy ran her hand over the arm of the wood and leather sofa. "It all looks new but has an old feel. Are they reproductions?" So they were off the Regency period and back to furniture.

Gabriella shrugged. "Yes and no. Except for one, my pieces are new, but they aren't really reproductions. The designs are old, but they've never stopped making them."

Amy nodded. "You said all but one piece?"

Gabriella walked over to the library table under the window. "This is a Gustav Stickley signed original."

"I don't really know what that means," Amy said, "but it sounds very special."

"It is. It was a gift from Emile."

As she said the words, a cold, foreign feeling washed over her. Emile had indirectly bought everything in this room—and everything she owned, from her La Perla underwear and designer clothes to her paperclips and Post-it notes. Not that he shopped for her bras himself. He only shopped online and at Pottery Barn.

As far as her fashion sense, it was Emile's fault she had such highbrow taste in clothes. The Lindells had been neither rich nor poor, but Johanna loved clothes and knew how to shop to make the most of her money. She'd dressed herself and Gabriella out of T.J. Maxx and high-end, last season sales, but no one in Buxton, North Dakota knew the difference. It was Emile who insisted they go to Paris for Gabriella's eighteenth birthday to shop for clothes. That was something both she and Johanna would have turned down, but Emile played the "if you won't go, she won't" card with both of them. In Paris, they might have started out a little country come to town, but they'd caught on quickly and returned with some fine wardrobes and refined tastes. Johanna had insisted on classic styles for most of what they'd bought and they both still wore most of the pieces.

Gabriella had been the best-dressed freshman at Buxton Junior College. While she was there, Emile had not only paid her tuition, but he'd also given her a very generous monthly allowance. With her apprenticeship, she'd begun to receive a small salary and had been given this apartment to live in rent free, but he'd continued the allowance, even raising it from time to time. When she'd asked him about it, he'd said being an apprentice was like being in school and he wanted to take care of her. She'd never thought much about it, because they were one. During the short time he had attended the University of North Dakota, she'd had a part time job and an allowance from Johanna and Paul. She'd paid for their movies and burgers then—because they were one. Wasn't that the same thing?

No. Not really. If she wanted to go skiing, she went. When she flew, she went first class. Her salary wouldn't have begun to pay for her lifestyle. And then there were the gifts he bought her—the library table last Christmas, the BMW SUV on her birthday, Louis Vuitton bags, and state-of-the-art electronics for Easter and her Saint's Name Day.

There was no doubt that Emile spoiled her, but that didn't make her a brat. She did enjoy her Versace, Armani, and Vera Wang, but she had never expected what Emile gave her, never took advantage of his generous nature. *They were one.* They had been poor and abused together. They had been orphans together. They'd basked in the warmth of Paul and Johanna's love together. Now they were rich together.

Except they weren't. Emile was rich. And inasmuch as Gabriella knew she wasn't a greedy little entitled sister, what would Amy think?

Apparently, right now she thought the Christmas present library table was pretty.

"Truly lovely." Amy stroked the table. "So when the time comes for me to furnish our house, will you help me?"

Gabriella hesitated. Amy would be better off with a professional. "Sure." Maybe she should tell Amy that that she didn't really know about decorating a house. She only knew what she liked, but that might sound like she didn't want to help. And didn't she owe Emile? She'd never felt that she owed him before, but now she did.

She had to stop this, stop it now, had to return to normal. She'd already spent too much time in irrational self-pity land. She wasn't going there again.

"Come and sit down, Amy. We still have some time before puck drop. Let's have some wine." That was a normal thing to say. She poured two glasses of Clear Valley Chardonnay—the wine that Emile represented and had shipped to her monthly.

"Sounds great."

"To you and Emile." Gabriella raised her glass. "And official congratulations, since I haven't had a chance to say so until now."

Amy looked puzzled. "Sure you did …" She trailed off. "We haven't talked, have we? I know Emile called you—but you and I?" She pointed to Gabriella and then herself. "I never called you did, I? Even though I told Emile to tell you I would."

"You called on the way here today." The words came out of Gabriella's mouth before she even thought. After years of being the good girl and trying to please everyone, it was automatic.

"Not the same. I meant to send you a picture of the ring and call you to talk about the wedding plans. There were so many calls to make—but that's no excuse. I'm a bad friend."

"It's all right. This is not about me. It's about you and Emile. I didn't think a thing of it." Pleasers always lied.

"Really?"

Amy was truly sorry. Gabriella welcomed the relief that passed over her. "You're here now. That's what's important. We have plenty of time to talk about the wedding." And that was true. Pretty soon, she wouldn't even remember why she'd been upset. Everything would be like it had been before. "But first, tell me what's been going on, other than the obvious." She gestured to her ring.

Amy took a sip of her wine. "Well, you know my family has a peach orchard and a store called The Peach Stand where we sell everything that can be made from a peach. So I made a lot of peach pies, peach bread, and peach chutney and salsa." She smiled. "I will never be the baker you are, but I can make decent peach pie."

"Maybe you can make us one for Thanksgiving."

Thanksgiving. Would she even be with them for Thanksgiving? What would happen? Did Emile have games? Or would he go to Georgia with Amy? If so, would she be invited, like some poor Regency-era maiden aunt who had to go live with her nephew, the duke, who didn't really want her there, but did his duty?

"I will. Thanksgiving is sandwiched between two home games. We'll have to make plans. Maybe you can make the pumpkin pie. I'm not so good at that."

We. That was nice to hear. "Emile likes pumpkin cheesecake." She shouldn't have said that—shouldn't tell Emile's almost-wife what he liked. She should have just smiled and said she'd make a pumpkin pie.

But Amy smiled. "Sounds delicious." Then her smile faded and she looked at her hands. "I suppose Emile told you about Cameron's wife coming to see me."

"What?" Any demons Gabriella was dealing with faded to the background. She was on the Emile/Amy team. "The woman your ex left you for came to see you? The nerve! I will hunt her down and kick her ass just like my brother kicked her husband's— though I guess I'll have to wait until she has that baby."

Amy laughed. "You might have been born in Quebec, but you are a Southern girl! But, no. It wasn't like that. Marley was very nice. Until Cameron and Emile had that fight after the Senators game, she didn't know Cameron had stolen everything I had and abandoned me one day and married her the next." She paused and looked up. "She made Cameron give my money back."

"Amy, that's wonderful. I only wish he would go to jail."

Amy shook her head. "Not going to happen. I'd given him control of my finances, so he didn't do anything illegal. But as my grandmother would say, he's going to get his."

"Starting with Emile beating him up on national television."

Amy nodded. "Starting with that. I don't think he will be able to start his big, multi-agent sports agency any time soon. He's losing clients right and left, and Marley has already filed for divorce."

"You're certainly up to date."

"Marley and I are going to stay in touch. We've already spoken on the phone a few times."

"That's good. Making new friends is always good." And it was. Certainly. "So what now for you?" Gabriella asked. "After the wedding, I mean."

"You know I signed a non-compete agreement when I sold Apple Pie Order, so I can't start another personal organizing business for four more years. Meanwhile, who knows? I have some ideas about some volunteer work I want to do. And there's the condo to sell and a house to find. Though Sharon Orlov is going to help with that. Emile called her right away."

Of course he had. It was of the utmost importance to share plans with a real estate agent—even if she was a friend—before one's sister. *No, Gabriella, Stop. Don't go there again. And don't think about how Amy had time to call this Marley person but not you.*

Amy went on, "And there's the rumor kicking around that the team could still be sold to Massachusetts."

That was something Gabriella did know about. Emile had assured her if that happened, he wanted her to move there, too, and open a bakery—with his financial backing, of course. Gabriella liked the South, and she wasn't even sure if she wanted to own a bakery, let alone in Massachusetts. But she wanted Emile to want it. Would he still, now that Amy made three?

Amy put her hand in the air. "But enough about me. What's been going on with you?"

"Baking, and there was the Harvest Festival. That was fun. But not much else. You know, you really weren't gone that long."

"True." What could only be the memory of heartache moved into Amy's eyes. "But it seemed like a long time. I missed him so much, even when I was so mad at him."

With that, the crazy, insecure pendulum swung back to normal. Amy really did love Emile. Gabriella took Amy's hand. "Hey. You're back. That's all that matters. And you're going to be together always and make beautiful babies." Because, of course there would be children. Unlike the dog, Gabriella knew Emile would want babies. He loved babies, always had.

Amy squeezed her hand. "I hope so. And the sooner the better. Though not immediately. I want to be able to have Champagne at my wedding! And about the wedding. Of course you know I want you to be my maid of honor."

Gabriella brightened. Maid of honor! That was the big job! Not just a guest, not even a bridesmaid, but the maid of honor! She *would* be part of things. And Amy had said *of course,* like she took it for granted—which Gabriella did not see as a bad thing. Sometimes being taking for granted was a comfort.

"Oh, Amy. Yes. Are you sure? I mean, you have friends you've known a lot longer …"

"I do. And they will be in the wedding. My friends Lulu and Cassandra will be bridesmaids, and my cousin Becky will be matron of honor."

So not really the top job. Co-top job. Okay. A few days ago she'd actually wondered if she'd be invited, so she'd be happy with that.

Amy glanced nervously at her phone.

"Expecting a call?"

"No. Emile will be on the ice soon." As if no one else could call her. "It's almost time for puck drop."

"Oh, right!" Gabriella handed her the remote. "Here. Put the game on and I'll get our dinner."

Amy made to get up. "I'll help you."

"Nonsense. Turn on the game. I know you don't want to miss seeing Emile skate out." And she meant that. She felt the generosity of it.

"Really?"

"Of course. And pour us some more wine. I'll be right back."

The puck was in play when Gabriella returned with the tray of food. It was easy to settle down and quietly watch. It was one of those fast and furious games with lots of shots on goal and lots of reason-defying saves by both goaltenders, but no score. Between periods, Amy pulled out her bridal magazines and they perused wedding and bridesmaids' dresses, and Amy asked Gabriella to go with her to the bridal shops in Nashville. It was very companionable and pleasant.

When the puck was in play, Gabriella found some time to ruminate. She had to accept that things had changed—maybe not even for the worse, but they were different. She had Emile were not one anymore and never would be again. It wasn't "and Amy makes three" like she'd thought earlier. It wasn't even Gabriella makes three. It was going to be baby makes three, dog makes four, with Aunt Gabriella as the poor relation in the threadbare castoffs mending socks by the fire. Hopefully, there would be a fire. Especially if they were in Massachusetts.

Gabriella laughed a little to herself, and that was a good sign. Clearly she'd been reading too much Regency romance. She wasn't going to be anyone's poor relation. She was going to be a world-class pastry chef, earn her own way, and maybe get written up in a cooking magazine someday. It wasn't money, material things, or wearing off the rack she was worried about. And it wasn't about Amy.

It was about not being half of a whole. She looked at Amy as her future sister-in-law leaned forward, intently studying Emile in the net. She loved Amy. It could be so much worse. She ought to be down on her knees thanking God and all the saints that Emile wasn't marrying some gold-digging puck bunny. With Emile's judgment, it could have easily gone that way. *And how would you have liked that, missy?* Not worth a damn.

"Yes!" Amy jumped to her feet.

Gabriella homed in on the television in time to see the instant replay. With three minutes to go in the third period, the Sound had scored!

"Finally! We have a goal here at the Pepsi Center," the announcer said. "And it's the Sound one, Avalanche zero, as number five, Bryant Taylor, puts it in!"

"Surely they can hold on for three minutes!" Amy was new to hockey.

"Maybe." Bryant was getting the hero's hug. Hugging him wouldn't be a hard job. "But I've seen it go bad in less time with more of a margin."

Amy dropped back to the sofa and put her hands on her head. "This is hard!"

But the next minute, it got harder. The Avalanche worked the puck down to the Sound goal, and all ten skaters from both teams were knotted together, like a maroon, navy, purple, and silver amoeba. In such instances, it was always difficult to see what was happening—but then there were gloves, sticks, and helmets flying. That was where the harder came in; it was always harder when there was a fight. Gabriella picked up *The Earl's Proposal* and read the same paragraph three times, retaining nothing.

"Get out of the way, Emile!" Amy yelled. Gabriella peeped over the top of her book. Emile moved toward the boards, as if he'd heard Amy.

"And it looks like we've got a fight, Kelton," the announcer said. "That's Bryant Taylor for the Sound, who just scored the first and only goal of the game, getting the better of Scott Alvin of the Avalanche."

At the mention of Bryant's name, Gabriella laid her book in her lap and trained her eyes to the screen. It wasn't easy, but it was easier than not knowing what was going on. A few years ago, Glaz had taken a skate to the neck in just such a pile up.

"Yes, Gino," the other announcer said. "It looked like Alvin shoved Giroux, the Sound goalie, and Giroux was definitely in the crease."

"You go, Swifty!" Amy waved her fist in the air. It hadn't taken her long to get bloodthirsty.

Gino chuckled. "And we all know that can't happen. The refs don't tolerate it; the goalie's teammates don't tolerate it."

Finally, the refs did their job and broke up the fight. Gabriella never understood why they let it go on at all.

"And it looks like Alvin gets a major and a game misconduct, while Taylor also picks up a penalty for fighting. So off to the box with both, though they won't stay there long with less than two minutes left in the game."

"That's not fair!" Amy said. "Bryant was only defending Emile."

"That's the way of it," Gabriella said. "Fighting gets you five."

Amy cut her eyes at Gabriella and not in a nice way. Surprised at Amy's response, Gabriella laughed.

"Maybe you want a whole set of NHL rules just for my brother."

"That would be great," Amy said and then looked back at the television. "Come on! Hang on."

And they did hang on. After the teams left the ice, it was Bryant who appeared on the screen with a microphone in his face.

"That was a hard-fought victory," the announcer said. "It must feel pretty good to claim a win after those disappointing back-to-back losses against the Senators and Hurricanes last week at home."

Bryant poured water down his throat. "A win always feels good." He was out of breath, sweaty, and looked like an angel returning from battle with the devil. "I don't think too much about what happened last week or last month." That was a canned reply. They'd been taught that good sport, no-controversy talk before they could tie their own skates.

Amy sighed. "Don't get me wrong. I only have eyes for Emile, but that is one fine specimen of a man. For a blond, I mean," she quickly added. "I am not so much about a blond."

Yeah, buddy. Definitely look, but don't touch. If Gabriella hadn't remembered that, the little cut on his chin would have reminded her.

"How about that fight in the last two minutes of the game?" the announcer said. "What happened? Did Alvin rough your goalie?"

Bryant leaned on his stick. "That's what the refs said. I'm going to go with that."

"Great game."

"Thanks, man." And he was gone.

Before Gabriella could ask Amy if she'd like another brownie, Amy's phone rang.

"Emile! Of course I watched."

He must have called before he even got to the locker room. What had he done? Strapped his phone to his helmet so he could call Amy immediately? Gabriella gathered the dirty dishes.

"Yes. I'm here with your sister." Amy took her phone from her ear. "Gabriella, Emile says hello."

"Tell him I said hello." She rose, picked up the tray, and headed for the kitchen.

"What? Yes. That sounds great. Just a second. I'll tell her."

Since she was the only other *her* in the room, Gabriella turned and looked at Amy. Apparently, from now on she'd get her news via Amy. It would take some getting used to, but it would be okay. It had to be.

"Emile said Pickens Davenport and his wife want to give an engagement party for us. Next Sunday, after the St. Louis game the night before. It's not a huge party. Just family, Sound people, and dates. Will that work for you?"

"Of course." Favorite words of a pleaser. *Of course* went beyond *yes*. *Yes* said, "I'm willing." *Of course* said, "Oh, yeah. Don't think a thing about it. It would never have occurred to me to want to do anything else."

So what if she'd had a weekend girls' trip to Atlanta planned for six months? She, Hélène-Louise, and Pam had good seats for *Hamilton* at the Fox Theater, but they could invite another friend, who would be glad to have a free ticket. Or they could use her empty seat for their purses and coats. What did it matter that the ticket had been so expensive?

Emile had paid for it.

"Wait!" Amy said as Gabriella left the room. She held out the phone. "Emile wants to speak to you."

She set the tray down and took the phone. "Hello."

"Johanna has taken me to task for not calling you. I hadn't realized. Please forgive me."

Relief flooded though her. She didn't have to be mad, hurt, or unreasonable anymore. This was enough—more than enough.

"Of course." There was that handy word again. "I know you've been busy. I haven't thought a thing of it."

"Good." There was relief in his voice that set everything right. "I told Johanna you knew I would never neglect you on purpose."

"Of course."

CHAPTER SIX

The Coyote game was in the books and Bryant was in a hurry.

He dodged the reporters, which wasn't too hard. He'd played decently with two assists, and he'd managed to stay out of the penalty box, but he hadn't been a standout tonight. In the locker room, he rushed through his cool down on the bike, declined a massage, showered, dressed, and headed toward the door.

Packi intercepted him and put a blue Gatorade in his hand. "Where are you going?"

"To the bus."

"Yeah? We don't leave for the airport for forty-five minutes. Nobody will be onboard yet."

"That's the idea. I need to make a call." It was a glamorous life he led, indeed—rushing to the cold bus with wet hair in order to make a private call. But he had put it off as long as he could.

"Uh huh," Packi said. "Woman trouble?"

"The worst kind—maternal."

Packi nodded. "All right, then. Better take this, too." He handed him two bottles of water.

Too bad it wasn't beer.

After taking his seat in the back of the bus, he drained the Gatorade, opened a bottle of water, and took out his phone. He briefly considered calling his dad or his brother, but that was the coward's way out. It also wouldn't help. He'd still have to talk to her.

The phone only rang once.

"Bry!"

"Hello, Ma."

"Two wins in a row now. This is a better week than last, for sure."

Depends on how you look at it.

"For sure," he agreed.

"Sure could be worse. I've got no complaints, don't you know, none at all."

Margaret Murphy Taylor considered it her God-given right to critique every game he had ever played in. After all, she'd birthed him, laced his skates when she was so pregnant she could hardly bend over, and saved grocery money to pay for his equipment and ice time. If he wasn't careful, she'd tell him all that again, and they didn't have time for that. But she was going to have plenty to sermonize about soon.

"Thank you, Coach Ma."

She laughed. "You bet, but don't say that." No matter what she said, she loved it when he called her that. "I want to talk about that Avalanche game. I hoped you'd call after."

"I'd already talked to you once that day." Not to mention every other Taylor and Kelly, blood and married-in.

"What? You can't talk to your mother more than once a day?"

"You could have called me."

"You know I don't bother you on the road." *Except when you do.* "But about the Avalanche."

"We won. You didn't like it?" Here it comes.

"Yes and no. Let's talk about the *no* first."

"You bet."

"Bry, why did you get in a fight with that Alvin thug? *Again?* If it had come two minutes earlier, you'd have been in the box and you wouldn't have scored the only goal in the game. You can't score from the box, as far as that goes."

"But I wasn't in the box." He absolutely was not going into how he had resisted Alvin's little dirty tricks the whole game until he shoved Emile. She knew no self-respecting D-man let his goalie get pushed around. "I *did* score."

"Yes, you did. It was beautiful. I don't like that Alvin kid. I never did. But the goal—we all thought it was perfection. We were all here together—your brothers and sisters, the kids, wives, and husbands, except Joanie. She had to work. Michelle wanted to invite the Dunlap boy, but I told her no. He's nice enough and they've been going out since August, but I thought it should just be family on Mary Philomena's birthday—though I did let David bring Casey. But that's different. He's almost twenty-one and Casey is practically family already. And the Kellys were here of course. I made lasagna—a whole big thing of it—and Beverly brought salad and garlic bread. The girls brought pans of cereal bars for dessert."

This wasn't news. When they had called him on Philie's birthday, they had all whispered, "How are you doing?" and then talked about who was bringing what to the big gathering. Mary Catherine was making Scotcheroos, Molly was making Special K bars, but with white chocolate chips instead of butterscotch, while Maria, Patrick Kelly's wife, was making them the traditional way. They had talked about getting a birthday cake for Mary Philomena, but decided that would have been morbid—like gathering on her birthday every year wasn't.

"It was really nice—all of us being together to watch you play on Mary Philomena's birthday. We couldn't have done it if you hadn't had this big room built on to the house."

It was a media room—good for holiday gatherings, watching hockey games, and holding never-ending funerals.

"You bet, Ma. Glad you enjoy it."

"Father Martin said he received a very generous donation from you for Mary Philomena's memorial Mass."

She paused. This was where he was supposed to tell her how generous, which he didn't intend to do. That was something he'd learned from living with Southerners. They didn't talk about money, especially blood money. According to them, it was tacky.

"Anyway," Maggie went on, "I'm sure he'll thank you in person when we see you next weekend."

And here it was—time to make the big confession for which there could be no penance big enough.

"Here's the thing, Ma. I'm not going to be able to make it next week."

Long, long silent pause. He'd been there. She intended to stay quiet until he reversed what he'd just said and apologized. It usually worked, but this time he was going to wait her out.

Finally, she caved. "Bryant." Pulling out the big guns, she was, putting the *ant* on his name.

"Still here."

"Did I hear you right?"

"If you heard me say that I can't come to St. Sebastian next weekend, you did."

"Well, see, if it was only that you weren't coming to St. Sebastian, that wouldn't be so much of a problem. But it's your wife's Mass you aren't coming for. That is *quite* the problem. The Mass cards have gone out. Father is planning on it. The notification has already been sent to the bulletin. It can't be changed."

"I don't want you to change it. I want you to go ahead without me."

She let out a horrified gasp, like he had suggested that they all renounce hockey and the Roman Catholic Church and take up badminton and naked, fire-dancing paganism.

"Bry, I don't know what to say."

That might be true, but it wouldn't last long.

"What on earth am supposed to tell Beverly and Alan? To explain why their son-in-law isn't coming to their daughter's memorial Mass?"

"You don't have to say anything to them. I'll call them myself."

"Am I allowed to know why you have chosen not to come?" It wasn't an accident that she wouldn't use the word *can't*.

"Emile Giroux has gotten engaged. Pickens Davenport is giving an engagement party at his house that night."

"Is that all? I know it's important to accept invitations from the owner, Bry, but he would understand this. Besides, you aren't some rookie trying to gain favor." She said all this like the problem—*her problem*—was solved. "Talk to him. Explain. Though I don't understand why, I know you don't talk about Mary Philomena to anyone down there, but you can say it's a Mass for a deceased family member. It won't be a problem."

"But, see, Ma. Here's the thing. I don't want to. I want to go to the party."

"You'd rather go to a *party* than Mary Philomena's memorial Mass?" She had that tone that said, "You'd better disagree."

He usually backed down at this point because it was easier, but not this time.

"Yes, Ma, I would. We had a funeral Mass for Philie, and we've had memorial Masses on her birthday and death anniversary every year since she died, complete with big multi-family meals afterward with every hot dish known to man. As far as I can tell, there are no plans to stop that. Emile is my best friend and he's only going to have one engagement party."

All that sounded perfectly reasonable, so reasonable that Bryant thought his mother had to accept it, if grudgingly. And she might have if he had only left out the word *best* when applied to *friend* and *Emile*.

"Emile Giroux is your *best* friend? Really? What about Patrick Kelly? Remember him? The one who had a crib next to yours in the church nursery—the one you played pond hockey with, and doubled-dated with to the prom? The one who stood up for you at your wedding—your *brother-in-law*? Where does this newfound friendship with Emile Giroux leave him?"

He wasn't allowed to move on from grief, and apparently now he couldn't have friends who didn't remember him from the cradle. Why, why, why had he used the word *best*? But why fool himself? It wouldn't have mattered.

"The same place he's always been—in St. Sebastian, where I am not. He's still my oldest friend and also my best friend. I text and talk with him all the time. Nothing is going to change that."

"So, now Patrick is your best friend. And Emile is your best friend. I might not have gone to Boston College, but I know what a superlative is and there can be only one."

"I didn't go to Boston College long—not long enough to learn anything." *Except that I didn't want to marry Philie.* He took a deep breath. "But, Ma, I'm not in St. Sebastian anymore with my old friends. They're still friends, but I need other friends."

"Fancier friends with more money, who don't work at the paper mill? Do I need to remind you that it was money earned at that paper mill that got you where you are?"

What the hell? "Ma, that's not fair. I don't think I'm better than anybody. I appreciate everything that you guys have ever done for me. I have tried to show it every way I can. If there's anything that you or any of the family needs, I'm happy to get it. You know that."

"This is not about money and things, Bryant. You can't buy your way out of mourning for your wife and baby."

He took a deep breath and counted to five. "I do mourn Philie, Ma."

"So this newfound bonding, with these newfound friends—I guess that means you've told them all about Philie, the baby, and what happened."

Only his mother would define five-year-old relationships as new. Partly because he'd wanted them to tell him it was okay, and partly because he hadn't wanted them to give him away, he'd told his family that he'd never told anyone in Nashville about his marriage and the rest of it.

They had not told him it was okay, but when they'd met his teammates at the road games they'd attended, they hadn't given it away either.

"No, I have not told. Just because I like to keep some things private doesn't mean they aren't real friends. If I could change what happened, I would. But I can't. Missing the party for Emile and Amy won't change anything. And I'm going."

"I don't even know what to say."

"I'm sure you'll come up with something and plenty of it."

"I can't believe my own son would talk to me like this."

"Look, Ma. I love you. I don't want to argue with you. I could have told you some bullshit lie about how this party was mandatory for the team. Hell, I could have told you a special mandatory practice had been called. But I didn't. I told you the truth."

"Is this what you've come to? Cursing when you're talking to your mother? And I almost wish you'd told me a lie. Then I wouldn't have to know you don't care."

"Good Lord, Maggie!" Bryant's father's voice boomed in the background. "Give me that phone. Son?"

"Hi, Dad."

"Hell of a game! Are you on your way back to Nashville?"

"Not yet. Soon."

"I just caught the tail end of that conversation with your mother. I take it you aren't coming for the memorial Mass?"

"I can't. There's an engagement party for Emile Giroux at the Davenports' house. It just came up."

"Well, that's a shame, but you have to do what you have to do. Team relations and all."

He was just going to go with that. "I'm sorry Ma is upset."

"Ah. You know how your mother is. She'll get over it. It's not just the Mass. She's disappointed you can't come for Thanksgiving. She wanted to see you." He coughed. "So do I."

And he wanted to see them—really. He just didn't want to see them at St. Joseph's doing it all over again—the whole funeral mass reenactment, complete with black clothes, crying, and grave visit.

"I have an idea," Bryant said. "We play Winnipeg the Friday and Saturday after Thanksgiving. I know Ma is set on cooking the turkey at home, but why don't I fly you down to Nashville the next day? Or even Saturday if Friday can't work out."

"I don't know, Bry. Nashville. The South."

"I've tried to get you to come a dozen times, and you always act like the South is a foreign country." They always traveled to see him when he played within driving distance of St. Sebastian, but they'd never been to a Sound home game.

"Well ..."

"If you'll just find out who all wants to come, I'll make all the arrangements—tickets, your own spectator ice suite at the arena, hotel rooms downtown, and limo service. Ask all the Kellys, too. Ask David's girlfriend and Michelle's boyfriend."

"Sounds pretty spendy."

"Not as spendy as keeping a growing boy in skates and sticks."

His dad chuckled. "I don't know about that ..."

"Come on, Dad. You know you want to."

"There are worse things than seeing my boy beat the Jets on home ice." He hesitated. "Bry, would you be willing to go to Mass with your mother that Sunday morning?"

Why not? A small thing to do for peace.

"Yeah, yeah, sure. The Cathedral isn't far from the arena. We can light a candle for Philie."

"Okay then. I'll give your brothers and sisters a jingle—the Kellys, too—and get back to you with a number."

"And, Dad?"

"Yeah?"

"Please remind them, I don't talk about Philie here."

"You bet."

After hanging up with his father, Bryant looked at his phone for a long time. He wanted to talk to someone who would make him feel better.

Without running it though his mind or analyzing why he did it, he scrolled through his contacts and called a number he probably wouldn't have even had if they had not planned a birthday party for Emile together two years ago. For all he knew, she might have a different number now.

"Hello?" Gabriella sounded perplexed. "Bryant?" She still had his number in her phone. That made him smile. He felt a little buzz of excitement in the pit of his gut. That was odd. Usually that only happened when sex was imminent.

Now it was his turn to talk, and what was he supposed to say? *Girl, you make my gut buzzy. And you definitely make me feel better.* Maybe he should have thought about what to say before he called.

"Yes. Bryant. Some call me Swifty."

"Some do," Gabriella agreed. "I don't usually."

"Why is that? You call Jake Champagne Sparks and Nickolai Glaz. I've heard you."

"I don't know. Do you want me to call you Swifty? Is that why you're calling? To tell me to call you by your nickname?"

"No. Bryant is fine. That's my name. Bryant is a saint's name, for Alexander Briant."

She laughed a little. "You don't say."

"He was fair of face and pure of heart, martyred at twenty-five. When he was tortured, he felt no pain." Why was he telling her this? The answer came loud and true in his head: he wanted to talk to someone, just talk for the sake of it about something other than hockey, memorial Masses, or how soon he and the puck bunny of the moment were going to have sex.

And she seemed to be going with it. "You know a lot about saints."

"No. Just mine. My mother drilled it into me. I used to think I would die at twenty-five, but my mother told me not to worry. Because I was no saint nor pure of heart."

"But you are fair of face," she said.

"Ah. That was nice of you to say." And nice to hear.

"I didn't say it. *Hot Nashville* said it. I'm just repeating what I read." But she had read it and she sounded flirty and happy.

"Michael was a saint, too. And an angel. He fought Satan," Gabriella said.

"Just like me. I fought Satan."

"I saw." Her voice went grim.

Time to change the subject. "Are you going to the party for Emile and Amy?"

"Of course," she said. "I'm the sister. Remember?"

"Would you like me to pick you up?" Holy hell! Where had that come from?

"What kind of sense would that make? You'd have to drive from Nashville to Beauford and back to Nashville again for the party."

"Doesn't have to make sense. A lot of times I don't. I wouldn't mind."

"No. I don't date hockey players."

What? She'd said *no*. No woman told him no. Anyway, he hadn't been asking her for a date.

"It wouldn't be a date. Just a pickup."

She laughed out loud. "And you think that's better? Good night, Bryant. Go be fair of face, pure of heart, and hold off on fighting Satan." She was still laughing when she hung up.

She hadn't even given him a chance to say goodbye!

Still. He sat smiling into the darkness.

CHAPTER SEVEN

"Wow. You could bring a dead man back to life."

That came from the valet when Gabriella stepped out of her SUV in front of the Davenport mansion—Greenwood Hall, it was called, though not because it was built of green wood, but because that was Mary Lou Davenport's maiden name and the house had been built by her ancestor in the 1800s.

"Sorry!" the valet said immediately and turned bright red. He couldn't have been more than twenty. "Ma'am, I am so sorry. I'm not supposed to talk to the hockey wives let alone say things like that. But it just fell out of my mouth. Mr. Davenport will fire me for sure."

"Only if he knows about it." She pressed her valet key into his hand. "And he won't unless you tell him."

"You won't tell him?"

She laughed. "No. And anyway, I'm not a hockey wife. I'm a hockey sister."

"Wow!" he said again.

She hid a smile as she mounted the steps and looked up at the massive double front doors. Her dress had had the desired effect—at least in the driveway. Inside might be a different matter. She had learned a long time ago that with her height, there was no way to fade into the woodwork. People were going to look at her, so she tried to make the best of it. Most of these hockey wives and girlfriends were all about some glitz, sequins, and glitter. To keep from becoming one of the tribe, she either had to out glitz them or go for an entirely different look. Since there was no way to out glitz them without diving into a tubful of glitter glue, she'd gone for what she hoped would be different, but not bland—a simple amethyst chiffon cocktail dress with a bit of silver embroidery on the bodice. The dress was short—mid-thigh—so she'd splurged on silk stockings that had just a bit of shimmer to complement her silver sling-backs and the embroidery on the dress. She'd probably be the only woman at the party who wasn't barelegged, but she didn't care. A casual skirt with sandals was one thing, but she had always thought a woman wearing a nice dress with bare legs looked like she'd left the house before she'd finished dressing.

She studied the doors. They were really something—huge, heavy, and ornately carved. They hadn't been built for mere function, to keep the babies in and the Yankees out. They were grand doors for a grand house to set the mood, meant to welcome or maybe intimidate. Gabriella wasn't the type to be intimidated by a house, but if she had been, this one would have done the job.

Located five minutes from Sound Town proper, Pickens Davenport's house, and a dozen or so other estates, was in a niche that was neither rural nor urban. And *estate* was the proper term. These houses were not McMansions sitting on too-small lots with waterfall pools. These houses—some new, some old—were the real deal, complete with stables, tennis courts, and who knew what else. Not Gabriella. Technically, she supposed plenty of the Sound players, including Emile, could have afforded a house like this. In fact, though she'd never seen it, she'd heard Thor Eastrom had one. She had a theory about why it was mostly the big money people from the pro teams and the country music industry who lived out here rather than the athletes and the entertainers. Most people who came from humble beginnings didn't have the capacity to think this big. Sure, she liked her designer clothes and Emile had that car he'd paid three million dollars for, but that was small time compared to how these people lived.

Davenports had no such limitations on what they could imagine in terms of luxury. According to Sharon Orlov, who seemed to know a lot about Nashville despite being from Massachusetts, there was plenty of Greenwood and Davenport old money. Aside from traveling, Mary Lou Greenwood Davenport had only ever left Nashville to attend the College of Charleston, where she'd met Charleston native Pickens, whose blood was at least as blue as hers.

All this meant nothing to Gabriella, but she understood nice digs when she saw them. From where she stood on the multi-columned porch, she could see what was probably a guesthouse. Why someone with a house this size needed a guesthouse, she couldn't fathom. Nor was there a world where she could fathom home bowling alleys, theaters, basketball courts, and fourteen bathrooms with solid gold fixtures.

Neither could Emile and Amy. Gabriella knew this about them because she'd gone with them to see the house they had their eyes on—a big, rambling Victorian in Sound Town that had been beautifully restored.

That had happened last week after Emile had returned from the Colorado/Arizona road trip. Things had been good, though Emile didn't seem to realize that it had been a full week since they had spoken—the longest ever. Even while she'd still been in Quebec and he'd been with Paul and Johanna, they'd talked on the phone every few days.

But it was what it was and she'd get used to the new normal. Amy had sweetly pointed out which of the nine bedrooms in the new house would be hers when she wanted to stay over, and they'd gone wedding dress shopping together. Luckily, Amy had found a dress at White Lace and Promises in Beauford that met her fluffy specification and only needed minor alterations. Unluckily, Gabriella thought the dress Amy chose overwhelmed her, but Amy had insisted that it was important to Emile that she wear what he termed "a big, fluffy dress" so it was, therefore, important to her. Hélène-Louise was hard at work on the lace for Amy's veil, but the question of getting bridesmaids dresses in such a short time had yet to be resolved.

But that was a problem for a different day. Tonight was all about celebrating the engagement.

And here she was—alone. To be fair, Emile and Amy had asked if she wanted to come with them to the party, but she'd said no. As the honorees, they'd had to arrive early and would have to stay until the last guest left. She didn't relish the thought of either of those things. Being here alone was bad enough without trying to look like she belonged there when it was only the hosts, honorees, and help.

Of course she supposed she *could* have come with Bryant. He'd offered to pick her up during that weird phone call he'd made to her from the road. She still didn't know what that had been about, but it had been amusing. She hadn't even realized she'd been half hoping he'd call again until she'd felt a little disappointment for the next few days every time someone else had called. But that had passed and it didn't matter.

She had considered bringing a real date to this party but had decided that even with a date, she'd feel alone. The only thing worse than being here alone was being here with someone to entertain. And there was no doubt—date or not, she'd be alone in a houseful of hockey players. There'd been a time when she would have been uneasy—afraid even—to be among so many hockey players. Thankfully she'd gotten past that. No one here would hurt her, but she still felt that phantom pain in her arm that haunted her now and then.

Time to go in. Past time. She opened the tiny beaded bag that hung from her wrist, turned off her phone, refreshed her lipstick, and finished climbing the steps to the porch.

"I wondered if you were going to stand at the foot of the steps forever," said a voice from the shadows.

"Who! What!" Gabriella's heart rushed to her head and pounded like a bass drum as she threw up her hands to defend herself.

• • •

Fuck, fuck, fuck. In that moment, Bryant hated himself. He *knew* she'd had an abusive childhood. Emile spoke freely about it. But he'd jumped out from behind that twisty little tree and scared the shit out of her. Would he never learn to think? Never learn to take care of people who needed taking care of?

"Hey, hey, hey!" He stepped into the light. "It's just me. I'm so sorry." To his relief, the fear left her face and his self-loathing lifted. He moved closer and gently laid his hands on her shoulders—and his hands felt at home, more than they'd ever felt on any other woman or even wrapped around a hockey stick. Maybe he was the one who ought to be afraid, but he wasn't. "You know I would never hurt you, don't you?" He gave her shoulders a little squeeze.

She looked at him blankly for a moment and then let out a shaky little laugh. "Of course. You just startled me. Why were you hiding behind that topiary?"

The truth was he'd been trying to recover from the latest round of pictures his mother had sent from the Official Day of Mourning for Mary Philomena. He beat back the memory of those pictures and concentrated on Gabriella.

"Just enjoying the view." He dropped his eyelids and gave her his best smile. "And I have to agree with that valet. You'd bring a dead man back to life—especially in that dress." And most especially *out* of it. But it wouldn't pay to think about that. He dropped one of his hands and dared to loop an arm loosely around her shoulders. She didn't pull back.

She laughed in a pleased kind of way. "You wouldn't tell Pickens Davenport the valet said that, would you? He said he'd get in trouble."

"Tell Pickens? Hell, I want to give the kid a trophy for his good taste." *But I also want to tie him up and throw him in the river.*

"You clean up pretty good yourself," she said.

"You think? I own this tuxedo, you know. I didn't rent it."

"I am impressed." She gave him a look that could get them in so much trouble—sexy, sweet, and curious all at the same time. "I made my dress."

"Really? You can sew?"

She laughed from the depth of her soul. "No!" That laugh was tonic for a tired heart. "I would be more likely to bake a dress than sew one."

"An edible dress? That's an interesting thought."

Her eyes danced and she opened her mouth to speak—but she never did, because Jake Champagne's red Lamborghini roared up and Gabriella moved away from him. Now he wasn't touching her anymore, and he'd never know what she'd been going to say. He might beat the hell out of Champagne at the next practice.

"I should go in." Gabriella arranged her little purse on her wrist and folded her hands like she was about to take communion.

He nodded. "Let's go."

She hesitated. "Why don't you let me go first?"

He could have pretended that he didn't know why, but he did. There had been electricity between them—the kind that hung on. If they went in together now, they'd look like the couple of the year. And that was something that would not amuse Emile.

He nodded. "I might go talk to Champagne a minute. Scottie's probably with him. Maybe I'll see you inside."

"Maybe."

He ran down the steps as his teammates got out of the Lamborghini.

• • •

What had just happened with Bryant? It felt like nothing and everything. Gabriella tried to shake it off as she rang the bell.

"Come right in, darling." Mary Lou Davenport always called Gabriella *darling*. She was pretty sure Mary Lou knew she was Emile's sister but doubted if Mary Lou remembered her name. In a foyer big enough for a family of twelve to sit down to Christmas dinner, the Davenports—Mary Lou, Pickens, and their daughter, Tradd, were lined up like Walmart greeters, only better dressed. Emile and Amy were next in line.

"Thank you for inviting me, Mrs. Davenport." She was wearing black sequins.

"We're just so glad you could come. Gabriella, have you met our daughter, Tradd?" Gabriella stood by her conviction that Mary Lou hadn't known her name at first. Probably had some little game to help her out. *Emile. Goalie, starts with G. Sister's name starts with G. Emile talks constantly. Gabby. Gabriella.* Her little exchange with Bryant on the front porch was fading now like a dream she couldn't quite remember. And there was good reason not to remember. It—like the phone call—was nothing.

"Hello, Tradd," Gabriella said. "We haven't met, but I heard you sing at The Café Down On The Corner in Beauford last summer."

Tradd didn't look delighted to be at this party, but she brightened a bit and smiled. "That wasn't me. That would have been Rita May Sanderson."

Pickens laughed. "Our Tradd feels like she has to have a stage name for her little singing hobby." *Ouch.* "Rita May" had sung backup in a few Keith Urban and Jackson Beauford videos and appeared here and there around Nashville, so Gabriella could only assume she wanted a real career. Figuring it was the kindest thing to do, Gabriella didn't look back at Tradd. Pickens hugged Gabriella, not in a creepy way, but a hug just the same. And there wasn't a damn thing she could do about it. "Tell me, young lady, how do you feel about your brother finally tying the knot? Did you think he'd ever do it?"

"I think he is incredibly lucky to have Amy—as am I to be gaining her as a sister."

"Oh, Gabriella!" Amy held out her arms—hugging again. She had definitely become a hugger. Amy and Pickens must get on like a house afire.

"The dress really works," Gabriella whispered in Amy's ear. And it did. It was silvery gray organza with a full, knee-length skirt and a heavily beaded strapless bodice.

"Thank you for helping me choose it. You were right. No one else is wearing this color. Lots of black, red, gold, bright blue, and bright purple."

"This ain't my first sequin rodeo."

Amy squeezed her hand. "And you look beautiful."

"She is always beautiful." Emile ran his hand over Gabriella's shoulder and she briefly covered his hand with hers. That was their answer to hugging and it felt good. "Your dress is pretty."

"Thank you. You bought it," she blurted out. Why had she said that?

He looked confused. "I did?"

"Never mind."

The door opened again.

"It's Sparks and Scottie!" Emile exclaimed and went to greet them. That would be his teammates Jake "Sparks" Champagne and Robbie MacTavish. Angels above and demons below. Robbie was wearing a full dress kilt.

But where was Bryant? Why wasn't he with them? Had he left?

Amy leaned toward Gabriella. "Does the noise level always go up with those two come in the room?"

"Every single time." Time to move on. Johanna had taught her not to linger too long in receiving lines at weddings and funerals.

This was neither, but it would apply. Besides, Bryant would be in soon. Maybe. If he hadn't left. "I'll leave you to the loud twins. And a word of warning. They will try to kiss you in the mouth—with tongue."

Amy laughed. "There's a bar in the grand salon, buffets in the dining room and the east verandah, and tables set up on the west verandah, the parlors, and music room."

"You sound like a tour guide."

"I got the tour," Amy admitted.

"I think I'll go find a drink."

"Try to find some fun, too."

"Don't I always?"

Grand salon, my ass. Gabriella made her way into the next room that was easily three times the size of her apartment. A waiter appeared in front of her with a silver tray of assorted drinks. She chose a martini because the glass went with her look. What did the Davenports do with a room this size when they weren't having a party? Roller skate? Fencing tournaments? Dog races?

Tonight there was a bar, a band playing "Brown Sugar," hockey players standing around the edges of the room, and a lot of sequined women dancing with each other. Krystal Voleck caught Gabriella's eye and small wonder. Who had thought it was a good idea to make sequined zebra print? Remembering Bryant's remark about her feet, Gabriella let her eyes drift there. Yeah, buddy. Bryant had been right. Those were some big feet, though Gabriella would not have called them clown sized.

"Why do you think women dance with each other? Everywhere I go where there's dancing, women dance with each other."

Gabriella turned to find Jarrett MacPherson at her side.

"I suppose because their men won't dance with them." Her smile came easily when she spoke. She liked Jarrett. He didn't have much of a sense of humor, but he was a solid guy and a loyal friend to Emile. She had always felt completely comfortable with him, even before she'd gotten over her fear of being around hockey players. After all, it was hard to believe a spokesperson for Walt Disney World would hurt a woman or child.

He sipped his drink and gave her a smile that was gone almost before it appeared. "Mikhail is dancing with Sharon. Glaz is dancing with Noel. Case is dancing with the flavor of the month." Jarrett was nothing if not literal. There were a few other men on the floor who looked familiar—probably Sound front office people.

"You could go dance with one of them."

He looked incredulous. "I'd rather eat. Do you want to eat with me? The food's good. There's prime rib, shrimp and grits, and some kind of seafood pasta. And I know where it is."

"Dining room and east verandah?"

"East verandah? I didn't know about that. Let's hit that. There might something there I didn't get my first time through."

Gabriella laughed out loud. He hadn't even meant to be funny. "Why not? We wouldn't want to you to be too weak from hunger to dance."

"Or eat again." He put his hand on the small of her back, then looked around. "Which way is east?"

CHAPTER EIGHT

In the short time it had taken for Bryant to do his duty in the receiving line, his phone had vibrated no less than five times. He reached into his pocket and turned it off. It was the only way to stop the incessant calls and text messages from his family and former in-laws.

And the pictures. If they'd been old-school Kodak prints, what they'd sent in the last hour alone would have been enough to fill one of those huge ten-pound albums that had always been on his grandparents' coffee table.

Determined to share the day with him despite his absence, the pictures and messages had started when they were at church—the flowers given in memory of Philie, the notice in the bulletin for her special Mass, the Mass card. It was a wonder they hadn't videoed the whole thing, but Father would have probably frowned on that. Then there were the family group shots in front of the church. Then they had moved on to the cemetery to put the flowers that had been at the church on Philie's grave. Pictures all around. None of this was new. He'd even expected it.

What he had not been prepared for were the ones he'd received as Gabriella had arrived. Someone had gotten the bright idea to dress a stuffed bear in an infant-sized Sound jersey and leave it on the grave beside the flowers—a memorial for his son who never was. His mother's text had said, "This is for you, Bry. None of us have ever had the heart to honor the baby, but it's time."

He'd almost hyperventilated.

They meant well. There was no doubt. And they had lost Philie and the baby, too. But the whole thing left him in a cold sweat—so much so that he'd scared Gabriella.

Then they'd moved on to the house for the big feed. They'd even taken pictures of the food. Apparently, no one except him thought it was right down spooky that they always made Philie's favorite foods—wild rice hot dish, Juicy Lucy burgers, strawberry fluff Jell-O salad, and chocolate Bundt cake.

He'd been half expecting some baby food and a bottle on an empty highchair, but no one had thought of it. Maybe next year.

As he stepped from the foyer into the room with the band, the bar, and a gaggle of dancers who looked something like a multicolored disco ball, he closed his eyes. He cleared his mind, willed himself to relax and let it go—which he could do. If he had a talent apart from skating backward faster than most could skate forward, he could put things in a box and lock them away. He imagined stacking all the pictures, all the texts, all the memories, in an iron box, locking it, and putting it on shelf in a room with hundreds and hundreds of identical boxes. There. Gone. The box would never be opened again. There would be more boxes to be sure, but all of today was gone. There was nothing left but this party.

Though he could use a beer.

"Hey, Swifty! Taking a nap?" The words were accompanied by a hard clap on his back and spoken in a Scottish brogue.

Bryant opened his eyes to a whole new world where things would happen that wouldn't have to be locked away. "Hi, Scottie. I closed my eyes hoping I would miss seeing you in that skirt."

Robbie MacTavish planted his feet wide apart and put his hands on his hips. "This is the formal attire of my people—same as that monkey suit you're wearing."

Bryant laughed. "Not the same at all. My legs are covered."

"Coach can force me into a suit and tie on game day, but it's not game day." He waved over his shoulder as he headed to the bar.

Bryant laughed at the memory of the first game of Robbie's rookie season last year when he'd shown up at the rink in a kilt. It had ended up all over ESPN. No one knew what Coach Colton had said to Robbie, but it hadn't happened again.

Robbie stopped and motioned. "Come on, Swifty. Let's get a drink."

Maybe he would. He really needed that beer and Robbie was always a good distraction.

But as he turned to follow, Bryant learned what a true distraction was.

There in the midst of a flock of sequined peacocks, Gabriella stood out like a swan with nothing to prove. Though he'd seen her earlier on the porch, he'd been up close and concentrating on her face. Now, from a distance, he got the full effect of her perfection.

"Go ahead, Scottie. I'll catch up." But he didn't say whom he'd be catching up to.

She was laughing at something someone was saying, just like she'd laughed with him earlier. He didn't like that she was sharing that laugh with someone else. From where he stood, Bryant couldn't see who, but he wanted to be the one who was amusing her. Her magnificent hair was caught up in swoopy, twisted braids, like a sweet secret that had gone into hiding for the night. She brushed some little wispy curls away from her face and laughed some more.

Gorgeous. If he'd had to name the color of her dress, he would have called it purple, but it wasn't exactly that—at least not like bright Nashville Sound purple. Lighter—like watered-down, see-through grape Kool-Aid. It was made of some kind of gauzy cloth like scarves piled on top of each other.

But the best part was where the skirt ended—over her thighs, but with inches and inches to spare above her knees.

The sight of her legs left him sweating and floundering for air. He'd never seen her legs before. How was that possible with as much time as he'd spent with her over past few years? Had she always worn pants? That had to be it, or he would have remembered. A man didn't forget a pair of legs like that, at least not this man.

She took a sip of her drink. And laughed again. Who the hell was she talking to? Just then, she took a half step aside. Oh. It was only Jarrett. He wouldn't be putting any moves on her—and he never said anything funny. So why was Gabriella laughing?

Maybe he'd better investigate. He took a step in their direction just as they headed toward him. Jarrett had his hand on the small of her back. That was no good.

"Follow me," Gabriella said to Jarrett as they came within earshot. "East is this way."

Bryant stepped into their path. "Going to Knoxville? Or China?"

"Perhaps." Gabriella said it slowly and bit her bottom lip. "But first we're going to the east verandah for food." She smiled. "Want to come?"

Oh, yes he did. Maybe he shouldn't. No. Certainly he shouldn't. *Bro Code. Emotionally unavailable.* Those were still facts of life. But they were only going to eat. What was the harm? "Lead on."

• • •

After they'd finished filling their plates, Jarrett wanted to find a table on the west verandah.

"It's a nice night and I'm hot," Jarrett said.

But Bryant vetoed it. "Then take off your jacket. I want to see what I'm eating."

And that was fine with Gabriella. She wanted to see, too—though she was more interested in looking at Bryant than her food. There was something about a man in a tuxedo—particularly this man in this tuxedo.

When Emile had needed to buy a tux for the first time, she had pushed him in the bespoke direction—and the result was impeccable. It had cost a fortune, but he would wear it for years.

Bryant would probably wear his for years, too, maybe without sending it to the dry cleaners. It was nice—if she had to guess, Ralph Lauren, but definitely off the rack. It fit him well, though not perfectly, so he wouldn't have bothered with having it tailored beyond having the pants hemmed. Yet, like his shaggy hair and the scar above his right eye, he wore it well. The whole look said, "I've got better things to do than get a $500 haircut or stand around while some tailor measures every inch of my body."

She wondered what those better things were.

"How about the winter parlor, then?" Jarrett asked. "Mrs. Davenport said there were tables in there."

"What?" Bryant quickly jerked around, and one of his miniature beef Wellingtons fell off his plate. "Whoa! Beef in a biscuit on the loose!" He caught it and put it back. "What did you say? Winner parlor? That's for us, for sure."

"Win-*ter*," Jarrett enunciated. "It's next to the music room."

"Hmm." Bryant shrugged. "Winter parlor. As opposed to what? Summer parlor? Beauty parlor? What does that even mean?"

"I'm hoping it means it's cooler in there," Jarrett said.

"I'm just guessing," Gabriella said, "but I would think it gets a lot of sun and has a fireplace so it's a nice place to sit on cold days."

"There are no cold days in Nashville," Bryant said. "These people don't know cold."

"That's for sure," Gabriella agreed.

"Tell me that when it hits zero in January," Jarrett said. "It might not last long, but zero is cold. I don't care where you're from." He led them through the door of the grand salon. "This way. We have to go back through here to get to the winter parlor."

There were not as many people on the dance floor now—no men and no women who weren't hockey wives. They were line dancing to "Wagon Wheel." The lead singer sounded remarkably like Darius Rucker and the dancers were remarkably in sync. Maybe they went to line dancing class together.

"I'm going to stop by the bar and get a beer," Bryant said.

"No you're not," Jarrett said. "There isn't any."

"No beer? What the hell? Who has a party without beer?"

"This is a fancy party. Mrs. Davenport didn't want beer. She wanted mixed drinks and wine served in nice glasses." Jarrett's tone of voice carried not a little measure of satisfaction, probably because he liked delivering facts whether he liked the information itself or not. Gabriella had no doubt the information was correct, though where he'd gotten it, she could not have guessed.

"No beer," Bryant marveled as if it was unfathomable. "No keg? You could put keg beer in glasses."

"You could," Jarrett agreed. "And some would. But others would have shot it straight into their mouths from the nozzle and—if we're going to be honest—at each other. Sparks and Scottie come to mind. Mrs. Davenport knows this. She's been down the liquor road with hockey players before." He headed for a door near the bar. "Through here."

"How do you know where you're going? Do you have a map of this house?" Bryant stepped back and allowed Gabriella to precede him into the room.

"I may not know east from west, but I notice my surroundings. It comes in handy."

The large room did, indeed, have not one, but two fireplaces and numerous windows, though the curtains were closed. It was furnished with a lot of ornate mahogany and multi-striped silk upholstery—not Gabriella's style, but pretty. Six tables for four were scattered throughout the room, far enough apart for private conversations—though only two of them were filled. Clearly, when entertaining, Mary Lou Davenport left nothing to chance. Jan and Krystal Voleck were sitting at a table with Mr. Klepacki and his wife. There were four young women at the other table who Gabriella took to be office staff.

"How about here?" Jarrett led them to a table in the far corner. "We can still hear the music."

"Because "Brick House" is my favorite," Bryant said.

Gabriella could only imagine what the dancing was like.

A waiter appeared immediately and placed two bottles of wine—one red and one white—on the table and poured water.

"Can I get you another martini, ma'am?" he asked.

"I'm fine," Gabriella said.

The waiter nodded. "Anything for you gentlemen?"

"Just water for me for now," Jarrett said. "Maybe later."

"I don't suppose it would do any good to ask for a beer?" Bryant said hopefully.

"No, sir." The waiter cast his eyes down like he'd failed. He was probably a pleaser, too. "We aren't serving beer tonight. Would you like a cocktail? Or can I pour you a glass of wine?"

Bryant sighed. "Can I get a Coke?"

"Of course."

"So you *can* take no for an answer," Gabriella said, "when it's not ice cream."

Bryant dropped his eyelids and gave her a smile that seemed to tell a secret—though she didn't know what that secret was. "I like ice cream better than beer," he said.

"I find that hard to believe," Jarrett said.

The waiter reappeared and set a glass before Bryant. "Your Coke, sir. Let me know if I can get you anything else."

Bryant sighed. "This is the worst party ever. I like to drink out of the can."

"Absolutely, the worst," Jarrett said. "If I had known there would be a plague of forced glass drinking, I would have stayed home. What could be next? Widespread cholera with bathroom privileges denied?"

"What's cholera?" Bryant asked.

"Something that requires bathroom privileges followed shortly by a coffin."

Gabriella laughed. This was proving to be fun. She had been silly to dread it. She didn't feel alone at all. More wedding festivities were bound to follow, and they would be fun, too, if she would allow it.

She poured herself a glass of red and gestured to Jarrett's wine glass. "Would you like some of this?"

"No, thank you," Jarrett said. "I've already had a scotch and water. I only have three drinks in an evening, and I drink two glasses of water between each one."

"Good thing we haven't been denied bathroom privileges. You must spend an extraordinary amount of time peeing." Bryant turned to Gabriella. "Of course, there's always the yard."

"No," Jarrett said. "If Mary Lou Davenport doesn't want us drinking out of cans at her party, I can just about imagine what she'd have to say about peeing in her yard. Besides, I wouldn't do that, anyway. It doesn't pay to get naked in public."

Bryant cut his eyes at Gabriella. "The Saint has a lot of rules."

Jarrett raised his water glass. "That why I'm The Saint. I never lose control of my faculties—or my pants."

Bryant looked somewhere over Gabriella's shoulder. "Well, if it's not the fair-haired child."

Gabriella didn't have to look behind her to know that Thor Eastrom was approaching. Though the big Swede had an abundance of very blond hair, he'd earned his nickname because he was a favorite of Pickens Davenport.

"Hello, fair-haired child," Bryant said. According to Emile, Thor didn't mind the nickname, but no one ever dared say it in earshot of Mr. Davenport or any of the coaches.

"Gabriella." Thor smiled at her. How could someone so charming off the ice be such a brute on? He was the Sound's enforcer and also, according to Emile, the most feared man in the NHL. He'd led the NHL in penalty minutes for the last eight years. "You're lovely. Do you mind if I join you?"

"Please. Our pleasure." *Only don't hit me.* What? That was a thought straight from Crazyville. Thor would never hit her. *And anyway, Bryant wouldn't let him.* What, again? And why Bryant and not Jarrett—Jarrett, who never fought on the ice and she had always felt completely at ease with? Angels above and demons below. She wasn't only a resident of Crazyville; she was the mayor.

"You didn't ask *our* permission to sit." Jarrett pointed to himself and Bryant.

"I don't care what you want." Thor set his plate down and sat in the empty chair. "I am only concerned with the lady's comfort." He smiled again, reached into the pockets of his tux, and came up with a Heineken in each hand.

"Hey, hey, hey!" Bryant said. "Where did you get that?"

"From the refrigerator in the kitchen." Thor produced a Swiss army knife from his pocket, popped out the bottle opener, and uncapped the bottles.

"Do you have free rein of this house?" Jarrett asked.

"Yes. Up to a point." He turned to Gabriella. "I have another. Would you like it, *lilla vän?*"

"No, but thank you." What had he called her? She hoped not a muddy pig, or something worse. But on the other hand, she didn't care.

"In that case, Swifty, do you want it?"

"You bet I do."

Thor passed him the beer. "You owe me."

"Sure thing," Bryant said. "I'll help you out next time you're getting your ass kicked on the ice."

"No help needed. Just give me first crack at that *skitstövel* Alvin when we face the Avalanche again in a few weeks."

"He's all yours," Bryant said. "I'd rather fight guys I like. I had enough of Alvin years ago."

Startled, Gabriella dropped her fork. "Guys you like? Are you serious?"

Without missing a beat, Bryant picked up her fork from the floor but handed her his. "I haven't used it yet. I'll eat with this one." He held up the one she'd dropped. "Fighting is part of the culture, part of the fun. There are no friends on the ice and—for the most part—no enemies off. You've seen guys fight and then hug and shout 'good job' to each other as they skate to the penalty box."

In fact, she had not. But she always looked away during fights.

Jarrett, who—as far as Gabriella knew—had never had a penalty for fighting, nodded. "There's a code. Everyone understands it. Not everyone lives by it, but everyone understands it. How do you not know this? You must have grown up at the rink."

"Emile's a goalie," Bryant said. "Always has been. She probably didn't grow up with a lot of hockey fighting talk. He's never had a fight on the ice in his life—probably had never had a fight at all until he knocked Cameron Snow into the middle of next week." He smiled at the memory.

Gabriella almost pointed out that she could speak for herself, but what Bryant said was true—though she hadn't known it until he voiced it.

Instead, she asked, "If you didn't want to fight that Avalanche player, why did you?"

"He had to." Thor paused and ate a bite of seafood pasta. "Alvin is a dirty player. He's been trying to get a rise out of Swifty for a long time. He finally found a way. You can't let your skill players get knocked around. It sends a bad message, makes you look soft—weak. And the goalie is absolutely off-limits. Nobody puts up with that. Alvin took a run at Emile. I wasn't on the ice. Swifty had to take it up. That's how it works."

That was food for thought. "So I assume there were no hugs," Gabriella said.

Bryant shook his head. "Not hardly. Usually, what happens on the ice stays on the ice, but not with that guy."

"I got it next time." Thor had a bloodthirsty look about him. "I've had enough."

Bryant finished off his Heineken. "I haven't had enough of this. Any chance you've got another one in your pocket?"

Thor laughed. "I'll get more when I finish eating."

Jarrett's head snapped up. "Here she comes. Don't look at her."

"Who?" Gabriella looked over her shoulder.

"Tradd." Jarrett looked at his plate, as did Bryant. Thor, however, did not. His ice blue eyes were high beams ahead.

Tradd Davenport led with her hips and marched toward them—on a mission with no time to waste. Gabriella hadn't noticed before, but Tradd wasn't dressed for this party. She wore black pants and a white silk blouse—not that it wasn't nice. On the contrary, the outfit was made of exquisite fabric and was a tailor-made perfect fit. You just got the idea that in an act of defiance, she'd refused to wear party attire—which meant probably she didn't want to be here.

She stopped at Gabriella's shoulder and looked across the table at Thor. "There you are."

"Here I am," he agreed and took another bite of his pasta.

Tradd let her gaze lightly pass over Gabriella and the other two men. "Hello."

They returned the greeting, but Bryant and Jarrett still didn't look up.

Then her eyes settled on the Heineken bottles. "Hey! Where did you get that beer? Mama didn't want to serve beer."

"She didn't," Thor said. "I served myself." He gestured to Bryant. "And Swifty."

"You could have put it in a glass," she said.

"Why?" Thor asked. "The bottle is glass."

"You are a philistine," Tradd said.

"No. I am a Swede." Thor smiled. "Did you want something, Tradd, or are you here to be the beer police?"

"No time to arrest you now. Here." She handed Thor a key. "It's almost time for the toast. Daddy wants you to let the caterers in the wine cellar and lock up behind them. He doesn't trust them."

"My pleasure." He rose. "I wanted to get up and get more beer anyway."

"Whatever. It's on you if Mama catches you."

"Are you going to tell on me?" His expression told just how much he cared—not at all.

Tradd shook her head and rolled her eyes. "Like I have time to be bothered with that. I've got to go. I have to check on the sparkling cider for the pregnant people and alcoholics." And she walked away with Thor behind her.

"Is she gone?" Jarrett asked.

"Yes," Gabriella said. "What was all that 'don't look at her' about?"

Bryant and Jarrett looked up and resumed eating. "The speech," Bryant said. "It's short, but intense. We all got it when we signed, and just in case we forget, Davenport repeats it every season when training camp opens."

"It goes like this." Jarrett made his face go even more no nonsense than usual. "'We are a family, but only up to a point. I have a daughter. You will, no doubt, run into her from time to time. She is off-limits. If she speaks to you, be polite. Otherwise, don't talk to her. Don't look at her. If you touch her, you'd better be jerking her out of the path of a speeding car or some other like situation that would save her from certain death. Failure to comply will result in a nullified contract regardless of your popularity with the fans or your prowess on the ice. Am I clear?'"

Bryant nodded. "Then we all mutter 'yes, sir' like bad Cub Scouts."

"Some of the guys are offended," Jarrett said, "like they think he feels like she's better than us. I don't think that's true. He just doesn't want a messy situation."

Gabriella nodded. "Emile made me promise when I was thirteen years old that I'd never date a hockey player. He said he didn't need that kind of trouble." *And neither do I.* Though the little exchange she'd had with Bryant on the porch earlier had felt more like a date than any she'd had in a very long time—or maybe ever. If he knew her thoughts, Bryant would probably find that hilarious. But he never would know.

Bryant narrowed his eyes. "Does your arm hurt?"

Gabriella had not been aware she was rubbing her arm. "Oh." She picked up her fork again. "No. Just a habit."

"So you've never dated a hockey player?" Jarrett asked.

"Never. Emile doesn't ask much of me."

"Emile's not wrong," Bryant said. "It can get messy."

So Bryant agreed with Emile. That was good—excellent, in fact. He wouldn't ask. She wouldn't go. There would be no mess. Best news she'd had all night.

Bryant continued to spew forth wisdom. "A couple of seasons ago, the Penguins had to trade Vasiliev when he started dating Clay Dempsey's ex-wife. Talk about a shitstorm. Nobody needs that locker room."

"Did she go with him?" Jarrett asked.

"Who? Dempsey's wife?" Bryant looked incredulous. "No. Of course not. He ended up alone, freezing his ass off in Calgary—all for nothing. So no one who doesn't want to be banished looks at Tradd."

"Apparently, Thor is allowed to look at Tradd," Gabriella said.

"But only that," Jarrett said. "Don't kid yourself. Even the fair-haired child wouldn't survive that."

"Not that he'd go there," Bryant said. "Or even want to. That is one high maintenance woman."

Gabriella laughed. "That's the thing with men. You all want a woman with particular trappings—the look, the intelligence, the personality, the ease in social situations. Then you're surprised when she has minimal expectations."

Jarrett got a blank look on his face. "I don't even know what you're talking about."

But Bryant studied her intensely with his eyes half closed. "How about you, Gabriella? Do you have 'minimal expectations'?" He spoke the last two words as if they were made of cotton candy and dipped caramel.

Oh, yes, I do. I want to be looked at the way you're looking at me right now. Choppy hair, pansy blue eyes, and a perfectly imperfect tux are only icing on the cake, but very sweet icing. Approved occupations: librarians, accountants, lion tamers, astronauts, chimney sweeps ....

She started at her thoughts. Good thing she didn't have a chance to answer, or she might have spoken the words aloud. That wouldn't have done anybody any good.

But Mary Lou Davenport saved her when she stepped into the room and rang a little silver bell.

"I'm sure y'all will forgive me for interrupting. If you'll please join us in the grand salon, it's time to toast Amy and Emile." Then she smiled at Gabriella and stretched out her hand. "Gabriella, darling, come with me. Emile's been asking after you. Family should be near one another for moments like these."

Elated, Gabriella bounced up, tucked her napkin under the edge of her plate, and joined Mrs. Davenport. It was going to be all right. It really was. Her lapse in good sense was over.

Was it bad manners for the groom's sister to give a shower for the bride? Seems like she'd heard that somewhere. She'd have to look into it.

CHAPTER NINE

Watching Gabriella Charbonnet leave a room might be one of life's finest moments, maybe only surpassed by watching her reenter it. Inasmuch as Bryant was an advocate of the "Bro Code," there was nothing wrong with looking at sisters as long as that was all you did. Of course, that had nothing to do with Gabriella herself. Watching her was like looking at Michelangelo's *David*—though not that exactly. Bryant wasn't really into statues of naked men, but art. Gabriella was art on two feet.

It was beyond him why Jarrett didn't seem to notice. "Coming?" Jarrett asked.

"Go ahead. I'll catch up. I need to pee." A lie. What he *needed* was to watch Gabriella walk away until she was out of sight. After all, you didn't go to the Louvre and glance at the Mona Lisa as you walked by.

"Nice party."

Packi. At least he hadn't appeared out of thin air this time—only from across the room.

"Nice for no beer. Hello, Mrs. Packi. Packi." He'd learned his lesson his first year with the Sound about speaking to Mrs. Packi first. Packi didn't like it if you didn't speak to her first, and you had damned sure better not ignore her if you wanted your skates sharpened—and you had better not call her Charlotte.

"How are you, dear?" She placed a hand on Bryant's arm. "Please excuse me. Krystal was having trouble with her dress. I'm going to see if I can help her."

"I'll meet you inside," Packi told her and Bryant noticed that Packi watched his wife walk away—and that Bryant noticed wasn't lost on Packi.

When she was out of sight, Packi tuned back to Bryant. "Not a bad pastime—watching a woman walk away. That is, if she's the right woman and you know she's going to come walking back to you."

"A damn sight better than looking at a grave." *Especially one with a baby bear hockey player on it.*

Bryant's heart skipped a beat and then went into overdrive. Had those things really gone through his head and come out of his mouth? He hadn't been thinking about that at all. No. Locked up and put away boxes weren't supposed to be able to get out on their own.

There were those on the team who said Packi was never surprised. But Packi's face was living proof that he *could* be surprised. Neither man spoke for few beats—it felt like an hour.

"Rough day?" Packi asked in a low whisper.

"Here and there." Bryant hadn't expected the *here.* He slammed the box closed again and double locked it this time. There was a crowd gathering in the grand salon, but Gabriella seemed to be lost among the people. How could that be?

"Some days are like that," Packi said. "You know, like when you're injured?"

Bryant shook his head. "I'm not injured."

Packi closed his eyes for a moment. "Not now. When you've been injured in the past."

"I've never been injured to amount to anything."

"Hypothetically. Boy, can you not just go with it?"

"Okay. Hypothetically." He tried to imagine it. "Where I am I injured?"

Packi shook his head. "I don't know. Your groin muscle. Let's say you pulled a groin muscle."

Bryant doubted that would happen since he was always careful to stretch, but okay. "I hear that's rough."

"Exactly," Packi said. "And if you rush getting back on the ice, you're likely to make it worse, if not reinjure yourself entirely."

Not sure where this was going, Bryant nodded.

"On the other hand, you can wait too long. That's easy to do because you're afraid of reinjury. So there comes a time when you just have to do it—or try. Have you heard 'if you rest, you rust'?"

"A rusty groin would be a terrible thing to have, don't you know?"

Packi laughed a little. "So would a rusty heart."

What was all this talk of rusty groins and hearts? He looked into the grand salon again. He could see Emile, but no Gabriella. But wait. There she was. Damn, she was beyond beautiful. And that dress. The sight of her made him calm, made the locked box fade into nothingness.

"We'd better get in there," Packi said.

"You got that right." *So* right. Bryant was already walking that way, walking toward Gabriella, away from graves with baby bear hockey players.

"And, Bryant? How you go about something is almost as important as doing it."

"You bet."

Who knew Packi was such a romantic? If only he wasn't emotionally unavailable, Gabriella was just who he'd want to take a chance with. But he was, so it wasn't possible. Still, he didn't have to be emotionally available to talk to her. Plus talking wasn't against the Bro Code.

He moved through the crowd.

• • •

Everything was lovely, and getting lovelier by the second—lovely enough to block out Bryant.

"Gabriella!" Emile and Amy held their arms out to her as she and Mrs. Davenport approached. It felt so good to be in Emile's familiar embrace—and Amy's, too. Her smell and touch were new, but were becoming more and more familiar.

"I am starving," Amy said. "But I survived the receiving line. You don't have a cookie in your purse, do you?"

"No. But I know where we can get you some miniature beef Wellingtons and seafood pasta."

"We three will sit down together and have some food soon, *non?*" Emile asked. "When the toast is over, I think we must dance, but then we will eat and visit together."

"Sounds perfect," Gabriella said.

"Here you are, ladies." Pickens Davenport appeared with a waiter at his elbow and handed crystal flutes of Champagne, first to Amy, Mary Lou, and Gabriella. Then he gave one to Emile and took one for himself.

Amy said, "Emile, don't forget. We aren't supposed to toast ourselves."

Emile raised his glass. "I toast you. I will toast you for the rest of my life, *chérie.*"

Pickens laughed. "I never thought I'd see this day. Did you, Gabriella?"

"I had hoped." And she had. But she'd learned something. Hoping in the abstract was very different than facing reality, because the reality was different from what she had expected— good but different. And the reality could have been terrible. There was terrible in this room.

Inasmuch as Gabriella thought everyone was too hard on Krystal Voleck, it was easy to believe that she had taken full advantage of Jan's youth and sweet nature. Word was that she hadn't made any friends in the front office when Jan's contract had come up for renewal and she'd coerced him into making unreasonable demands.

And Gabriella just plain disliked Mike Webber's girlfriend, Wyoming. (Yes. Wyoming.) She was sneaky and a mean gossip. Sharon Orlov swore the woman had not only changed her name, but she was also a habitual and chronic liar, always making up outlandish things that had absolutely no purpose—like she used to teach chemistry and had been a massage therapist for the New York Yankees. Gabriella didn't doubt that she was a liar. Not only was Sharon usually right, but she was also like a dog with a bone she couldn't put down and had spent an extraordinary amount of time fact-checking the things Wyoming said. She'd shown Gabriella her spreadsheet.

There was no reason to fact-check what happened to Sparks Champagne; it was no secret. His wife had been nice and well liked by everyone, but with absolutely no warning, she'd left Sparks for a music producer. Now, Sparks was a walking broken heart, running wild with Robbie MacTavish.

Amy would never do that to Emile.

"Where's Tradd?" Pickens asked his wife. "Should we start without her?"

"She's making sure no Champagne gets on the cider tray," Mary Lou said. "We've summoned everyone in here, so we should go ahead."

Pickens directed them in front of the portable stage. "Amy, Emile, stand in the middle," he said. "I'll stand here by Amy. Mary Lou—on the other side of Emile." He smiled at Gabriella. "And don't you leave us. Stand on the other side of me. And don't run off when we're done. We'll want pictures."

"Do you want my bell, Pickens?" Mary Lou held out her silver bell.

"Thank you, honey, but I don't have my man card on me to surrender." He picked up a microphone from the stage, tapped the side of his glass with it, and the chatter in the room ceased.

"Mary Lou and I would like to thank you for coming here tonight to celebrate Emile's engagement to Amy Callahan. We gather tonight as a family—not only the Sound family, but with Emile and his beautiful sister Gabriella." Pickens turned and smiled at Gabriella. "We celebrate the family that Emile and Gabriella will be forming with Amy." Amy reached across Pickens and squeezed Gabriella's hand. Emile put an arm around Amy and blew Gabriella an air kiss. This was truly one of life's sweetest moments. How could she have thought she wasn't part of this?

Pickens continued, "It seems that up until now, Emile has been as successful at keeping women at bay as he is at keeping the puck out of the Sound goal." Laughter drifted through the room. "Though I'm not sure how Emile managed to capture Amy's heart, we are so glad that he did. For all that Emile has meant to us for his talent and commitment to this team, he is to be commended even more for bringing this lovely lady into the Sound family— which it will always be, regardless of changes that time might bring about." Gabriella wondered if that was in reference to whether the team would be sold to Massachusetts. In this moment, that didn't scare her so much.

Pickens lifted his glass. "Now let's raise—"

But just then, there was a commotion and what must have been twenty people entered the room.

Amy gasped and ran toward them, with Emile right behind her.

What the hell? Noise filled the room, some from people who were also wondering what the hell, but most from Emile, Amy, and the newcomers expressing delight.

Pickens laughed and said into the microphone, "Ladies and gentlemen, welcome Amy's family."

Her family. Of course. Gabriella hadn't even wondered why they weren't here. If she'd thought about it all, she would have assumed they'd made the same decision Johanna and Paul had—it was too far when they were coming for the wedding next month.

"They flew in to surprise Amy and Emile, but missed their connection in Atlanta. Haven't we all been there?" *Surprise?* Why did Emile and Amy need to be surprised? And even so, why had it had to be a surprise to her as well? But she knew the answer. It hadn't, but no one had thought about telling her.

Pickens moved closer to Mary Lou and put an arm around her. "Cliff, Amy's father, called and said to carry on, that they would get here when they could. I promised him we would party late to make up for what Atlanta did to them." Applause—weak, weak applause. There ought to be a rule. No clapping when holding glassware. "We are so glad they made it in time for the toast. Could someone get these people some Champagne?"

Waiters came out of the woodwork and the newcomers had flutes in less than two minutes. But Emile and Amy didn't come back to the front of the room. They stayed in the bosom of Amy's family. There was still a good bit of hugging and handshaking going on.

"To Amy and Emile. To family." Pickens raised his glass, as did Gabriella from where she stood beside him—forgotten. Again, with the weak, flute-impaired applause. Wasn't that as bad as a feeble handshake?

Pickens nodded to the band. "We're going to let our happy couple lead off this dance and then invite their family to join in while the rest of us honor them by enjoying the music. I have it on good authority that this is one of Amy's favorite songs. It's also appropriate because Emile must have done something right—though we still don't know what that was."

The band struck up "Must be Doing Something Right," and everyone stepped to the edges of the room to make way for Emile to lead Amy to the dance floor.

Gabriella found a place in the corner completely against the wall.

Emile tenderly ran his knuckles down Amy's cheek and Gabriella could practically see the sighs floating above the heads of the women in the room. And why not? She felt like sighing herself. Emile was handsome, Amy was pretty, and they were both so clearly drop-dead in love—so together, so one.

Ever the showman, after the first chorus, Emile swung Amy out, brought her back to him, and motioned the family—Amy's family, soon to be *his* family—to the floor. What was that old saying? "A son's a son until he takes a wife, but a daughter's a daughter all her life." No son/mother relationship here, of course, but the meaning was clear—clear and true.

Amy's family filed onto the floor in pairs. She counted. She'd been wrong. Not twenty, fourteen. Seven couples. The parents and grandparents were easy to pick out. There was a young man, who Gabriella took to be Amy's brother, dancing with an older woman, maybe the other grandmother, maybe an aunt or great aunt. As for the others—Gabriella had no idea. They were of an age with Amy, so they were probably cousins. For sure, one of them would be her co-honor attendant.

She wasn't going to start feeling sorry for herself again, even if the whole family except for her was dancing. She *was* family so she had, therefore, been invited to dance. It wasn't their fault she didn't have anyone to dance with. So no more mayor of Crazyville. No destitute Regency-era maiden aunt with three hand-me-down dresses and a pair of mismatched knitting needles that she had to make do with. Utter silliness.

Emile loved her and would never leave her behind. Amy not only loved her, they were friends.

But things had changed, she had no one to dance with, and she was sad. Even though she was pretty sure there would be no pictures and no sitting down to dinner for the three of them like they'd arranged before the toast, Gabriella couldn't leave the party. Soon she would mingle and smile. *"I'm Emile's sister. So glad you to meet you,"* she'd say.

But for now, she wanted to be somewhere else—just for a little while before someone noticed she wasn't on the floor with the rest of the family of the bride and groom. There was a door at the back of the room not far from where she stood. She'd take her chances with it.

But as the chorus ended, a hand closed around her elbow from behind and slid down her arm to her hand. There was something about the warmth and pressure of that hand. She knew it was the same hand that had touched her shoulder before on the porch; she knew it was Bryant before he turned her toward him. There was too much fire in that touch for it to be anyone else.

He looked at her the way every woman wants to be looked at least once, and there wasn't a trace of pity there. "Dance with me."

She answered him by moving into his arms and letting him move her to the floor.

CHAPTER TEN

Bryant couldn't believe his luck.

He would not have expected to see Gabriella standing against the wall watching the dancers. Every other man in this room was stupid. Didn't they know this was a dance for Emile's and Amy's families and Gabriella didn't have a partner? He couldn't get to her fast enough.

She moved in his arms like they'd been practicing for *Dancing With the Stars*. But it was more than just good dancing; there was a warm buzz between them. He felt it the second he touched her. Was that what people meant by chemistry?

She looked sad and he wanted to make her smile. "This is the sexiest song ever written. I know because five backup singers and a kangaroo told me so."

"A kangaroo? Really?" She blessed him with that smile.

"Don't kangaroos dance? Isn't dancing that thing they do?"

"I don't think so. At least none I know. I think *boxing* is that thing they do."

"Yeah, that's it. Must have been a dancing bear."

"I thought as much." She nodded and the light bounced off little diamond-like gems in her hair. He hadn't noticed that before. "Your head twinkles."

"It's the jeweled pins holding my braids in place."

He twirled her under his arm and pulled her in closer. The song demanded it.

"Jeweled pins, huh? You ought to let a guy think your head twinkles naturally. Never give away your secrets."

"I don't." She leaned her head back and looked up at him, though she didn't have to look far. He'd never had much opinion on the height of a woman until now. Now, he liked tall—especially when dancing. "But the pins weren't a secret."

"No?"

"Do you have secrets, Swifty?" That was the first time she'd ever called him by his hockey nickname, and it was wrapped in a bit of a laugh. The warm buzz got buzzier. She felt it, too. Every once in a blue moon, he was sure of something and, for this blue moon, this was it.

"Secrets?" He leaned in and whispered in her ear. "You bet. So many. You have no idea."

"Is that right? I don't see any jeweled pins." And she ran her hand slowly through his hair. "No. Don't feel any either."

And just like that, he went from soft to raging, pounding hard like this was an erection he'd been saving all his life. He hadn't had time to distance his pelvis from hers. There was no way she didn't know, but she would probably pretend she didn't.

But he was wrong and she didn't move away, either. "Well, hello," she said.

What a woman. He shook his head and smiled. "I am a bad, bad boy."

"But an incredible dancer." She moved in closer. "Did you have lessons?"

"Hardly. Unless you count getting passed around by the older girls at the annual smelt feed the spring I turned fifteen because I'd gotten some height on me."

She raised one eyebrow and tilted her head. "I doubt it was only because you were tall if you've always been this pretty."

She might have a point. He hadn't lost his virginity to Hope Zielinski in that VFW hall cloakroom, but she'd taught him some things that still served him well today.

Bro Code or not, he'd like to show them to Gabriella. And that wouldn't have anything to do with emotional availability.

The song would be ending soon. Bryant felt a little panic. He didn't want to let her go, but if he didn't, he might never. Gabriella was the kind of woman a guy would think about for the rest of his life after he'd settled for someone else. He didn't want to be that man—which meant he ought to run.

But on the other hand …

"Song's almost over." She sounded wistful—as wistful as he felt.

He locked Emile and the Bro Code in a box and put it on the shelf with every other bad or distasteful thing that he'd ever encountered.

He ran his knuckles down her cheek and she sighed, all sweet-like. "It doesn't have to be for us."

"I don't date hockey players. Ever."

"I'm not asking you for a date. And I'm emotionally unavailable. Seven good women and a puppy dog told me so."

"Are you physically available?"

He twirled her to give himself time to process. "Is that what you want?" he said close to her ear.

The song moved into the chorus. It would be the last.

Gabriella leaned her head back and looked at him through half-closed eyes. "I have a feeling you might do something right."

"You still haven't answered me." He moved his hand to the small of her back. "What do you want, Gabriella?" If she was just flirting, fine. He'd walk away, no regrets. But he didn't think she was.

"I'm not looking for a man. I'm looking for a friend." She moved the hand on his shoulder up to his neck. "And if that friend happened to be the most beautiful man in the room, a moment in time with him wouldn't be amiss."

He laughed and hugged her to him as the song faded away. "And this is what I would say to the most beautiful woman in the room: It won't be a moment. I'm only Swifty on the ice."

• • •

The music was over. The correct thing to do would be to step away from Bryant, applaud, and let him escort her off the floor.

But just then, Gabriella wasn't into correct. From the moment Bryant rescued her, she'd felt something warm and wanting. Despite her flirting, she wasn't sure she would have gone through with it—*it* being what she was about to go through with—but when Bryant had stroked her cheek the same way Emile had stroked Amy's, any contemplation she'd had was over.

That sweet, tender gesture had made her feel a different kind of longing—not to be alone, not to be sad. It had made her want some semblance of what her brother had now—even if it was brief and imitation.

"This way." Bryant took her hand and moved slowly toward the spot where he'd found her. She wondered if he was going to leave her there—but she didn't need to wonder long. "Through this door," he said quietly and headed toward the same door that she'd been going to use for her escape route earlier.

"Where does it go?" For all she knew, it might open into a fiery pit of hell. The Davenports had everything else—grand salon, multiple parlors, music room, verandahs for every direction. Why not their own private hell?

"No idea where it goes." But he surged on as if he did. "The Saint probably knows, even if he couldn't tell if it was south or west. Should we find him and ask?" He tilted his head until his hair fell in his eyes. "Or should we just go with it, then? Huh? Just you and me?"

"That door could be a trap. There could be a ledge on the other side. We could be tricked into falling into a dungeon."

He laughed and moved them closer to the door. "I've got to say, I'd be all right with that if it was a private dungeon—because Gabriella Charbonnet, I can't wait to kiss you." He brought his face very close to hers, and for a moment, she thought he wasn't going to wait. "Have you ever done anything crazy, Gabriella—really insane? Like go through a door without knowing if it was bedroom or a kitchen?"

"I don't think houses like this have bedrooms on the ground floor."

He smiled squeezed her hand. "Then I guess we'd better find some stairs." And he opened the door.

Not a ledge with a dungeon or a fiery pit. Just the dining room, with servants replenishing the buffet. The hungry hordes couldn't be far behind. There were also two huge floor to ceiling china cabinets full of crystal—hundreds of pieces.

"Beef Wellington? Highball glass?" Bryant asked as he rushed her toward another door—one that led to a wide sun porch, that led to the outside, which is where they landed before Gabriella could catch her breath.

She almost told him she couldn't leave the party, had to stay, meet Amy's family, be charming. All that was true, but she could do it later. Pickens had said the party would go late.

But there on a dark terrace with more than a little nip in the air, Bryant folded her against him and his mouth was on hers.

She got lost in his mouth, lost in his arms, lost in everything about him. She wanted him. Not with a forever kind of want. Probably not even with a tomorrow kind of a want. But not just a sex-tonight kind of want, either. This was different. She'd wanted men before—wanted sex, though it had been longer ago than she cared to consider. It wasn't just about the warmth in her loins, though there was plenty of that and—angels above and demons below—this man could kiss, oh yes, he could.

There was a steady, familiar, belonging feeling to being in his arms—all backlit with fire.

He lifted his mouth from hers. "It's time to go." His voice was shaky.

"Where?"

"No idea, but we're going there." With that, he took her hand and rushed her toward a door across the way that led inside. "If I were building a house and I put the dining room there"—he seemed to be talking to himself—"I'd put the kitchen *here.*" He opened the door. "Yes! Stairs."

He pulled her inside and they were in a tiny anteroom with a staircase and built-in glass case after case of every kind of drinking vessel known to man.

Bryant noticed, too. "Mary Lou Davenport sure does love her some glasses."

"I can see why she didn't want us drinking out of cans and bottles at this party. She has to justify owning all this crystal. These probably aren't even her favorites—stuck off like this under the stairs."

"The Harry Potter of barware?" He pulled her to him and kissed her again. Now she'd had an outside kiss and an inside kiss—and they both had turned her inside out.

Gabriella pulled away. "The kitchen's right through there. I can hear the pots and pans banging. Do you want me to sneak in there and get you a beer?"

"Tempting, but no. I want you to go up those stairs with me. Come on." He took her hand and in a flash they were halfway up.

"Wait!" Gabriella said.

"What?"

"This is the part where I'm supposed to say, what if we get caught and that we aren't supposed to go upstairs without being invited, let alone in the house of the man who owns your team."

He smiled—part amused, part sexy, all "come and get me."

"So, are you going to say any of that?" He smoothed some escaped wisps of hair off her face.

Not a chance. She felt his smile reflected on her own face. "No. I'm not. I just wanted you to know—"

"That you've never done this kind of thing before?"

She laughed. "I really haven't. Not that I expect you believe it."

"Oh, I do believe it." He kissed her again. Stairs kiss. Just as good. "But what right would I have to give a damn if you had?"

The door opened below and they heard footsteps. It was a good thing they both had legs long enough to take two steps at a time or they would have gotten caught. Finally, they were upstairs in a long hallway.

Bryant put his hand on the first doorknob he saw.

"Bryant?"

"What?" He looked over his shoulder at her.

"Not the master bedroom. That would be taking things too far."

"Agreed." He opened the door and looked inside. "I don't think we have anything to worry about." He pulled Gabriella inside and locked the door. He was right. The room was pretty, but not overly plush and on the small side. Definitely not a master. "No way Mary Lou would sleep in here. Not a glass in sight."

Gabriella dissolved in laughter and held her arms out to him.

CHAPTER ELEVEN

All kind of sloppy, corny thoughts went through Bryant's mind when he looked at Gabriella.

Goddess among women. Eyes like the sky. Skin like silk. Lips like— well, he didn't know about that one. Maybe it was a good thing he'd been more interested in his slap shot and right hook than tenth grade poetry. If he'd preserved any more poetic thoughts, his brain might turn to rose petals and Cupid poop. The puzzling thing was, why had he only noticed her lately? It wasn't like she'd turned from a gawky fourteen-year-old to a woman who'd come into her own. She'd been a woman five years ago.

She took a step closer to him. "We don't have a lot of time. We'll be missed."

"Right." And she was. "I'm going to touch you." He ran his hands up her arms, over her shoulders, and cupped her cheeks. She looked surprised. No doubt, she'd expected him to touch her in more interesting places—and he would. He'd get to that. But it had been a very long time since he'd made love to a woman he'd taken the time to touch. "I want to touch you in your public places."

She laughed and placed a hand over his. "I have public places?"

No. Come to think of it she didn't. Public places would imply that she had places that anyone could touch. Unacceptable.

"Only as opposed to private places." He lifted her chin and kissed her—gently teasing her lips and drawing her tongue into his mouth as he stroked the back of her neck and her arms. It had never struck him before that kissing was such an intimate act. She tasted like red wine, which he'd never liked until now. Just when he thought he couldn't become more aroused, she let out a low moan and his penis set a personal best record. He opened his mouth wider because he wanted more, wanted to give her more—and he did for a long time, until breathing wasn't optional.

"If this hockey thing doesn't work out for you," Gabriella said against his mouth, "you could give kissing lessons. If kissing were an Olympic sport, you'd be the winner. Then you could go on to coach other winners."

"You're good for a guy's ego." He reached into her hair and started searching for those little twinkle pins. He was going to take that hair down.

"Don't take my hair down," she said.

"Why not?"

"Because I can't fix it again. I had it done at a salon. We have to go back to the party, so you can't take it down unless you know how to put it back up. Do you?"

"Yes. I do. I can fix it up way better than before." He put his hand on either side of his head and wiggled his fingers. "I can put in flashing lights—got some in my pocket for such emergencies."

They laughed together and hugged, friendly and sweet-like. He kissed her brow.

"So no hair taking down?" he asked.

"Afraid not. How about if I let you take off my dress?"

"You would win the Olympics of best ideas." Suddenly, he couldn't wait to get her naked—naked and next to him. There was a time and place for public touching, but that time had passed. He reached behind her, expecting a zipper, but found buttons—tiny buttons and about four million of them. He leaned his head on her shoulder. "The maker of this dress has true hatred in his soul for me. So I'm guessing if you won't let me take your hair down, tearing your dress off is completely off the table."

"I'll do it." She reached behind her and in a matter of seconds, her dress was in a puddle around her feet on the floor.

"How—" He was going to ask how she had undone the buttons from hell so fast, but the sight before him left him speechless.

She was oblivious. "There's a zipper hidden under the buttons," she said—just stood there talking like the mere mortal that she could not possibly be.

Apart from getting it off as fast as possible, he had never concerned himself with an opinion on women's underwear before, but he'd never seen any like this. It was a fair bet it hadn't come from an outlet mall like the one his mother and sisters shopped at for school shoes, Easter hats, first communion clothes, and the like.

No. Gabriella's underwear was that watered-down grape Kool-Aid color like her dress, but see-through and lacy. The bra was low cut and covered the lower half of her small, perfect breasts, and the thong was little more than a triangle of lace and some strings. None of that was unusual. But above the thong, just below her belly button, sat a wide band of lace with ribbons and hooks that attached to her stockings. The whole outfit sparkled like magic, but it was probably just the little beads sewn onto the lace.

The sight of it all sent his cock into a frenzy, not unlike a rabid dog being chased with a water hose. That dog wanted out of his pants.

Her spectacular body would have been more than sufficient to drive a man to beg, but it was mostly that lacy stocking holder that put him into a completely senseless state of mind. If he wasn't careful, he'd start drooling. Women didn't wear stockings anymore—or if they did, they wore panty hose, the singularly most unattractive item anyone could wear. But this lace thing— that was a different story.

Garter belt. That's what it was. No wonder he couldn't think of what it was called. Hockey players wore garter belts to hold their socks up, but this was no Bauer or Shock Doctor version.

He let his eyes drift to her legs. What legs—miles and miles of perfect legs, plenty to wrap around him with some to spare. The parts he'd already seen—knees, ankles, calves—had made promises about the secret parts. And those promises were well kept.

His voice was shaky and he was sweaty. "I have to say, I never saw anything like you in the VFW cloakroom in St. Sebastian, Michigan."

"No?" She stepped closer and brushed the hair off his face. "I don't have a twin in St. Sebastian, Michigan?"

"Girl, there's no equal to you in any VFW hall on any planet." He ran his hand over the garter belt. It felt soft from the silk and rough from the lace and beads. "Do these little beads hurt you?"

"No."

And he could stand it no more. He grabbed her against him, filling his mouth with hers, grinding her pelvis against his. Oh, yes. A tall girl had her advantages. They fit together like Legos.

"I want you, Bryant Taylor," she whispered again his ear. "I want you more than I've ever wanted anything in my life."

"That's a lot of want." When he cupped her breast, he was shaking like a fifteen-year-old virgin man-child who'd just been given the go-ahead from the girl he'd just been hoping to dry hump. "You are the most beautiful woman in this world, or any world."

"That's a lot of beauty."

"Uh huh." That was all he could say with his mouth on the soft part of her neck.

She sighed, shuddered, and stroked the same spot on his neck. "How did you know about that spot? Perfect ... perfect."

His hand drifted from one breast to the other, stroking lightly until her nipples were hard. Only then did he bend his mouth to suckle her there through the silk.

She moaned and reached for the buttons on his shirt. "Tell me again why we looked for a bedroom and not a closet."

"Because it has a bed."

"Yet, we're standing up and you're still wearing everything you started out in."

"You don't have to tell me twice." He picked her up, laid her across the bed, and stripped completely while she watched.

"Oh, my." She smiled with appreciation.

"I work out." He found the condom in his wallet and threw it on the nightstand.

She smiled. "You're good at it."

"I'm going to take your fancy little bra and panties off you now. But will you leave on the rest of it?"

She laughed. "The garter belt and stockings?"

"That would be the ones."

"If you won't mess up my hair."

He gave her an evil little look. "Which hair?" And he stripped off her thong. That's when he discovered the only hair she had was on her head.

She burst out laughing. "If you could see the look on your face!"

Then he was entwined with her, skin on skin, silky legs against his, her hands everywhere, stroking, urging him on. He did his best to return the favor, and from the sounds she made, he wasn't doing a half-bad job. He almost lost it completely when she took his cock in her hand and stroked it against her garter belt.

"I might have a garter belt fetish," he said into her ear. "Yes! Do that again."

"Really? I could take it off and leave you alone with it."

"Hell, no!"

"Then it's not a fetish."

He grabbed her hips and stroked his penis between her legs.

"Bryant! Bryant!" She pulled away from him and pushed his hands away when he tried to stroke her there. "All this is good—really, really good. But I really need it. I don't want to come until you're inside."

"Thanks be to the patron saint of hockey and all his buddies."
He rolled to his back and pulled her to straddle him. "I didn't
want to be Swifty."

"I need you to be Swifty. Do you want me like this?"

"I want you any way—every way. But you said not to mess
up your hair." He stroked her now bare breasts. "Hand me the
condom, please."

"My pleasure."

"That's the idea."

After he was sheathed, she stroked him lightly. "Let me do it."
And she guided him inside.

This was life's perfect moment—joined, tight, and pounding.
He would have said so if he could have spoken. Then he discovered
that wasn't life's perfect moment. That happened when she began
to roll her hips.

"I'm going to come very fast." Her words were punctuated with
breathlessness. And just then she did—she cried out, bore down
on him, shuddered. Determined to make it the Stanley Cup of all
orgasms for her, he stroked her breasts, thighs, and belly—and the
garter belt and tops of her stockings. That was for himself.

Finally, she calmed. He pulled her down until they were chest
to chest, but willed himself not to come, to continue thrusting.
He kissed the tender spot below her ear. "Come again?"

"No," she whispered. "Can't stand anymore. Can't ride Niagara
Falls twice. Come, Bryant. Come for me."

"I try not to disappoint a lady." He just managed to get that
out before he had the orgasm of his life.

It would have been poetic to say they lay together, entwined for
a long time. It would have also been a lie. Usually, Bryant was the
first up and gone, but not this time.

"Do we have to go back to the party?" he asked.

Gabriella had already found her underwear and was reaching
for her dress. "I do. That's a decision you need to make for

yourself." She backed up to the bed where he was still naked and reclined. "Here. Zip me up."

He sat on the side of the bed and reached for her zipper with one hand and her hip beneath her dress with the other. He was already stirring again. He'd just part his legs a little more and press her lovely, lovely bottom there …

"Stop that!" She pulled away. "Do you *want* to be the object of a search party?"

"No one would look for me."

"Do you want *me* to be object of a search party? Because right now, that's the same thing, and eventually Emile is going to wonder where I've gotten off to."

The Bro Code jumped out of its locked box and slapped him in the face. She was right.

She dug in her little handbag and pulled out a lipstick.

"Wait, Gabriella." He got up and gathered his clothes. "We're going to do this right. I'll go first. You follow in five minutes. Just let me get dressed."

"Why you first? I'm already dressed."

"Because I'll go find Emile. If he's looking for you, I'll defuse it—tell him you had a dress malfunction while we were dancing and went somewhere to fix it."

She looked surprised. "That's actually a good idea."

"I have some sometimes." *This, tonight, in this room for an example.*

Once dressed, he went to the mirror and ran his hands through his hair.

"Do you want my comb so you can fix your hair?" Gabriella asked.

He smiled at her in the reflection. "This *is* how I fix it." On the way to the door, he stopped and stroked her cheek. "Five minutes. Don't go back the way we came. That's sneaky looking. Go down the main staircase like you own the place."

"Right." She hesitated. "How do I get there?"

Good question. "I don't know exactly, but go the opposite way that we came. South. That should get you there."

She smiled, amused. "Jarrett would never get out of here."

"Jarrett would never be somewhere he wasn't supposed to be." He couldn't help himself; he touched her face one more time. "See you down there." As he reached for the doorknob, Gabriella spoke.

"Bryant?"

"Yeah?" He looked at her over his shoulder.

"You didn't just do something right."

"No?"

"You did *everything* right."

That pleased him a little too much. "So did you, baby. So did you."

Too bad this had been a one-time occurrence. When was the last time he'd wished for a repeat occurrence? Maybe never.

But it was for the best. He could make her happy in bed, but beyond that, he had nothing to give.

CHAPTER TWELVE

Five minutes.

As anxious as Gabriella was feeling, she'd likely follow Bryant too soon if she didn't time it. She removed her phone from her evening bag, turned it on, and set the timer.

Uh oh. A text from Emile twenty minutes ago.

Where are you? Amy wants to introduce you to her family.

Then five minutes later:

???

Should she answer him? Tell him she was mending her dress and she'd be along soon? No. Then she'd have to explain why she hadn't answered earlier. Better to just go find him, pretend her phone had been off this whole time, and tell the dress malfunction lie. Or was it a lie? What was it, if not malfunction, to throw a two-thousand-dollar dress on the floor?

She should look around to make sure they hadn't dropped anything. Good decision. One of her jeweled hairpins was under a pillow sham. After tucking it back into her braid, Gabriella smoothed the duvet and straightened the pillows. There. No one would ever know.

You'll know. Yes, she would. And she was realistic enough to know it would be a while before she'd forget it, if ever. She might have known—sex she'd never forget with a hockey player. She'd gone where she'd sworn she never would—and with Emile's best friend no less. It was hard to tell if it had been a gift or a punishment. It had to be her imagination, but it seemed she could still feel the aftershocks.

And angels above and demons below, she'd thought he was beautiful before. If *Hot Nashville* could have seen him naked and lusty, they'd name him most eligible single of all time and put his picture on every cover. *That* would sell some magazines.

Why couldn't he be a baker? They could exchange recipes and debate the best way to stabilize pastry cream. Or a plumber? Plumbers didn't get enough credit, because you never thought of them until you needed one, and that was usually when something had gone very bad. A plumber would be great to have around.

But it was done now—one and done. That's how it had to be. Even aside from her personal vow, she'd done the one thing Emile had asked her never to—*don't date a hockey player*. Of course, technically, there hadn't been a date, but she doubted if Emile would see it that way.

The phone alarm went off.

Five minutes. Time to go back out there and act like nothing had happened.

And really, nothing had.

● ● ●

Bryant had been right. South took him to the grand staircase, which he named himself because it ended up in the grand salon. Very fancy. There was a balcony-like structure that curved around so you could approach the steps from the right or the left. The whole Sound starting line could stand shoulder to shoulder in full gear on one of these steps with room to spare for the mascot. Maybe it should be called the Sound staircase.

From above, he could see people milling around below. There were even a few folks standing on some of the lower steps chatting and drinking, though they probably hadn't been upstairs. He ought to be able to slip by since he didn't know them—they were probably office staff and dates or spouses. He put his hands in his pockets and pretended to study the carving on the handrail. He even stopped halfway down and ran his finger over the wood. If anyone noticed him, he'd claim he had an artistic interest in staircases, and wasn't this one a humdinger?

Time to finish his descent. Almost at ground level. The band was taking a break and waiters were circulating with drinks and little bits of food. It would be easy to blend in. There. On the floor. Now, he'd go find Emile.

That's when he heard the voice behind him. "Swifty! Have you been upstairs? You aren't supposed to go upstairs in someone's home without being invited."

Fabulous. Captain rule follower. Bryant turned. "I swear, Jarrett McPherson. If you don't think there are enough rules to follow, you get nervous and start making up new ones to make yourself more comfortable and torture everybody else." Though he was probably right. Gabriella had said something about that.

"I didn't make it up. Everybody knows that. You're supposed to stay out of private rooms—especially upstairs. I'm just trying to keep you from getting in trouble with the team owner who might not want you going through his underwear drawer."

"I did not go through his underwear drawer." He needed to get away—and get Jarrett away before Gabriella showed up. It wouldn't be long now. "Let's go find Emile. Do you know where he is?"

"Not upstairs. What were you doing up there anyway?" Jarrett got a peculiar look on his face. It reminded Bryant of how his mother used to look at him when he hadn't exactly told her the whole story. "Please tell me you haven't been upstairs in Pickens Davenport's house having sex."

"No! I have not!"

Jarrett stepped closer to him and sniffed.

"And don't smell me!"

"You have. You smell like sex. I am so disappointed in you."

"That's ridiculous. There *is* no smelling like sex. That's something they say in books to out people who've been having sex. Anyway, what would you know about it since you've never had sex?"

"I've had sex more times than you've read a book."

Debatable, but no time for debate. Gabriella would come down those stairs any second.

"You bet. You're a regular love god. Let's go find Emile."

"Who was it?" Jarrett hissed at him like a nun who had found her two star pupils naked in the confession booth. What next? Was he going to pull a ruler out of his pocket and start rapping knuckles? "There are only wives, girlfriends, and office staff here. I don't know which would be more inappropriate. Please tell me you have not been up there having sex with one of our teammate's wives."

Bryant was incensed—and insulted. "Who do you think I am? I would *never* have sex with another man's wife." *Don't look at the stairs,* he told himself. *That will give it away. Get out of here and take him with you.*

But that didn't help. Jarrett looked at the stairs and Bryant let his gaze follow.

Ah, hell.

There she was—on the landing, looking aloof and beautiful.

Jarrett swung his head around, met Bryant's eyes, and shook his head. "No!"

"No. We were looking at Mary Lou's glassware collection."

Jarrett didn't even bother to respond to that—not that Bryant blamed him. It was lame, so lame.

"Not wives, huh? But sisters? Not just any sister, but Gabriella?" Jarrett was dangerously close to sputtering. Popping an eyeball out of its socket wasn't out of the question. "Emile is going to *kill* you."

"No, he's not. He doesn't hit people."

"He hit Cameron Snow."

"That was different. Snow did something spectacularly bad."

"And you think this isn't?"

Good point. Not that Bryant feared being hit. He'd been hit by a lot worse than a goalie who had no stomach for fighting. But it would be bad if Emile knew—bad for everybody.

"Bryant, I—"

"Stop." There was no point in continuing to deny it. Gabriella was halfway down the staircase now, looking like she owned the world. And she might. "Just stop it. Now. Don't you embarrass her. I mean it, Jarrett. If you embarrass her, I swear to God I will beat you like eggs for an omelet. You know I can and you know I will. I don't care if you are the Mouse and Cinderella Ambassador. When I get through, there won't be enough of you left to be Disney World spokesperson."

"At least I'm not the Big Brew Beer Ambassador. But I won't embarrass her." Jarrett glanced up the stairs and lowered his voice. "But not because I'm afraid of you. I like Gabriella. But this stops now. Do you hear me, Bryant?"

"It's already stopped." Bryant hesitated. "And you're right. I shouldn't have done it. It was stupid." All correct, but it didn't sit well in his gut.

Jarrett nodded, mollified. "That's something. Okay. But you'd better be telling the truth. Because, Bryant, I don't have to tell you—"

"You don't. I know—I know what this could do to the team, to our friendships—everybody mad and picking sides." Bryant put his hand up. "I swear. It won't happen again. I mean it."

And he did. It had been stupid, so stupid to violate the Bro Code—even if he hadn't misled Gabriella, even if they had been in agreement.

But it had been incredible.

CHAPTER THIRTEEN

"I wish you'd come back to the condo and spend the night," Amy said. She and Emile were standing at the front door beside the Davenports again, but this time they were saying goodnight to their guests. "It's so late. There's plenty of room."

In fact, there was *not* plenty of room, even for a condo the size of Emile's. With the Kelly clan staying over, there were barely enough places to bed everyone down, even doubling up in every bedroom and making use of the pull-out sofa in the den. Besides, with such a full house, life at Star View Towers was likely to be an extension of the party—and Gabriella had had enough party.

"Yes," Emile said. "Come back with us. It's so late."

"I have to work in the morning. Besides, I'm sure Amy would like some time with her family."

Amy nodded. "True. But that includes you."

The words were so simple, so sincere. For whatever reason, Gabriella believed it. In fact, her previous paranoia had either vanished completely or been eclipsed by something else on her mind.

When she'd come downstairs earlier, it hadn't felt natural to walk by Bryant without some kind of communication, but it had been necessary. It was obvious that Jarrett had detained him and Bryant hadn't had a chance to find Emile, but that didn't matter. She'd known from the text that Emile had been looking for her.

When she'd found him in the music room, he hadn't blinked at the torn dress story, and the next several hours had been taken up with meeting Amy's family—who were nice, but exhausting.

She hadn't seen Bryant at all. Maybe he'd left.

Now everyone was leaving.

"Are you sure you want to drive back, Gabriella?" Emile placed an arm around her. "I can call an Uber for you."

"Thank you, Emile. Really. But I'm not sleepy at all and I haven't had a drink since the toast."

He nodded. "But you will send me a text when you get home. *Oui?*"

"*Oui,*" she agreed.

"I will go out and ask for your car to be brought around." Things really were back to normal. Gabriella felt that old, familiar annoyance she'd always felt when Emile hovered too much.

"No need," a voice behind her said—the same voice that had recently whispered in her ear. "I'll help Gabriella get her car." His hand closed on her upper arm.

Emile broke into a smile. "Thank you, Swifty. You'll stay with her until it's brought around?"

"You can count on me."

Once the door closed behind them, Gabriella said, "I am capable of getting my own car, you know."

Bryant gave her a smoky look. "I doubt there's anything this side of Mars you aren't capable of. I wanted to talk to you." He turned to the valet who approached. He wasn't the same one from before. "Silver BMW crossover. Black Porsche Cayenne."

"How do you know what I drive? I didn't know what you drive." It struck her odd that she'd had sex with someone without knowing that. Wasn't that a basic fact? And she'd had so few lovers. Four, to be exact, if you counted Bryant—and none who could even begin to compare with Bryant.

And it wasn't just the sex. No one she'd ever been involved with spoke her language the way Bryant did. Come to think of it, none of them had even been hockey fans. Was that the difference? She'd been born into the hockey life. It was part of who she was.

How could she spend her life with someone who cared nothing for something that was so fundamental to her essence? Maybe she needed to look for a hockey fan who wasn't a hockey player. But were there any who hadn't played at least youth hockey? And once a hockey player, always a hockey player.

The hockey player she could never have spoke. "I went with Emile to pick up your car at the dealership when it came in last year."

Right. She'd come out of work on her birthday to find it out front, complete with a big bow. Emile liked to do things he'd seen on television.

Bryant took her hand. "I wanted to say thank you for tonight. It was not my intent to ignore you after we came downstairs."

"I didn't feel ignored. I was busy. As I said before, we had a moment in time. Not a whole evening." That sounded good.

"Good. Gabriella, I know my reputation. I know we might have done what we did lightly, but I don't *take* it lightly. I loved what happened—"

There was a *but* coming and she wanted to be the one to say it. "But it needs to be our secret, and it shouldn't happen again. I understand and I'm glad you do. It would be a huge mess."

He looked relieved, and though it wasn't rational, that disappointed her just a little. But if he looked relieved, he looked sad, too. He squeezed her hand. "Here's the thing, Gabriella. What happened shouldn't have, but I'm not sorry. Does that make sense?"

She laughed. "Perfectly. If you asked if I had it to do over again, if I'd still do it, I know what my answer *should* be, but I doubt if that would be the honest answer. At any rate, I don't have any regrets."

"I do."

Her gut caught until she saw his smirky expression.

"What would that be?"

He reached into her hair and took out one of her jeweled pins. "I didn't get to take your hair down. So I think I'll just keep this." He put it in his pocket.

That might have been the most romantic moment of her life.

"BMW?" The valet held out the key and opened the driver side door.

"Thank you." She took the key, slid behind the wheel, and never looked back.

Usually, Gabriella enjoyed the drive between Nashville and Beauford and the forty-minute trip flew by. Not tonight. It seemed an eternity before she pulled into her parking space behind Eat Cake. Before getting out, she texted Emile.

Home.

He didn't answer, which meant he was in bed or—more likely—playing host to any Kelly who would sit up with him all night long. She paused to try on for size that he didn't answer. It was okay. Yes. Crazyville was a thing of the past.

And so was Bryant. He'd been there for her in a very low moment—seemed to have even helped her snap out of it. But no more, and that was for the best. He'd go back to his puck bunnies and she'd go back to her baking and dating who she wanted to— twice. It was rarely more than twice before she got bored. It was hard to imagine Bryant boring her.

Well, no more of this. She didn't have time. Five o'clock came early and somebody had to make the scones.

She went in the back door, reset the burglar alarm, and marched up the stairs. She knew she had no business drinking caffeine at this time of night, but she popped the top on a diet Coke anyway, took a long drink, and kicked her shoes off.

That was when the back doorbell rang, startling her. *No need to be afraid,* she told herself. The door was solid steel with a peephole and there was a floodlight out back that made the back alley bright as day. She grabbed her phone and went downstairs. She would call the police if she didn't like what she saw.

But she did like what she saw. Bryant stood on the step wearing shorts and a purple Sound T-shirt. He was shivering. Even distorted by the peephole, he looked like everything any sane woman could ever want.

She deactivated the alarm and threw open the door.

He smiled slow and sexy. "Good. I got here in time."

"In time for what?" Her heart raced.

He stepped inside, took her against him, and reminded her why his kiss would never get old. "You haven't taken your hair down," he said when he lifted his mouth from hers. "And I intend to do it."

And she intended to let him.

CHAPTER FOURTEEN

Bryant stood over Gabriella holding a mug of coffee.

It was four thirty in the morning and she had to be downstairs in the bakery in a half hour. He ought to wake her right this second, but he took just another minute to look at her. It was doubtful that he'd ever see her this way again—sleeping with all that glorious hair swirling around her like a mermaid. Well, not really like a mermaid. She had feet. And those legs. Couldn't forget them.

Couldn't forget the time in her bed either. Turned out he hadn't needed her in fancy underwear and stockings to rock his world. Everything about her was new every time.

And there was something in his gut that told him that would always be true, even if they were together fifty years—which they would not be.

He sat on the side of the bed. "Hey." He touched her face when she didn't wake at his voice.

She opened one eye and then closed it again. "You're mean. I thought you were nice."

"I am nice. I made you coffee."

She groaned and sat up. "What time is it?"

"4:34." He handed her the coffee. "Drink this."

"Good thing my commute is thirty seconds." She took a tiny sip. "Thank you."

"I didn't know how you like it, so I put in cream and sugar so it would cool down faster."

"Good thinking. The faster it hits the better." She took a deeper drink. The little grimace she tried to hide was not lost on him.

"But that's not how you take it, is it?"

"No. Not usually. I take it black. But I appreciate it."

He sighed. "I don't know how you take your coffee. You didn't know what I drive."

"Yet, here we are." She gestured to the bed, their scattered clothes, and the empty whipped cream can. "That's not who we are, is it?"

Bryant shook his head. "It's not who *you* are. It's exactly who I am. And, Gabriella, I'm sorry."

"Sorry?" She gave up on the coffee and set it on the nightstand.

"Not exactly sorry. I was not and will never be sorry that we had some more time last night. But I apologize. You clearly told me this couldn't happen again. I agreed. But I came here anyway." He laughed a little. "Seems like I do what I want instead of what I should—at least where you're concerned. I was about to get in bed. Then a thought ran through my mind: I wished you were there with me. That couldn't happen, but I figured I could be where you were. I didn't even take time to dress for the weather. I came straight here in the shorts and shirt I was going to sleep in."

She nodded. "It's not all on you. I could have sent you away."

That was true. He'd been afraid she would. "Why didn't you?"

Please say because you couldn't stand to, because it was more than sex, that you like things about us. Though he had no right to wish for that when he had nothing to give.

But she didn't. "Let's just consider it an extension of what happened earlier."

"So it was still just one time."

"Hmm." She raised an eyebrow. "One time, part *b* ..."

He laughed. "And *c, d, e?*"

"Something like that. It was great. We had fun. But it's behind us now and we didn't break our resolve. It was still just once."

"I don't know if I've ever heard a rationalization that good."

"Thank you. I specialize in rationalization. I'd put it right up there with my *pain au chocolat.*" She picked up her cell phone and looked at the time. "But you need to scoot. My commute may be nonexistent, but I do have to go get clean."

"Okay." He didn't move.

"Then, go. I can't get up until you leave. That wouldn't be productive."

She had a point.

"I guess I'll go pack. I'm leaving today …"

"I know. You'll be gone all week. Pittsburgh tomorrow, Philadelphia Wednesday, and Toronto Saturday."

"Right." Of course she would know her brother's schedule. He wished she knew it because of him instead of Emile. "Well. I'll see you."

"Sure," she said. "Wedding stuff. And at The Big Skate after games, like usual."

"Right. And we'll all be at Mikhail and Sharon's lake house for Thanksgiving Day."

"And that's next week."

"So, goodbye."

"Wait!" she called out.

His heart leapt and that made no sense—maybe for other people, but not him. Still, he turned too quickly. "Yes?"

"The security code is 7830. Don't forget to punch it in."

"Right." At the last second, he turned back to her. "Gabriella?"

"Yes?"

"You said you weren't looking for a man—that you were looking for a friend. I can be that."

She smiled. "I'd like that."

Yes. That was just the thing. Friends, pals, confidants. Perfectly innocent with no Bro Code betrayal.

And there was the other thing—the more important thing. Despite what had just happened, Gabriella was not a one and done kind of woman, and he was never going to be emotionally healthy enough to pull his weight in a real relationship. Maybe he should get that tattooed on his arm, because he'd been losing sight of that lately.

CHAPTER FIFTEEN

It was the Tuesday before Thanksgiving.

The Sound was playing Tampa Bay at home. Gabriella knew she shouldn't go. She was exhausted.

She had not recovered from her all-nighter with Bryant last week before the wedding errands started. With Emile gone, she and Amy had spent a lot of time when Gabriella wasn't working going back and forth between Beauford and Nashville, making wedding plans and watching hockey.

They had firmed up the menu, music, and flower selections with Emory at Beauford Bend. Gabriella had been relieved to learn that Amy didn't want to go with the predictable Christmas wedding trappings: poinsettias, plaid taffeta, and a red and green color scheme. Instead, she wanted a winter theme—blue, silver, and all white flowers. Emory hadn't blinked when Amy had said Emile wanted an ice sculpture. Gabriella only hoped it would not be of Olaf from *Frozen*.

They had also attacked the bridesmaids' dresses dilemma. Gabriella wasn't too sure about the solution, but what was done was done. Finding a wedding dress for Amy on short notice had been one thing; it was one dress. Getting four identical dresses was another. Finally, they'd chosen a Vogue pattern, purchased fabric, had Gabriella measured by a professional tailor, and shipped the whole lot to Amy's aunt in Georgia, who was going to make the dresses. Amy assured Gabriella that her aunt, a home economics teacher, was very much up to the task. Gabriella hoped so. The fabric was a lovely ice blue silk shot with silver threads, and it would be a shame to see it ruined.

Now it was Thanksgiving week—an incredibly hectic time at Eat Cake. Tomorrow, Thanksgiving Eve, would be the worst.

The plus was she hadn't had time to think about Bryant—at least not all the time. The team had earned two wins and one loss on the road, with a shutout against Toronto. Bryant had fought once in Pittsburgh and had a little skirmish in Philadelphia, but no gloves had come off. It had been hard not to think about him while watching—and for a few hours after. And to be honest, a few hours leading up to puck drop. Aside from that, he hadn't been on her mind at all.

She really might have taken a miss on the Tampa Bay game tonight if Amy hadn't asked if they could meet beforehand at Foolscap and Vellum to choose wedding invitations. The shop was even willing to let them in after hours since Gabriella had to work until five o'clock. So there was no saying no to that—especially after all her self-whining about being excluded from wedding plans.

And since she was in Sound Town anyway, she might as well go to the game. But no Big Skate after. Definitely not. Tomorrow, Eat Cake should be called Eat Pie, because they had hundreds of orders for pies—not to mention rolls, pumpkin bars, cheesecakes, cookies, and a few odd birthday cakes. They'd be baking until midnight and opening for two hours Thanksgiving morning for pickups.

When Gabriella tried the door of Foolscap and Vellum, it was locked, but a pretty redhead immediately unlocked the door.

"Welcome!" she said. "I'm Merry Sweet."

Gabriella hesitated. "You look familiar, but I've never been in before."

"Maybe Bridgestone?" She gestured to the Sound jersey Gabriella wore. "I work as a suite attendant there when I'm not here. You know—s-u-i-t-e. Not s-w-e-e-t, like my name."

Gabriella said, "Then you've seen my brother play."

And Bryant. Did this woman know Bryant? Was she a puck bunny? Was that why she worked at Bridgestone when she also had a job here? To meet hockey players? If that were true, she would certainly want Bryant. Who wouldn't? She'd probably slept with him, probably yesterday as soon as he got back from Toronto. She was definitely pretty enough. Apart from that golden copper hair—which looked natural—she had eyes the color of emeralds and, unlike Gabriella, she wasn't a Jolly Green Giant of a woman with huge feet.

Gabriella hated her, hated her, *hated* her. So much.

Merry Sweet—and what kind of stripper name was that?—sighed. "No. Sorry. I don't really watch the hockey games or know who the players are. When I'm not fetching beer and nachos, I try to get a little studying in. I'm taking an online law school class." She smiled. "But now that I know Amy is engaged to one of them, I'll be sure and notice him."

And Gabriella hated, hated, *hated* herself.

What had she just turned into? She'd never been mean and judgmental. And never once in her life had she had one disdainful thought about her height—though she had wished from time to time that her feet were smaller.

Must be because she was tired—all that *pate brisee* she'd made this afternoon for tomorrow's pie marathon. Yes.

"Amy's right back here." Merry led Gabriella toward a table at the back of the shop. "Amy is one of our favorite customers. We're going to move heaven and earth to get these invitations here as soon as possible."

Amy, also dressed in Emile's jersey, stood and embraced Gabriella. "I've narrowed it down to five—unless you think they're awful." They were all black on white or ecru with traditional wording. Really, it was just a matter of the font.

"What do you think?" Amy asked.

"All lovely, but I like this one best." Gabriella picked up one of the pure white samples. "It's easy to read. The ecru paper is pretty, but your dress is white."

"That's the one I liked, too," Amy said. "You don't think it's too plain?"

"Not at all. Some things are meant to be plain. It's traditional."

Merry laughed. "So true. Where I grew up, there was a rash of weddings one summer at the Beaver Crossing Baptist Church—eleven, I think. The first bride of the season sent out an invitation with little plastic gold rings tied to the top with a ribbon. The next girl's had a foldout paper honeycomb bell. After that, all the mamas got into a competition to see who could come up with the most elaborate invitation."

"How funny!" Amy said.

"It was," Merry said. "Of course, the mamas got secretive about it, and everybody sat around waiting for the mailman to get there with the surprise of the week. We didn't have a lot to do in Beaver Crossing. I remember one that was so big it came in a box. It had a framed picture of the bride and groom and a CD with a recording of them verbally issuing the invitation. And there were a couple of the mamas who each claimed the other had stolen her idea for pop-up hearts. They didn't speak until the next spring revival when the visiting preacher delivered a sermon on the evils of envy and competition."

Gabriella gave Merry the warmest smile she could to make up for her mean thoughts. "Emile would have probably wanted at least a honeycomb bell, and probably a recording."

"Why do you think he's not here?" Amy asked.

"If you want a little whimsy," Merry said, "you could do a wax seal."

"I would love that!" Amy clapped her hands. "A snowflake! Gabriella, do you think we could do a snowflake?"

Gabriella saw hours and hours ahead of her with dripping candles and snowflake wax stamps. Fire—there would be fire involved. Amy used to be such a sensible, practical woman.

"Of course." What did it matter if they burned down a building or two in the process?

"Since your schedule is so tight," Merry said, "you can get the supplies and make the seals ahead of time. After you address the envelopes, you can attach the seals with a drop of glue." She walked across the shop and came back with a handful of white sealing wax sticks and two stamps. "Now, how many invitations are you sending?"

Amy looked chagrined. "Two fifty," she whispered. "We didn't have time for save the dates, but we sent emails and made calls. So everyone knows, but we have to have invitations. Otherwise, my grandmother would blow an artery and take a few of my aunts to the grave with her."

Hopefully not the aunt who was sewing the bridesmaids' dresses.

"I understand. Sending an invitation in the mail is just what you do." Merry nodded. "But I'd better get you some more wax."

"Oh, Gabriella!" Amy said. "We can do them Thanksgiving afternoon. Can't we?"

"Great idea." Better to burn down the house on the lake where they could all jump in the water and save themselves.

"I'll get a third stamp," Amy said. "Sharon will help."

Sharon would not help. She would be too busy digging up intel on Krystal Voleck and Wyoming, whose last name Gabriella did not actually know.

"We'll get it done," Gabriella said.

• • •

"Are you ready for your food?"

Bryant looked up from his stall to where Packi stood over him.

"Yes. Thank you." It had been sweet having his pregame snack appear like magic, along with the other things Packi had been doing for him. Packi still hadn't caught on that he didn't need any extra looking after. He was fine.

Packi handed him a banana and a sandwich. "It's peanut butter. I made arrangements for the spectator ice suite for your family for both Friday and Saturday night."

"Thank you. I appreciate that. We're at fourteen right now, but we could have a couple more." Or a couple drop out. With his family, who knew? Sick kids, double shifts at the mill, and broken water pipes had been running their lives for years.

While he was on the road, his dad had called with the definites—his parents, Philie's, Patrick, and nine assorted siblings, spouses, and kids. Honestly, he hadn't even tried to keep up with who. The number and list would change daily, if not hourly, so *definite* was a very loose term. "I told them that I absolutely had to know exactly by Thanksgiving Day." He'd bought some plane tickets, but there would be more to get sorted out.

"I asked for one of the twenty-person capacity suites for both games and arranged for catering."

"Great. They'll send me a bill?" He had to pay for this, but that was fine.

"They know where you live. Since it's Thanksgiving week, I thought I'd also better call the Hyatt. I know a guy. He's set aside a block. When you know exactly what you need, with who in each room, tell me and I'll firm it up."

That was a surprise. "Packi, that was really over and above. I didn't expect that."

"That's why I didn't mind doing it. Also, I dropped your name."

Bryant laughed. "For what that's worth." He peeled the banana.

Packi turned like he was going to leave, but then he said, "She's here." Oh, hell. Pretending to leave had been a trick to throw Bryant off track.

"Who?" he asked, but he knew, could feel it in the vibe coming from Packi. Maybe the man did have a little magic about him like Glaz claimed.

"I saw her come in with Amy."

"Oh?" He busied himself with unwrapping his sandwich. "Good to hear. The more fans the better." But he was pleased—more pleased than was healthy. A week on the road hadn't cured him. He'd made arrangements to see Brianna in Pittsburgh and Kayla in Philadelphia, but he'd ended up canceling on both. By Toronto, he'd known better than to bother, so he'd never answered Maya's texts.

"The best way to handle this would be to be straight with your friend." Packi let his eyes drift across the locker room to where Emile was talking to Glaz and Jarrett.

Oh, right. *Emile, I felt it only right to tell you I had sex with your sister. I took her upstairs at your engagement party and had my way with her in the first bedroom I came to. And if that wasn't enough, later, I drove to Beauford and kept her up most of the night even though she had to be at work before God got up. And I did all this knowing I am unfit for a relationship. But you don't worry. I'm going to stay away from her now, honest Injun.* Wait. He couldn't say that word. As far as he could remember, he'd never said that, but it must be highly insulting to Native Americans. Or was it people from India? Hell if he knew, but it didn't matter. He would not want to insult anyone. *Scout's honor,* then. As far as he knew, that referenced Boy Scouts. Having never been a Boy Scout, he'd never said that either, but swearing to the Boy Scouts of America that he would stay away from Gabriella would make that little speech A-OK with Emile.

Yeah, right. And where had A-OK come from, anyway? Did he think using words he'd never used before would fool Emile into thinking he was someone else?

Not that he was ever in a million years going to make that speech.

He looked Packi in the eye. "There is no *this* and there's nothing to be straight about, nothing to tell."

"She's in love with you. I wouldn't consider that nothing."

The hair on the back of Bryant's neck stood up. "That's not true. Your magic is failing." A part of him rejoiced at the thought. A bigger part wanted to run because if were true, he would fail her, as he'd failed Philie and his son. "She has a strict rule against dating hockey players."

"Uh huh." Packi handed him a bottle of water. "Well. It was just a thought. It's game night. We won't talk about it anymore—now. I wanted you to know she was here. It's always good to know when there's some good inspiration in the house."

Bryant laughed. Packi might be spooky-wise, but he had that all wrong. His game had never depended on who was there to watch. It never entered his mind.

But even so, he went out and played the game of his life.

CHAPTER SIXTEEN

There was a pecking order in the Player VIP Suite, or as it was more commonly known, the WAG suite—for wives and girlfriends.

The front row was reserved for the royalty—top players' wives, Noel Glazov and Sharon Orlov among them, plus any visiting parents. Amy would move up after the wedding. For now, she sat in the second row with Gabriella, the rookie wives, and the long-term girlfriends who were probably going to be wives. In the back were the new girlfriends and Krystal, no matter that she was a wife and Jan was a top dog.

This hockey life was a crazy and wonderful one, one Gabriella knew and understood. As Emile's sister, as long as he played, she would always have one foot in this world, but she was never moving up to that front row. She'd never thought about that before, but now that she did, it made her a little sad.

"Ready?" Amy stood up. Gabriella sat paralyzed in her second row seat, though not because of her pecking order musings.

It was because Bryant had played the game of his life. Gabriella knew it was true, not because the announcers had said so, not because all the women in the suite said so, but because hockey ran in her blood and she knew great moments when she saw them.

She had not intended to watch him specifically, had promised herself she wouldn't. But how could she not, when he was having the game of his life?

She hadn't needed the numbers to confirm his prowess tonight, but the numbers were there—a hat trick and three assists, in a 6-0 win. That meant he'd had a hand in every point scored and was part of the defense in a shutout game. Also, no fight, not a single penalty minute.

Powerful. He was so powerful on the ice—which made her think of his power in other areas.

Bad plan, bad thoughts.

"Gabriella?" Amy was still waiting on her. And no wonder. She was the only one still sitting down. "Are you okay?"

"Tired. And I have a big day tomorrow."

"I know you aren't planning to go to The Big Skate, but you didn't eat a single thing tonight. I'm going to ask the suite attendant to get you something before you have to drive back to Beauford."

Gabriella opened her mouth to thank Amy, but instead she said, "Wait, Amy. I'll go with you to The Big Skate." After all, she did need to eat. "Time wise, what's the difference between eating there and eating here?"

• • •

"The guys will be forever and you're hungry." Amy pushed a menu toward Gabriella. "Go ahead and order."

They were seated at a large round table. Usually they sat in the booth directly under Emile's framed jersey and pictures, but unlike usual, Sharon and Mikhail had left their children with a sitter and were joining them tonight.

"Maybe I will." Gabriella studied the menu as if she didn't know it as well as her recipe for ganache. She really didn't feel that hungry, but if she didn't eat, she'd be ravenous in the morning and fill up on pastry. That would not make for a good day. It would be best if she ordered, ate, and left before Bryant was finished with interviews, cool down, massage, shower, and the rest of it. Yet, she dawdled, debating between the black and blue burger and Cobb salad, the steak quesadilla, and the Buffalo chicken mac and cheese. Or pizza. That would be good—it took a while, but they didn't make a half-bad crust here.

"What can I get you?"

Gabriella looked up at the waitress, and her stomach turned over. Like the rest of The Big Skate waitstaff, she wore a Sound jersey. Unlike the rest of them, hers had a 5 on the shoulder—Bryant's number. It shouldn't bother her. It wasn't as if Bryant had given her the jersey. It was a replica and everybody wore a different one every shift. Emile yesterday. Bryant today. Sparks Champagne tomorrow. And even if he had given it to her, what of it?

Still, Gabriella hated her.

"Go ahead, Gabriella," Sharon said.

What? What had she decided?

The girl smiled. "Miss Charbonnet, our soup tonight is chicken corn chowder, and we also have a barbeque stuffed baked potato that's not on the menu."

What was wrong with her? Hating women because they might know Bryant or wore his jersey? First, Merry Sweet, who worked two jobs and took classes, and now this nice girl, who had waited on them numerous times and remembered Gabriella's name. She'd heard Emile call the girl by her name. He knew everyone's name. She should make it up to the girl by ordering quickly and calling her by name. She willed herself to remember it.

Megan, the deep part of her brain threw out.

"Thank you, Megan. Large pizza with Italian sausage, mushrooms, spinach, caramelized onions, olives, and extra cheese. Iced tea to drink."

"Will that be for the table?" Megan asked.

"No," Sharon said. "Mikhail will want a steak. I'll wait to order when he gets here. If I have to wait for him to finish, I might as well eat with him."

"Good idea," Amy said, "though Emile will want blackened salmon and pasta. But I'll have an iced tea now."

How could they be so sure what Emile and Mikhail wanted to eat?

"Iced tea all around," Sharon said. "No alcohol for the guys when they get here, either. They play at one o'clock tomorrow afternoon. They'll have to do their boozing on Thanksgiving at the lake."

When the waitress had gone, Amy said, "Thank you for inviting us for the holiday, Sharon."

"It wouldn't be Thanksgiving without a houseful of hockey players. The schedule is so tight that they seldom make it home for turkey. I haven't been back to Boston for Thanksgiving since I got married. My parents are not over it yet, but will they come here? No. Though we're going there for Christmas—flying out the morning after your wedding."

Amy's eyes went wide. "Oh, no! You could have left a day earlier. We never considered that the timing of our wedding would keep people from their families! The break is short enough as it is."

Sharon laid a hand on Amy's arm. "Don't be silly. Remember we have the whole off-season to travel. We're going to Russia to see Mikhail's family for a month, and then we'll have a good long visit in Massachusetts."

"I still feel bad. We were just thinking of ourselves for a little while there. I like to think we've snapped out of it. As much as we'd love to have you there, if you want to go ahead and leave, we won't be offended."

Megan brought their drinks and Gabriella gave her an extra sunny smile.

"We wouldn't miss your wedding for the world." Sharon added lemon to her tea. "Emile is family—and so are you. Hockey wives have to stick together. That's how we get through those long road trips when we're pregnant, an ice storm knocks the power out, and the toddler has an ear infection."

As bad as that sounded, it sounded nice, too. Gabriella could imagine them all having a huge slumber party at a house that had a generator and a fireplace. Of course, Krystal and Wyoming would probably have to make do together the best way they could somewhere else.

"So if the team is sold, you'd get to go home," Amy said. "I'm sure that would make you happy."

"No, not really," Sharon said. "I'm from Boston, and the team wouldn't be there. I don't know where. They are very hush, hush about that, though my money would be on Springfield. But aside from all that, I like it here. My real estate business is doing well. My kids have never known anywhere else. And after Russian and Boston winters, Mikhail and I have learned to enjoy the occasional ice storm and snowfall."

"Do you think Mr. Davenport will sell?" Gabriella asked.

Gabriella didn't mean to picture Bryant in Massachusetts, but she did. And she didn't like it.

"I don't know," Sharon said. "Mary Lou told me at the engagement party that he has too many irons in the fire and something needs to go. That's all she said, and I didn't pick."

"That's hard to believe," Gabriella said.

Sharon laughed. "I know, right? *Me.* But really, what does it matter? We like it here, but we could be traded tomorrow. Any of us could. I could find myself in Winnipeg wishing for a Boston winter." She sipped her tea. "Go, Jets. Right?"

Gabriella didn't mean to picture Bryant as a Jet—or a King, a Penguin, a Bruin—but she did. And she didn't like it.

Amy waved across the room. "Sparks, Isak, and Case."

"Our guys can't be far behind," Sharon said.

Gabriella's stomach turned over again—in a good way, in a bad way, in every way. She should leave, just say she didn't want her food—what was it she'd ordered? She didn't even remember. She should drive through Sonic, get two corndogs, and eat them on the way back to Beauford.

Of course, Bryant might not even come. He might have a date. He often did. Not that she thought his dates ever involved dinner and a movie.

And of all the things she hadn't meant to picture, she definitely did not want to picture *that*. But she did.

Maybe he *would* get traded. That would be best. Maybe some team owner had seen his magnificent performance tonight and called Pickens Davenport and asked—no, begged—for the trade. Maybe they offered five D-men, fourteen forwards, twelve goalies, and all their first round draft picks for the next eight years. Maybe when Pickens played hardball, they threw in four ice girls and a washer and dryer and that sealed the deal. Bryant could be on a plane to the frozen tundra of Winnipeg right now.

Except he wasn't. The door opened and the noise level in The Big Skate went up—way up. Gabriella had her back to the door, but she didn't need to turn around to know it was him. She recognized Game of Your Life noise when she heard it.

Sharon and Amy laughed and clapped along with everyone else. Gabriella turned. He was making his way across the room like a prince warrior returning from battle, with Emile and Mikhail flanking him like lackeys. He shook hands, clapped people on the back, and accepted hugs. There was something primal about the way he moved—like a hunter who had just made the kill that would feed his village for the winter, but he was going to be humble about it.

Finally, the three men approached the table. Emile and Mikhail kissed Amy and Sharon.

And Bryant stood before Gabriella. He was still wearing his game day suit.

Unlike Mikhail who looked like something out of *GQ* and Emile who looked like he had invented *GQ,* Bryant looked like he didn't give a damn. So why did he look so much better than them? His blond hair was a damp mess, his silvery gray tie was loose, his navy blue jacket unbuttoned.

"Great game," Gabriella said. "And that's an understatement."

"Thank you."

The moment was awkward, though they were both smiling. Or maybe the awkwardness was *because* they were both smiling.

Bryant stretched his hands out, fingers open, as if he was going to touch her, but then pulled back and looked at them as if they were foreign objects. He didn't know what to do with his hands.

She knew this because her own hands were knotted in her lap without purpose. It wasn't natural. Last time they'd seen each other, they'd known very well what to do with their hands—sweet and wonderful things. Now, without an icing spatula, a hockey stick, or each other, what were they to do?

Finally, Bryant patted her shoulder, much like you would pat a baby's back and—just like that—that image moved through her and shook to the core. Her ovaries shouted to her, "Now! Do it now. We need a baby!"

Ridiculous. She'd never thought much about children one way or the other. That was way into the future, if ever.

Just then, Megan brought a huge pizza and set it down on the table. Bryant burst into pleased laughter and the awkwardness evaporated.

"My pizza!" Bryant said. "Now, that's service."

The men, except Emile, were removing their jackets, rolling up their sleeves, and taking the vacant chairs.

"Your pizza?" Megan asked. "No. That's Miss Charbonnet's pizza."

It was? Angels above and demons below, it was. She'd just ordered—ordered without thinking. But why one the size of a wagon wheel?

"Oh." Bryant rested his forearms on the table, close enough to Gabriella's shoulder that she could feel the warmth. "That's the exact same pizza I order every time—Italian sausage, mushrooms, spinach, caramelized onions, olives, and extra cheese."

Was it? She hadn't known that—at least not consciously. But she must have absorbed it somewhere along the way.

"Gabriella," Emile said, "you must be very hungry."

"Not this hungry. I didn't realize it would be so big."

As the others were giving their orders, Gabriella gave Bryant a sidelong look. "I can share."

"Are you sure?" He looked longingly as the pizza. He was hungry. She had known he would be, because they always were, but something in her subconscious had wanted to feed him, hadn't wanted him to have to wait. It would have been nice if her subconscious had shared that information.

"Sure," she said lightly. "Dig in."

"Thanks. I thought Packi might have called it in."

"And how would Packi know what kind of pizza you like?" Emile asked.

"Hell if I know," Bryant said around a mouthful of pizza. "He knows things."

"Magic," Mikhail said. "He has magic."

"Bah!" Emile slipped an arm around Amy. "There is no such thing."

"I don't know," Sharon said. "We were in the middle of moving and there was a thunderstorm. I had no idea where the kids' raingear was and Packi showed up with new boots and raincoats for them. And they were the right sizes, too."

"Or," Emile said, "he could have looked outside, seen the rain, and figured you didn't know where everything was packed. He had kids, so guessing the sizes wouldn't be that hard."

"Maybe," Sharon said, "but it seemed like magic at the time."

Emile turned to Amy. "Did I tell you Swifty is getting the Packi treatment right now?"

"It's sweet, too," Bryant said. "Pregame snacks, coffee ready for me at early skate, and nobody can sharpen skates like Packi. I'm dreading when he realizes that I don't have anything going on and moves on to somebody else."

"Maybe Packi knows something you don't," Amy said.

"I don't know about that, but I know this. My family is coming for the weekend games the day after Thanksgiving and he made all the arrangements. I didn't even ask him."

His family was coming? That would make for a full weekend. She should get a date for that weekend. It wouldn't be hard. There was Heath's new apprentice, Shannon, at Spectrum. Either he'd be willing or he loved pineapple upside down cupcakes more than any man should.

She tried to imagine Shannon on a pond teaching a toddler to skate, putting a hockey stick in his hand. The image wouldn't come—and not because no pond in Tennessee was likely freeze hard enough to skate on. Shannon wasn't the hockey type, and therefore not her type. She was damned if she did and damned if she didn't—couldn't have a hockey player, couldn't settle for anyone else.

Her whole life was tangled up in hockey—it paid for her lifestyle, filled her free time, and dictated her vacations. Even her love for baking was tied to the hockey life—she'd discovered her talent in a hockey-centered household. She'd learned from Johanna when they'd baked cupcakes for team parties, cookies for long road trips, and birthday cakes for Emile's friends who were far from home.

Maybe it was like the children of career military parents who couldn't be happy outside of the military culture. It was all they'd ever known, so they joined the military and/or married soldiers.

Though her brain remembered, it was getting harder for her heart to remember her reasons for refusing to have a relationship with a hockey player—at least this hockey player. What was it Bryant had said on the porch before the engagement party? *You know I would never hurt you, don't you?* She had said *"of course,"* like the pleaser good girl that she was, but had she believed it? Did she believe it now?

She waited for the phantom pain in her arm to set in. It did not come.

But it didn't matter if she believed it or not. It wasn't as if Bryant wanted her. And there was Emile.

She shook it off and focused on what Amy was saying to Bryant.

"Maybe you're getting traded to Boston," Amy teased, "and Packi is making your last days as good as they can be."

"I might have to quit if that happened," Bryant said. "I have no wish to go north."

"What we wish is not always what happens, my friend," Mikhail said. "We might all end up in Massachusetts." He gestured to the table. "All except Gabriella. She will be here laughing at us as we shovel snow."

"Let's not talk about that," Sharon said. "Let's talk about Thanksgiving. The kids and I are going to head to the lake house as soon as the game is over tomorrow. I want the rest of you to come as soon as you can so the fun can start. I thought we'd have Mexican food tomorrow night and watch movies."

"That sounds like fun, but I can't," Gabriella said. "I have to work late tomorrow night, and we're opening for two hours Thanksgiving morning for people to pick up their orders. I'll get on the road by ten. That'll get me there by noon—with the desserts."

Bryant swung his head around. "But you're coming to the game?"

"No. No game for me." He looked disappointed and the pleaser in her screamed—but she took some satisfaction in it, too.

"I do not like this, Gabriella." Oh, great. Emile had his big brother voice on. "It's two hours there, much on a narrow road. There will be lots of holiday traffic. It might rain."

"Emile, be reasonable," Gabriella said. "I can drive in the rain, and there isn't going to be a lot of traffic once I leave the highway."

"Non." He raised his hands. "Amy and I will wait for you."

"No," Amy said. "Feel free to stay and go with Gabriella. That's fine. But I'm going tomorrow to help Sharon with some of the precooking."

Emile gasped. "Be parted from you? I just got off the road!"

"I tell you this is not necessary!" Gabriella raised her voice.

"Emile, Sharon is having us all for Thanksgiving," Amy said. "I will not leave her to do all the work."

"Really. It's okay," Sharon said.

"No, Sharon," Gabriella said. "Amy's right. If I didn't have to work—"

Bryant raised his hands in the air. Finally, they had a purpose. "I'll wait," he said quietly. Everyone turned and looked at him. "Really. With my parents coming in, I have some things to take care of here. I'll wait for Gabriella."

Gabriella looked at him wide-eyed, searching his face. "I don't need—"

"It'll be fun to drive together. You just come to my house when you're finished working and we'll go from there. I'll drive. You'll be tired. You can sleep on the way."

"You are a good friend, Swifty," Emile said, "to help me take care of my little sister."

Yeah, buddy. He took care of me all right, and I took care of him. Do you want to hear about that, Emile?

Bryant ducked his head and took another piece of pizza.

"So, that's settled. Thank you, Bryant," Amy said. "Who's coming besides us?"

"Let's see," Sharon said. "Sparks, Robbie, Bryant, and Jarrett are coming. I invited Thor, but he's going to the Davenports'. That's it, unless you guys know someone else who has nowhere to go."

"Krystal and Jan," Gabriella said. "I hear they are going to be all alone."

For a second, Sharon's face went white. "You are lying. Miss Corn Pone Princess is from Murfreesboro. They'll be at a big hoedown over there with fried turkey, fireworks, and a lot of 'hey, y'all, watch this.'"

"Ouch," Gabriella said. "Don't you think that's a little harsh?"

"When she goes to a road game and knocks on your guy's hotel room door at two o'clock in the morning, you can come talk to me about how harsh it is. And I might add she was fooling around with Jan at the time, too."

"I don't have a guy," Gabriella said.

"No hockey players for my sister," Emile said.

Sharon rolled her eyes and ignored Emile. "Still, you get my drift, Gabriella."

Unfortunately, she did get it. She tried not to look at Bryant.

"Simmer down, Sharon," Mikhail said. "I sent her away."

Sharon laid a hand on Mikhail's cheek. "And he called me immediately after it happened." She pointed to Emile and Bryant. "And that's the way to do it. If a puck bunny comes knocking, send her away and call home. Believe me, your wife will want to be wakened for that news and it had better come from you. Don't let it wait for the sin bin telegraph."

"I don't have a wife," Bryant said.

"You will, my friend," Emile said. "Some day. And we'll have to get a bigger table."

No we won't, brother. No way I will ever sit at a table with Bryant's wife. In fact, on that note …

Gabriella rose. "Five o'clock comes early, so I'll vacate my chair now." She smiled and winked at Bryant, just to show what a good sport she was. "You can get started on that wife-hunting."

He did not smile.

Emile said, "I'll walk you out."

"No." Bryant rose from his chair. "Here comes your food. I'll see Gabriella to her car."

Emile narrowed his eyes and stopped smiling. "You seem eager to spend time with my sister—driving to the lake with her tomorrow. Walking her out now. Should I be worried?"

Hell!

But Bryant played it perfectly. He nodded emphatically. "You absolutely should. I am sick of hockey. I want to quit and make cake. I have this plot to make Gabriella fall in love with me and steal her chocolate cake recipe. Then I'm going to start a chain of chocolate cake stores along the California coast. *Swifty's Chocolate Cake,* I'm going to call it. Catchy, huh?"

For a moment Gabriella froze, but everyone laughed.

"Emile, what's wrong with you?" Amy asked.

Emile shrugged. "I don't know. Sorry, Swifty."

"Nothing to be sorry for," Bryant said. "A man has to look out after his sister. With four, I ought to know."

"I can look out for myself," Gabriella said. "I don't need anyone to walk me out."

"No," Emile said. "Swifty should walk with you."

"Keep your hands off my pizza," Bryant said. "I'll be back for it."

• • •

As they moved toward the door, Bryant walked a step behind Gabriella—partly because he figured Emile was keeping an eye on them, and partly because he wanted to watch her walk. She moved like a ballet dancer. Why had he never noticed that men watched her when she walked—not that he blamed them, the way she looked tonight. Okay the way she looked every night.

Oh, hell, no. That damned rookie forward, Marcus Olsson, was undressing her with his eyes and Bryant blamed him—blamed him very much. Bryant gave him the stink eye. The kid looked down at his nachos. Good boy. He could be taught.

But he needed a lesson right now. To hell with Emile. Bryant put a hand on Gabriella's back. She didn't respond. Maybe she didn't feel the buzz there.

As they stepped onto the sidewalk, Gabriella looked over her shoulder and smiled. "Sorry about Emile."

"Better that he got suspicious tonight than a few other times I could think of."

"Yeah."

"Yeah." He almost said they were going to have to be careful, but then he remembered that there was nothing to be careful about. Nothing else was going to happen.

"Thank you for seeing me out, though it's not necessary."

"I'm your friend." He moved beside her. "Friends don't let friends walk into parking decks late at night alone."

"I'm not parked in the deck." She pointed down the street. "I actually got a place out front."

"Oh." He took her hand and why not? It was just a hand. Toddlers held hands. Whole families held hands when they said grace. Strangers on airplanes held hands during turbulence. Nothing sexual about any of that. "Friends don't let friends walk down the street alone."

"Do friends hold hands?" There was a smile in her voice.

"In November? You bet! Friends don't let friends slip and fall on icy pavement. Emile would approve."

"The pavement isn't icy." She laughed and he wanted to capture that sound and save it in a bottle for later.

"No?" They were beside her SUV now. "Where I come from, the pavement is always icy in November."

She leaned against the passenger door, but she didn't take her hand away. "You're in Nashville, Tennessee."

"You bet I am." And right now there was no place he'd rather be. He leaned beside her so they were facing each other.

"Do you miss it?"

"Miss what?"

"Where you come from—home with the icy pavement. I know you were exaggerating when you said you'd quit hockey before moving north again, but don't you miss home?"

Where had all that come from? How had they gone from joking about icy pavement to a conversation he didn't want to have?

"What?" He smiled, hoping to distract her. "The land of wild rice and *dontcha know*?"

She smiled, but she was clearly waiting for an answer. "But do you miss it? Or *dontcha know*?"

"I miss the lakes. I'd like a lake house someday."

"But your home, your family, the way you grew up—do you miss that?" Damn. She should be a reporter—or maybe a military interrogator. Anyone would feel compelled to answer, with the way she smiled and twinkled her eyes when she asked the questions, all the while acting like she was only mildly curious. Or maybe she was only mildly curious. "You must miss it."

Did he? "Sure. Parts of it. At one time I thought it was the best place in the world. You know, I didn't leave home to play juniors like Emile did—didn't see why I should. There was a world-class team in St. Sebastian. They wanted me, so I thought it would be crazy to go live with people I didn't know when I could be with my own family."

"You must love your family. You seem happy they're coming this weekend."

"I do. I am."

"But?" Where had she gotten that there was a *but?*

And why was he driven to answer? "I don't like how they won't let me go."

She shook her head, puzzled. "Won't let you go? I don't understand."

And for some reason he wanted her to understand—to understand and tell him it was all right. "It's almost like they want me to hate my life here—or anywhere that's not St. Sebastian, where they are. They would say they don't want me to be miserable, but I think it would bring them comfort if I were. It would give them assurance that I can't wait to get back there."

"And do you want that? To go back there?"

He hesitated. "I used to think I would. I thought when my career was finished that's what I'd do—go back there, build a house, play men's pickup, and coach a local team—maybe my son's." But any possibility of that was gone. If he ever married, it would be far into the future, and it would have to be to someone who wanted nothing from him that he wasn't able to give.

"Would that be a bad life?"

"I don't know, Gabriella. It wouldn't have to be. But I don't think it would be enough for them for me to move back. And, though they probably don't know it, I don't even think it's the physical distance that bothers them. They do not want me to have changed. They want me to be the same kid I was when I was riding high in the youth and junior leagues, with my mother in her hockey mom shirts and my dad pacing on the sidelines." *And Philie in my jersey, reigning princess of the rink.*

"Everybody changes, Bryant. Everybody grows up. They know that."

"Yes. I'm not saying it very well. They want an older version of that me. They want to recreate the memories of those times. And I understand on some level. Those were good times. And I can't give them that again. They invested a lot in me—money, time, emotion. I can't give them any more hat tricks or championship highs."

She frowned. "Weren't they watching tonight? And the Stanley Cup championship is the fairest championship in all the land."

"It's not the same. I can't explain." Or maybe he could. He took a deep breath. "When I was *all that* on the ice in St. Sebastian, it was like I was capturing something for the home team, like they were part of it—*we* were winning and that included them. Now, *we* means something else."

Gabriella was silent for a moment. She opened her mouth and closed it again, like she had something to say but was reluctant.

"What?" Bryant asked. Even if he didn't like what she was going to say, he had to know.

"Then that's on them. If they can't move on to be part of the new *we*, that's sad for them."

Of course, there were extenuating circumstances. If Philie had lived and was sitting in the stands with their son, maybe it would be different. Maybe they would all embrace this new life. But he wasn't going to tell Gabriella that.

She covered his hand with hers and he wanted that moment to never end. "Bryant, every bit of joy you find in life, every friend you make, is not a betrayal of your roots."

"Thank you for that." She did understand, maybe with good reason. "Do Paul and Johanna make you feel that way?"

Gabriella shook her head. "Not even a little. They love it when we visit, love it when they visit us. But they never expected us to stay. They loved it when we were all together, but they grew with us. It's still *we*. Your family can find their way back to we."

He doubted that, but he was done. "Deep conversation for a late night when somebody has to bake pies at five o'clock."

"And somebody has early skate at six."

He laughed. "Yeah. That'd be me, wouldn't it? Let's get you on the road." He led her to the driver's side and helped her inside.

"Thank you." She started the engine.

"A friend wouldn't let another friend drive off into the night without saying 'be careful and watch for snowdrifts.'"

She laughed. "You'd better get back inside before my brother catches you standing on the sidewalk. Good night, Bryant."

And a friend wouldn't kiss a friend good night if she were never going to be more than a friend. So he didn't.

Damn it.

CHAPTER SEVENTEEN

Pumpkin.

It was everywhere. It had been fun in October, smelled heavenly in early November, but now it was old, so old. Pumpkin pies, pumpkin cheesecakes, pumpkin bars, pumpkin this, pumpkin that, and pumpkin everything. Gabriella had already had enough when they started this morning at five o'clock. Now, four hours later, she was longing to make Christmas tree cookies, Yule logs, and coconut cakes. That would come soon enough, but for now and many hours to come, it was pumpkin, pumpkin, pumpkin all the time.

She was taking loaves of pumpkin bread out of the oven when Quincy stuck his head in the kitchen.

"Swap with me, Gabriella, and go watch the front with Marcy. You have a visitor. I'll get the bread."

"A *visitor*. Like someone wanting to pass the time of day? Who would come here today of all days?"

"I don't know." He took her hot pads and began moving pumpkin bread to the cooling rack. "Could be a customer. He just asked for you."

"I'll be right back to decorate those," she said to June and Haddie, who were icing pumpkin—of course—cupcakes.

Gabriella barreled through the door without taking time to wonder who it might be, but stopped short.

"Bryant. What are you doing here?" The game was in four hours. He ought to be having his pregame nap. "You're supposed to be at the rink in an hour." He was wearing sweatpants and a Sound hoodie, as if he'd just come from morning skate and stretch.

"I know." It was then she noticed that he was not smiling and he looked about as harried as a man could look.

And her stomach revolted. "What's wrong?" She flew from behind the counter past Miss Sticky and Bradley Stanton who were here for their morning doughnuts. "Has something happened to Emile? Amy?" It had to be that. Otherwise Bryant wouldn't be here.

"Oh, no, no, honey." He wrapped her in his arms and let her tremble against him. He had not had a shower, but she didn't care. "No. They're fine. I'm so sorry I scared you." She willed herself to calm down. "The thing is," he said close to her ear, "I need a bed. I'm desperate."

Angels above and demons below! She pulled away from him and moved him across the shop out of earshot of everyone. "Really? Right *now?* When you need to be at the rink and I need to be working? You haven't even had a shower. Besides, I thought we'd settled that. No bed! Flattering, but you have lost your mind?"

Shock washed over his face. "No. I mean … no. I need a bed— by Friday. I don't know how to make that happen, with the game this afternoon and tomorrow being Thanksgiving."

Well, assuming he wanted sex was embarrassing, not that she had time for embarrassment. She moved him all the way to the corner. "What are you talking about, Bryant?"

"It's my mother. See, they were all going to stay at the Hyatt. Packi had it all arranged. But I had said to invite my little sister's boyfriend. They're seventeen. He wasn't coming, but now he is. My mother says she, my dad, and Michelle have to stay at my house because Michelle can't be at a hotel with Stephen."

"Why not? I wouldn't expect they would want them in the same room, but …"

"I know! That's what I said. But Ma says, what would people say and it has to be that way. I would give my parents my bed and sleep on the couch, but I don't have a couch. And then there's Michelle." He looked into space. "I guess Michelle could have the couch but still, no couch."

"So really, you need two beds or a bed and a couch."

He swiped his hand over this face. "Yeah. And I have no time. Their plane gets in at three on Friday."

Gabriella could have spent a lot of time dissecting Bryant's mother's logic—or illogic as it were—but it was a waste of time. For that matter, she could have asked why Bryant hadn't just told his mother he didn't have any furniture or why the boy couldn't stay with Bryant in a sleeping bag on the floor. But there was no time for that. She'd learned a long time ago to skip the whys and get on to the solving.

"Calm down, Bryant."

He nodded. "I knew you could fix this."

"I haven't fixed anything yet." But she would. He'd come to her when he needed something. Wasn't that better than wanting sex? She would not let him down. "Do you want two beds? How many bedrooms do you have?"

He seemed to be counting. "Five. It's five. And yes. Two beds. Little tables and things if I can get them."

She took out her cell phone. "I'm going to call my friend Pam Anderson at Halfway Home."

• • •

Gabriella had some frosting on her cheek and Bryant wanted to lick it off, though he doubted that would go over very well.

Why had he come here? He needed help, needed it bad, but he could have called.

He'd come off the ice after morning skate to his mother's frantic and demanding voice mail and called her back, thinking he could reason with her. He should have known better. The minute she said, "Well, Bry, if you don't *want* us there with you…" he'd been lost. He'd never told her he didn't have any furniture except a bed, recliner, and electronics. In fact, he might have led her to believe he wasn't living like an animal.

All he could think of was to drive to Beauford as fast as he could. It had never even occurred to him to call. Now, Gabriella was talking into the phone and nodding. She met his eyes, smiled, and gave him a thumbs up.

She was saving him. No one had saved him in a very long time.

"Thank you, Pam," Gabriella said. "You have a good one, too. Definitely. Lunch next week—on me. I owe you for this, owe you big."

She owed someone for his favor. That was nice.

"All right." She was all business with a serious face. Clearly she didn't know about the icing. It was brown—probably chocolate. "This is what you're going to do. You're going around the corner to Halfway Home. It's next door to Sparkle, Neyland Beauford's jewelry studio. Pam will be waiting for you. You are going to give her your credit card number and some idea of what you want and how much you want to spend. Work out how she can get into your house early Friday morning since I assume you'll still be at the lake. She will make this happen."

Relief settled over him. "I don't care what it costs. I don't care what it looks like. And I can leave her a key."

"Settle that with her." She took his arm and moved him toward the door. "Just tell her what you need—sheets, towels, lamps. She has everything in her shop except big pieces of furniture, and she has connections for that."

They were on the sidewalk by now. "Sheets! I didn't think."

"You don't have to. Pam will think for you. Now, go. Then go to the rink. I'll text you in the morning before I head your way—probably about ten o'clock."

"Thank you, Gabriella. I really thank you. You're much better than Packi."

She laughed.

That did it. He couldn't stop himself. He quieted her laughter with a kiss. It wasn't a deep kiss or a sexy kiss, but it was nice—and the nicest thing about it was that when it was over she put her fingertips to her lips as if she wanted to keep it there.

CHAPTER EIGHTEEN

Stepping onto Bryant's front porch was like coming home. It was jarring—so much so that Gabriella almost forgot to congratulate him for the Sound's win the night before.

But only almost. "Good win last night."

"Good for the team." He stepped aside and motioned for her to come in. "Not great for me. I sucked."

"I'm sure you didn't suck."

"Did you see the game?" he challenged.

"No. I was baking."

"Trust me, I sucked. I got the ass-chewing of my life. It's happened before. It'll happen again. Hopefully not too soon." He smiled. "There's always tomorrow—literally, tomorrow. Winnipeg."

Time to change the subject. There was no reasoning with a hockey player who was convinced he had played poorly.

"I didn't know you lived in a Craftsman cottage." She gestured to the wide foyer with the built-in hall tree and leaded windows.

"Me neither. Is that what this is?" He looked around like he'd never seen his house.

She stepped from the foyer into the main part of the house, knowing what she'd find: hardwood floors, built-in cabinetry with glass doors, tiled fireplaces, and window seats. He didn't offer a tour, but she kept walking. Mesmerized, she had to see it. Her furniture had been built for this house. And there was plenty of room for it, too. The large living room held only a recliner, a giant flat screen television, and a TV tray. Unlike Emile's home, which was a Pottery Barn catalog on steroids, none of Bryant's other rooms had any furniture at all. She could see her prized library table in the room that would have been an office/library if there had been any books on the empty shelves.

The kitchen was a dream—a mix of modern convenience and respect for the past, with oak flat panel cabinets. And, angels above and demons below, he had four ovens—a Wolf range with two, and two more wall units. She could run a bakery out of this kitchen. Sadly, there were no smells of cinnamon and vanilla. Only soap and bleach—and with good reason. Everything was immaculate, but the table of the built-in banquette was piled high with mail, newspapers, and hockey equipment catalogs—all neatly stacked. Gabriella suspected the person—not Bryant—who had cleaned had also made these ordered piles for lack of knowing what to do with it.

Bryant followed her quietly as she made her rounds. Finally, she stopped by the staircase and laid her hand on the newel post. It was oak done right—smooth with a satiny matte finish. None of that thick, high gloss luster with a yellow cast. She looked longingly up the stairs, aching to see the bedrooms, but her tour had to be over.

"You like the house," Bryant said. It wasn't a question.

"So much. You have no idea. I can't believe you can own a house like this and not know the style. Do you know when it was built?"

He shrugged. "Sharon probably told me when she sold it to me, but I didn't pay any attention. I'm guessing a while back. What are you, some kind of house witch?"

She laughed. "No. I just have an interest in this particular era. I have some pieces of mission furniture."

He frowned. "Like church furniture?"

"No. It's—" She stopped. If he hadn't known the architectural style of his house, he likely cared even less about furniture. "Never mind. It's from the same time period as your house." She almost told him when that was, but since she didn't know who won the Stanley Cup during those years, she couldn't have given him a frame of reference.

He leaned on the railing and glanced up. "Aren't you going up to see the rest?"

She shook her head. "One should never go upstairs in someone's home without being invited." *Are you inviting me?*

"I might be able to arrange that. I know the owner." He was flirting, for sure. And he meant it.

"That might make us late for the turkey."

They were at a crossroads and they both knew it. If they went upstairs, they wouldn't stop going upstairs and behind doors until everything was a mess spewing forth like a dynamited septic tank. But if they didn't, this would be the third time they'd seen each other and displayed restraint and it would be over. Before long, they'd forget there had been any attraction. That realization came with a feeling of relief—until a big ball of sad moved in and chased it out. Relief couldn't stand a chance against sad. It never could.

"Maybe some other time?" He half smiled and dropped his eyelids.

She shook her head. "Probably not. I like this house so much that if I see upstairs, I might be tempted to lock you in the attic and take it for myself. So it's best if I don't see any more."

He read the double meaning there. She could see it in his eyes. If he invited her again, she wouldn't have it in her to say no. But he must have seen the wisdom there.

He slapped his forehead and gave a fake groan. "I hate it when a woman locks me in the attic! It's the worst." Some of the relief and sadness running around in her must have seeped out because it landed on his face.

"Yeah?" She tried to interject amused playfulness into her smile. "Does that happen a lot?"

"Ooh." He cocked his head to the side, widened his eyes, and gave his nod a little circular motion. "More often than you would think."

She turned to mush. He wasn't just gorgeous. He wasn't just funny, smart, and amazing in bed. He was so damned cute. Cute was always going to outlast gorgeous, and it was hard to walk away from.

But she didn't have to walk away from him, not completely. They were friends. She just couldn't walk up the stairs with him.

"We'd better get on the road before the temptation to take this house from you drives me to criminal behavior."

He nodded. "I agree—though you would look fetching in an orange jumpsuit."

She followed him out and unlocked her hatch. "I just have a bag and a cooler with the desserts."

"Pumpkin pie no doubt."

"That and pumpkin cheesecakes."

He lifted both things into the back of his SUV and set them beside his battered suitcase. Battering is what happened to road trip bags. Emile bought a new one every year. Bryant had probably had this one since juniors.

He slammed the back. "Thanksgiving is the worst dessert time of the year."

"I might have made some apple pies and a chocolate almond tart, too."

"Chocolate? Well, that's a piece of luck! The day is looking up."

He opened the passenger door and she settled in and fastened her seatbelt.

He didn't need to know luck had nothing to do with that tart. She had remembered that he didn't like pumpkin.

CHAPTER NINETEEN

Every Thanksgiving, Bryant swore he wasn't going to eat until he was miserable, and every year he did it anyway. It was an hour after the big feed and he could still barely breathe—though it wasn't just his jam-packed stomach causing him discomfort.

He was about to roast.

It was too hot in Sharon's giant lake house living room—and with good reason. Though it was a mild fall day, flames blazed in the massive fireplace. Bryant wasn't sure whose idea that had been. Probably Sharon's. She was running this show. After eating, he'd changed into shorts and a T-shirt, but he was still sweating like a whore in church.

He glanced across the room at Gabriella.

On the way over, she'd conked out before they'd gotten out of Sound Town and slept until he'd shaken her awake when they arrived. He'd briefly wondered if she'd been pretending to sleep. They'd come close to having sex before they left his house—never mind that they hadn't kissed, or even touched. He could tell and so could she. But she had probably really been asleep. It was reasonable that she would have played possum to avoid conversation and temptation, but she wouldn't have carried it to the extent of drooling and snoring a little from time to time.

He glanced across the room at her. She wasn't drooling or snoring now. She was sitting at a game table with Amy and Sparks Champagne where they were all melting wax and making something to do with wedding invitations. Did she know that she drooled and snored? Probably not.

Don't worry, sweetheart, your secret is safe with me. I would bust right through that glass wall and throw my Stanley Cup rings in the lake before I'd tell anyone you snore. Well, if he had his rings with him. And really, would there be any point in running right through the glass and making a bloody mess when there was door? Sharon had bought this house for the view of the lake and the trees. She probably wouldn't like it if somebody caused her to have to put up plywood, even temporarily.

Besides being hot, there was a lot of noise in here.

In this end of the room, he and the guys were watching football. Green Bay was losing and Jarrett was not a happy man. If it was possible that he loved something more than a rule, it was the Packers. Though he gave Bryant a knowing, disapproving look sometimes, Jarrett had been true to his word and not mentioned Gabriella to him again, which was a relief. You could always count on The Saint to keep his word. Of course, he didn't know about round two after the party was over—or the hand holding outside The Big Skate or the kiss outside Eat Cake.

Mikhail and Robbie were on the floor playing Legos with the two older kids, Dennis and Erik. The baby wasn't anywhere to be seen. Fresh hell washed over the room in the form of a new wave of heat. It was a wonder those Lego blocks hadn't melted into plastic puddles.

Bryant knocked back the rest of his beer, but his mouth was the only thing that was cool. "Emile, for the love of my sweat glands, stop poking at that fire."

Emile turned, and when Bryant saw his expression, he nearly jumped off the couch. He looked like the devil possessed. *"Non.* Man was made to have dominion over fire. I am asserting my supremacy over the flame."

"It's hot."

Emile shrugged and turned back to the fire. "Go to the other end of the room."

He glanced that way. Why was Sparks doing crafts instead of watching football? It wasn't natural. Just then, Sparks said something—though Bryant wasn't close enough to hear what—and Gabriella laughed. That was it; Sparks was down there to be near Gabriella. That was no good.

Bryant slowly rose and stretched. "I hate to leave a good ballgame but—"

Jarrett gave him a murderous look.

He moved to the other end of the room. It *was* cooler. Bryant dropped to the couch where Sharon was sitting.

"Welcome, Swifty." She didn't look up from her iPad, but Gabriella glanced his way.

"Amy, are you inviting Wyoming to your wedding?" Sharon asked.

"Not specifically." Amy pressed a little metal thing into a circle of hot wax. "We're inviting Mike Webber and a guest. It's up to him who he brings."

Sharon groaned. "That means Wyoming. She'll steal something and lie about it. Wait and see. She'll steal your going away dress and tell people she made it."

"What about me?" Sparks asked. "Do I get a guest?"

"Of course," Amy said.

"And I can bring anyone I want?"

"Anyone who will agree to come with you," Amy said.

"I pick you, Gabby," Sparks said. "I want you to be my date."

Oh, not just no! Fucking *hell* no!

"No," she said without missing a beat. "I don't date hockey players, especially ones who call me Gabby."

You tell him, Gabriella. Note to self: never call her Gabby.

Sparks sighed. "A guy has to try."

But did a guy? If it violated the Bro Code and the wishes of the lady in question? And most especially if a guy was certain to fail her?

"So, what does your going away outfit look like, Amy?" Sharon asked.

Amy looked up and glanced at Emile, presumably to see if he was listening. "It's very simple but pretty—sapphire blue. Gabriella helped me choose it. She has the best taste. It's a wool and silk blend, with a fitted bodice and a full skirt."

"But not *too* full," Gabriella said. "It has pin tucks at the waist. Not gathers. It looks wonderful on her."

"I had a *suit,*" Sharon said. "Beige. Can you believe it? It was so matronly. Everyone tried to talk me out of it, but I was so young. I thought I needed a suit to look like a wife. I never wore it again."

Wedding talk. Bryant got an uncomfortable feeling in the pit of his stomach. He was remembering another Thanksgiving afternoon dominated by wedding talk where he hadn't been able get away. Except it had been a two-day notice wedding, and there had been talk about which relative's dress would fit Philie because there was no time for new dresses, and which friends could be counted on to make hot dishes because there was no time for caterers. Yet, everyone had been joyful except him. Of course, he'd thought he was coming home from school to let Philie down easy.

"What are we eating?" Sparks asked. "I like to know what I'm going to eat—also, if it's something really good, it might help me get a date."

"We're having a buffet with a good variety," Amy said. "Salmon, beef tenderloin, chicken breasts stuffed with prosciutto, spinach, and smoked provolone. Then there's a vegetarian pasta dish. As for the sides …" She went on, naming dish after dish, optional sauces, salads, and then she started on the wine list.

With every word she spoke, Bryant's heart beat a little faster and his head spun a little more. And when they were done talking about food, they moved on to wedding music, wedding cake, wedding flowers, and wedding, wedding, wedding.

Bryant thought he was going to pass out.

There was commotion at the other end of the room. Halftime. And from the look on The Saint's face, things hadn't gotten any better for the Packers.

Emile came and put his hands on Amy's shoulders. "So do you have all your little wax seals made for the invitations?"

"Not yet, but soon. It's coming along," Amy said.

"We must go to the jewelry store on Monday," Emile said. "The book I read said we should have had our wedding bands in August."

Bryant and Philie had gotten married with borrowed rings, which they'd had to return after the ceremony. He'd bought Philie a big diamond and matching band with his signing bonus, but he'd never had a ring. She hadn't been happy about it, had never believed that he wasn't trying to hide his marital status, when the truth was he just didn't want to constantly have to take a ring on and off for hockey.

Everyone was laughing now and Amy looked at Emile adoringly. "We didn't know each other in August, so we couldn't have very well bought wedding bands."

Now, Sharon was waving her iPad in the air. "Look, Amy! We can get this hockey player and bride wedding cake topper from Etsy!"

"*Oui!*" Emile cried. "It is wonderful! Is he a goalie?"

"No!" Amy and Gabriella said in unison.

Mikhail, carrying the smaller boy, Erik, came to sit on the couch arm beside Sharon. Now they were all talking about hockey pucks printed with a picture of Emile and Amy for favors.

The older boy began to bang on the baby grand piano.

"Dennis!" Sharon called. "Stop that." He did not.

Bryant couldn't breathe.

"I've got him, Sharon," Robbie said. "Come here, laddie. I'll play. You sing."

And just when Bryant thought it couldn't get worse, Robbie sat down at the baby grand piano and began to play wedding songs.

Dennis stood on the bench singing made-up words at the top of his little lungs.

Bryant *had* to get out of here.

Praise the patron saint of hockey and all his buddies, his phone rang.

"Excuse me," he said, but no one noticed when he went out the door and collapsed on a bench overlooking the lake.

• • •

Something wasn't right with Bryant. He'd left the football game to join them, but he'd gone quiet and detached. Gabriella got why he had changed into shorts. It was warm in here, but he'd gone outside, where it was too cool for workout clothes. Why hadn't he gone to another room to take his call?

And who was calling anyway? His family? That made sense. It *was* Thanksgiving, but they were coming tomorrow, so why call? Maybe it was a puck bunny who wanted a little Thanksgiving treat. Maybe he'd head back to Nashville. Not that it was her business.

"Do we need to make rice bags?" Sharon asked over the cacophony coming from the piano, courtesy of Robbie and Dennis. "Do people still do that? I went to a wedding where they shook ribbon wands. It was stupid. Not a bubbles fan either."

"I thought we should have glitter," Emile said, "but Emory will not allow it at Beauford Bend."

"I'm amazed you thought she would," Amy said.

"I'm amazed that you have an opinion on glitter or rice," Mikhail said.

"Don't throw birdseed," Sparks said. "We had birdseed. That's what ruined my marriage."

"We're having rice," Amy said. "It doesn't hurt birds. That's a myth. And my aunts are making the bags."

Gabriella made a few more wax seals, all the time picturing people ripping them off the envelopes and tossing them in the trash. Would Robbie never stop playing that piano?

"Is anyone hungry?" Sharon asked. "I can put out snacks."

Surely no one was hungry after that monster meal.

"I am," Jarrett said.

"Did you make pigs in a blanket?" Mikhail asked.

"And cheese dip." Sharon rose. "I'll get it."

"I'll help you," Mikhail said.

"No, you just occupy Erik," Sharon said. Just then, wails burst forth from the baby monitor. "And can you get Lucya?"

"I'll get her!" Emile sprinted for the stairs.

Maybe since Jarrett and Mikhail were hungry, Bryant was too. Should she tell him Sharon was serving snacks? Was that what a friend would do? She glanced out the window. He was cold, shivering so hard he was shaking. Did he have a jacket down here? She looked around. She didn't see one, but her eyes landed on a throw on the back of the sofa where Sharon had been sitting. She should take it to him. That *was* what a friend would do. She wouldn't intrude, wouldn't stay around long enough to find out whom he was talking to. She'd just hand him the blanket and come back inside.

She rose, snatched it up, and headed to the door before anyone could ask what she was up to.

CHAPTER TWENTY

"Hello, Ma. Happy Thanksgiving." It was cooler out here than Bryant had expected. He reveled in it for a full minute before the breeze off the lake chilled his sweat-soaked body.

"Happy Thanksgiving to you, too, Bry! Everyone wants to say hello."

It would do no good to tell her to put him on speakerphone. She wouldn't do it. By the time he'd talked to his dad for a few minutes and said a few words to everyone else in the family, he was officially cold.

"You sound cold," Maggie said once she was on the line again.

"How can you tell?" he asked.

"I'm your mother. I know things."

"I'm all right. I'm outside in shorts. It was hot inside."

"Outside in shorts! It's November!"

"This is the South, Ma." She didn't live in a world where it could sometimes feel like spring in the winter—though he had to admit it didn't feel so spring-like here on the water. "You need to remember that when you pack for the weekend. Check the weather forecast for Nashville."

"I'm already packed."

"Of course you are." He laughed. No one had said a word about Philie, and it felt really good to be connected with home. "Never let it be said Maggie Taylor is unprepared."

"You have seven kids and see how it works out if you don't plan ahead."

"Seriously, Ma. Plan for the climate here. I want you to have a good time. You won't if you're overdressed."

"You bet. I got it. Do you know what I'd like to do?"

"No. But I'll make it happen for you if I can." He was feeling pretty nostalgic right now.

"I'd like for all of us to go to the Olive Garden for your pregame meal on Saturday." So much for the Butter Factory brunch reservation that he'd had to pull some strings to get for such a large party on a holiday weekend. But he smiled. She loved Olive Garden and there wasn't one in St. Sebastian. As a kid, he had loved it, too. For road games, they'd always gone to Olive Gardens for his carb-up meals when there was one available.

"For sure, Ma."

"Now, tell me what you ate for Thanksgiving."

"Turkey, cornbread dressing, sweet potato casserole, macaroni and cheese, corn casserole. You know, the usual stuff." *Chocolate almond tart.* He didn't mention that, because he wanted to keep it to himself.

"That's not our usual stuff. No Snickers apple salad or wild rice hot dish?"

"No, but we had a strawberry Jell-O pretzel salad."

"Interesting. Lisa Tervo brings that to church potlucks. It's good for summer. But for my money, you need Snickers apple salad for Thanksgiving."

"For sure."

"I don't know about that cornbread stuff. It sounds terrible. I use good old plain white bread."

"That's the best." He had really preferred the cornbread dressing that Amy had made, but he didn't dare say that was a large part of why he was still so stuffed. No need to get Maggie cranked up. Things were going so well. He wasn't about to ruin it over cornbread.

"You don't worry. I'll make you some when you come home for Christmas. And I'm bringing your favorite bars on the plane tomorrow—Rice Krispie Scotcheroos."

"Sounds good, Ma." Time to wrap this up while everybody still felt good. Besides, he was shivering in earnest. "I can't wait to see you. Remember, I have to be at the rink before your plane gets in, but I have arranged to have you picked up. They have all the instructions about where to take you. And I'll see you after the game."

"Yeah, you bet. I printed out your email with all that. But just one more thing."

And here it comes. He felt it in his gut.

"About the Mass on Sunday morning at the Cathedral."

Fuck, fuck, fuck. This was not going to be good.

"Yeah?" The shaking increased and it wasn't just from the cold anymore. She was loaded for bear, and he was the bear.

"I have a surprise for you." She was nervous, and that paired about as well with surprise as lutefisk with chocolate milk. This was going to be beyond *not good*; it was going to be *bad,* so bad.

"Yeah?"

"I know how disappointed you were to have to take a miss on Mary Philomena's birthday Mass—but you couldn't help it."

Doom, absolution, and rewritten history all in one breath. Maggie could make one sentence do a lot of work, that was for sure.

"So we—Beverly and I—spoke to Father Martin. It was short notice, but he was able to arrange to have another Mass for Mary Philomena on Sunday in Nashville."

Bryant's brain shut down. His senses took over and he settled into taking in his surroundings—the fancy outdoor kitchen with a fireplace and built-in grill, the trees on fire with orange, yellow, and red, the lake that looked like blue glass. Pretty. Serene. It would be nice to skate on that lake, but it would never happen, would never freeze hard enough, if at all. Maybe he could get Sharon to build a fire out here later. It was stacked with wood and ready to light. Emile could poke at it all he wanted without turning the world into an incinerator.

"Bry?" She sounded anxious. Good reason. This was the part where he was supposed say, *"Whatever,"* and let it go.

"No," he said.

"What?" Could she really be surprised that he said *no?* She knew he had never brought that piece of his old life to his new one.

"I said, *no.* No birthday Mass. I will be more than happy to light candles for Philie with you, Beverly, and anyone else who wants to in a private moment of remembrance. In fact, I would like that, but that's as far as it goes."

"It's all arranged. Father Martin went to some trouble."

"Then Father can go to some more trouble and unarrange it. I mean it, Ma. There will be no memorial Mass for Philie in Nashville this week or any other week."

"It's done," she insisted. "I suppose you can refuse to go, like you did before."

"So now I refused. A minute ago, I couldn't help it. Which is it, Ma?"

"Does it matter?"

"Not really. But it's not happening. I *am* going, like I said. I will be at Mass at the Cathedral Sunday morning, whether you go or not. I will go if I am the only one in that church, if the Bishop runs off to Las Vegas, and the Holy Father calls off Catholicism. I'll break in if I have to."

"Bryant! Do not blaspheme!"

He ignored her comment and plowed right on, "But there is *not* going to be a Mass for Philie. You can put a stop to it in your own way, or I will. If I get there and it's happening, I will shout the house down. Don't think I can't and don't think I won't. I will act so bad that I will be excommunicated from the Church and heaven. The Pope himself won't be able to save me from hell, and that will be on you."

"Bryant Michael." Ah, there it was—the full name. "Calm yourself. Are you overwrought because you didn't play well last night?"

Holy Saint Sebastian, patron saint of hockey!

"No. I wasn't overwrought at all until you started this emotional blackmail crap again. Ma, why can't we just be a family?"

She gasped. "We *are* a family. We planned this Mass for *you.*"

"No, you did not. Look, Ma, I don't understand all this myself and maybe you don't either. But in some weird way, you're trying to tie me to you, the family, and St. Sebastian with this eternal, damnable martyrdom of Philie. You just need to realize you don't *need* to tie me to you. The only thing that's driving me away is that you won't let me move on."

"Well, if you think honoring your dead wife is not moving on …"

"This is not about honoring Philie." *And Alexander. They had been going to call him Alexander.* Nobody alive knew that except him.

"Maybe we shouldn't come. It's clear you don't want us to."

He came very close to cursing at his mother, something he had never done. Deep breaths, deep breaths. There was a flock of birds flying overhead. He had no idea what kind, except not roosters or penguins. He didn't know birds.

"Did I say I didn't want you to come? Have I not been trying to get you to visit me in Nashville since I've been here? Have you repeatedly refused?"

"Bryant, I—"

He cut her off. "No, let me finish. Have you refused, like if you don't come, Nashville or anywhere else in the universe besides St. Sebastian where I might want to be, won't exist? Of course I want you to come. You are my mother; they are my family. I love you all and I want to see you. I want to show you a good time. I want you to see me skate on home ice. What I do not want is a Mass for Philie. And it isn't going to happen."

Some of the wind must have gone out of her sails, because when she spoke again, she sounded a little beaten, but she made one last-ditch effort to get her way and save him from the world outside of St. Sebastian. "It does seem that Mary Philomena's family should have some say in whether the Mass takes place."

"Maybe. But at the end of the day, I'm the husband. That trumps family. And I say no."

There was a pause. She was waiting for him to speak, to recant. He waited her out.

"You bet, Bry. If that's what you want."

Now, Ma, how did you figure out that was what I wanted? He wouldn't say that, of course. That would be uncalled for snarkiness.

"It is what I want. And I want you to come."

"All right. I'll call Father. I'll explain to Beverly."

"Then I'll see you tomorrow night. I love you, Ma."

"I love you, too."

After hanging up, he sat for a moment numb, but the moment passed and with it the numbness. That's when he got the sense that someone was looking at him. And somehow, he knew that someone wasn't just anyone. He turned slowly and looked over his shoulder.

Gabriella stood like a statue, eyes wide and as blue as the lake. She held a little blanket in her outstretched hands as if she were about to hand it to someone. One foot was in front of the other like she'd frozen in mid-step. Her hair, stirring in the breeze, was the only thing about her in motion.

"I ... I was only bringing you this." She lifted the blanket upward a few inches. "You looked cold. I didn't mean to overhear. Really. I was going to give you the throw and go back inside."

"What did you hear?" He could hope, but doubted if hearing him tell his mother he loved her would make her incapable of movement.

"The first thing I heard—and the most remarkable—is that you're the husband. I'm not sure I heard anything after that."

He nodded. "I see." Clearly he was going to have to tell the story. On some level maybe it would be a relief to tell her. "You surely don't think that I have a wife hiding in the attic or squirreled away in St. Sebastian."

She shook her head, but he got the sense that it meant, *"I'm confused,"* rather than, *"No, I don't think that."*

"I don't know what to think," she said.

He moved to make room for her on the bench. "Then I guess you'd better come here and sit down." He had no idea how she would react. The only thing he was sure of was that his secret would now be their secret. She would never tell and there was comfort in that.

CHAPTER TWENTY-ONE

Husband? That meant there had to be a wife. And how could that be? She certainly wasn't in Nashville.

Gabriella willed herself to take the steps to close the distance between her and the bench where Bryant sat. She felt like the tin man who'd been caught in the rain. Then Bryant looked at her beseechingly and she noticed his lips were blue. He needed the throw. That got her moving—that and she wanted to know what the hell was going on.

"Here." She wrapped the throw around him and sat down.

"I'll share." He covered her legs. They were close together, but there wasn't much warmth coming from him. "I suppose you're wondering what that was all about."

"It would be hard not to."

He met her eyes full on. "First off, I know my reputation—and you know I deserve it. But no matter what you might think of me, I would not cheat. That's not who I am. I don't have a wife. But I did. For a short while."

"So you're divorced? It happened before you came here?" That didn't make sense if he was still the husband. And what had he been arguing with his mother about? "You would have been so young. You would have been—" She paused to do the math.

"Nineteen when it happened. I was twenty when I came here. But it wasn't a divorce." He looked at his hands and then back at her. "She died."

Gabriella's hair stood on end and her mouth went dry. "Died? Your wife died?" She had to say it to make it real, but still it wasn't. "Emile never said anything."

Bryant shook his head. "He wouldn't—couldn't. He doesn't know. I never told anyone here. Until now."

"So *no one* in Nashville knows?"

He shrugged. "I don't know for sure. I was a rookie who hadn't seen much ice time. It hardly made the local news, much less national. Packi might know. He seems to. The brass might. Who knows what the Red Wings's top guys and coaches told the guys down here. But they've never said anything."

"I see," she said, though she didn't. "She would have been young, too. An accident?"

"No. Not an accident." He closed his eyes. "I guess you want to know what happened."

Damn straight she did. "If you want to tell me."

"She—Philie—was pregnant. She had preeclampsia. I was on the road. She died while I was gone. That's pretty much it."

"So your wife *and* your baby? Oh, God." The horror of it all washed over her like lava down a mountain. "Bryant, I am so *sorry.*" She laid a hand on his arm.

"Don't put a whole lot of energy into feeling sorry for me. She tried to tell me she was sick. She wanted me to drive her to St. Sebastian, but there was no time. I should have insisted on flying her mother in or hiring a nurse. But she didn't want it. When I left, we were mad. I thought that's why she wasn't answering the phone. And when I came back she was dead."

And there was fresh horror, fresh lava. "You mean you found her?"

"Uh huh." He looked at the lake.

"And you blame yourself for this?"

"Who else is there to blame?"

"Sometimes there is no blame."

"Not this time."

"Bryant, you were nineteen. And it sounds like you tried to find a solution to keep from leaving her alone."

"Not hard enough. And deep down, I didn't really believe she was that sick. Philie was eighteen. She could be pretty dramatic."

"Being dramatic is a vocation for an eighteen-year-old girl."

He gave a half laugh. "I guess. And I guess it's pretty obvious she was pregnant when we got married."

"I don't know about obvious, but there aren't many teenage marriages these days."

"No. She was my high school girlfriend. The Red Wings drafted me out of juniors, but I also got a scholarship to Boston College. I decided to go to school and put off signing with the Red Wings until I graduated. But Philie got pregnant, so I quit school, signed the contract, and there we were. After it happened, I asked for a trade. So I came here. That's the story."

Gabriella doubted if that was even half the story.

"What were you arguing with your mother about?" All he could do was tell her it was none of her business.

He sighed and ran his hand over his face. "That's a whole other thing. You have to understand, St. Sebastian is small—small and tight. Everybody goes to the same school, goes to the same church, works in the same paper mill, skates on the same pond, goes to the same corn feeds, smelt fries, and chili cook-offs in the same church basement or VFW hall. Philie was friends with my sisters. Our mothers were on altar guild together. Our dads worked the same shift at the mill and played men's pickup together."

"A lot about that sounds nice." She'd grown up in a small hockey town like that, too, but their family had never been part of it—isolated because of the abuse. Her father hadn't wanted them close to anyone.

Bryant looked surprised. "A lot of it was—is. It's like I told you the other night outside of The Big Skate. There's a lot to love about home. And you remember how I told you my family—my mother primarily, though she's just the spokesperson—didn't want to let me go?"

"Yes."

"I'm sure that it wasn't anyone's top choice for Philie to get pregnant first and the wedding to come later, but they weren't that upset either." To Gabriella's surprise, Bryant took her hand under the blanket. It was odd to hold his hand while he talked about being married to someone else, but she didn't pull away. "To my family, marrying Philie cemented me to St. Sebastian and them. Sure, they knew—or hoped—I'd play in the NHL and make a name for myself. But they always wanted me to come home when it was all over and be one of them. They knew Philie would make that happen. She was St. Sebastian through and through. She hated Detroit, was just serving her time out until she could go back home. When she died, all bets were off. They didn't know what I'd do. They'd lost Philie. They'd lost the baby. And now, they might lose me, too. I'm sympathetic to that. I really am."

His tortured expression took root in her heart. "But?"

"*But* every time I turn around, we have to have a big, public, Philie mourning. There's always a birthday Mass, a memorial Mass, a grave visit on holidays. And that's what led up to the row with my mother today. I always go back for those special Masses and the big family meals afterward where they make all of Philie's favorite food and bring out the picture albums."

"My sweet Lord!" Gabriella clapped her hand over her mouth. "Sorry."

"No. You're speaking my language. So, anyway, I couldn't make it back for the birthday mass this year because of the party for Emile and Amy. All day they sent me pictures." His eyes went hollow and haunted. "This time, they put a bear wearing a little Sound jersey on her grave. You know." His voice dropped to a whisper. "For the baby. They'd never done that before."

Pure pitch black moved in and overtook her. Gabriella had felt such despair before, but never for another person. Who were these people? How could they be so insensitive? Clearly, Bryant loved them, so maybe they meant well, but sometimes meaning well wasn't worth a damn. Her mother had meant well. And Bryant had been living with all this since he was nineteen years old. No wonder he constantly distracted himself by having sex with every puck bunny who shook her cotton tail at him, and no wonder he'd had sex with her—Gabriella—the night of the party. Oddly, she wasn't offended. In the face of such heartbreak, if she'd offered him any comfort at all, so be it. Besides, she'd needed solace herself that night for reasons much more trivial. So it was no different.

"Oh, Bryant. Oh, sweetheart." She would have taken him in her arms if they hadn't been sitting in full view of everyone inside. The best she could do was offer a term of endearment.

He waved his hands. "I don't want to talk about that. But on to getting into it with my mother today. I had said I'd go to Mass this Sunday at the Cathedral and we'd light candles for Philie. But my mother set up a whole new birthday Mass without discussing it with me. That's what you came in on. I said I was the husband, and it wasn't going to happen."

"Good for you. That's not good for anybody." And he was the only one who could put a stop to this morbid way of life.

He didn't seem to hear her. He was on a roll. "On Philie's *actual* birthday, I was in Colorado. They all called to tell me they were thinking about me. *All.* Consider what *all* means. I have parents and six brothers and sisters. Most of them have spouses. Philie had parents and five brothers and sisters. They all have spouses. Do you know how many phone calls that is? And it was game day. Pretty soon, the nieces and nephews will be old enough to call. Then they'll get married and there will be more spouses. And I just want some peace." He stopped abruptly. "I sound like an unappreciative bastard, don't I? Whining because my family cares about me. There are lots of people who would love to hear anything at all from their families." He stopped abruptly. "I'm sorry. I'm sure you'd love it if your family called you all the time."

For the barest second, she was confused. "My family *does* call me all the time. There was a short time there for a bit when I wasn't hearing from Emile as often as usual, but it passed."

"I didn't mean Emile."

"I know." She took a deep breath. Inasmuch as Gabriella never talked about the abusive home she and Emile had grown up in, everyone knew it because Emile had no secrets. But maybe it was time to give a little piece of herself away—just a tiny piece. That's all she could spare and this wasn't about her. "But Johanna and Paul are my parents. Wishing things had been different doesn't do any good. It only robs you of the present. My mother died. I'm sorry. I mourn her. My father is in prison. I don't hear from him. I don't wish to. I don't have baggage about it—or at least very little. A lot of people would. But I chose a different path. I chose to let Johanna and Paul be my parents. Bryant, it is possible to move on."

"I wish my family knew that."

"It's been, what? Five years?"

He nodded. "Five years. Nearly six."

"For what it's worth, I don't think you sound like an unappreciative bastard. You sound like a man who wants to put his grief in its appropriate place and move on."

He let his eyelids drop to half-mast and looked at her for a long minute. "Yes. You get it. You get it exactly. And why not? What happened to you was as bad … worse."

"No. You can't compare. Bad is bad. Everyone has it. You just have to find a way to live with it. The only difference is, I have found a way and you haven't."

He nodded. "I'm a grown man. I should have found a way."

She got the feeling no one had ever validated him before. "Bryant, what you're feeling is appropriate. There's no timeline to finding your way."

"Do you really think so?" Just for a split second, he was a little boy who wanted to be sure his finger painting was good enough.

She squeezed Bryant's hand under the blanket.

"You just have to let it go. Sure, you'll always mourn. There are days that it's on your mind. But you can't live with it day in and day out. It's not natural. What you're feeling *is* natural. I'm sure your family loves you and they mean well, but this needs to stop."

"They really do and it really does."

"But I don't think they are the ones making you hang on to your guilt and grief. You're doing that yourself."

He opened his mouth, probably to protest, but seemed to think better of it. "You might be right."

"I never wanted to hear from my father after he murdered my mother, and Paul, Johanna, and Emile all told him that. But he kept trying to contact me. This rocked on for a few years. But do you know what it took to end it? I had to write him a letter and tell him. You're the only one who can get control of this situation."

"I'll give it some thought."

She didn't tell him that sleeping with every lithe young thing in a Sound jersey was no way to cope either. That would seem too much like she wanted him for herself.

But there was something she was going to ask. "Is this why you are emotionally unavailable? Because you loved Philie so much?" Her voice was a scared whisper.

If possible, his face became more miserable. "No." He shook his head. "Because I didn't."

She didn't believe that for a minute. If there had been no love, he wouldn't be so haunted. but she wouldn't insult him with platitudes.

In that moment, she knew beyond a shadow of a doubt that he'd been telling the truth when he said he would never hurt her. He was safe, sensitive, and utterly incapable of hurting someone.

"You're a good man, Bryant. That's really all that matters. And you deserve to be happy."

"It means a lot that you think so, Gabriella, even if it isn't true."

"I can't make you believe it. You have to get there yourself, just like you're the only one who can stop your family from putting you on this eternal emotional roller coaster."

He nodded.

They both gazed at the lake for a few silent minutes. The sun was setting.

Finally, she spoke again. "If I can help, I'm here. Anything I can do, I will."

His head snapped up. "Do you mean it?"

"Of course. We're friends. Remember?"

"How do you feel about a Tour of Italy?"

"As appealing as it might sound, I don't think running away to Italy would help."

He gave her the old Bryant smile. "No. It's an item on the Olive Garden menu. Would you go with me to meet my family Saturday? I need a friend."

Angels above and demons below, hell no! "Of course," she said. Because that's what friends say—especially friends who are pleasers. But somehow, she knew she would have wanted to please Bryant even if she hadn't been a pleaser by nature.

She stood. "Come inside, Bryant. You need to take a hot shower and put on some warm clothes.

"Can you persuade your brother to let the inferno die down?"

"I'll try." And she would. She would have tried to fly to Egypt by flapping her arms if he'd asked it of her.

CHAPTER TWENTY-TWO

Confession is good for the soul. Bryant had heard that all his life. He wasn't sure about the soul, but it was good for the shoulders.

He felt lighter. It seemed as though the secret between him and Gabriella had caused them to drift together. He'd come down from his shower to find that everyone had moved to the deck to sit around the outdoor fireplace. He'd gone straight to the little couch for two where Gabriella sat like he had a homing device strapped to his back and she was home. It never occurred to him to sit anywhere else. Likewise, she had unfolded her long legs from the space beside her and moved over to make room for him as if there wasn't another empty seat available.

And as far as he was concerned, there wasn't. Though it didn't make a lot of sense, the buzz between them was still as strong, but it was softer, too—like a solid shot of the puck to the net wrapped in finesse. The place above her knee was comforting against his hand, but it was more—full of expectation. No one would have noticed that he was touching her even if she hadn't had a blanket over her lap. How could they with all the s'mores making, wedding talking, and fire poking? And let's not forget the reveling because the Packers had pulled it out in the last quarter.

But Gabriella noticed. When he settled her hand on her leg, she barely turned her head in his direction, but her expression was clear. She felt what he felt. They were going to have sex—tonight—and they both knew it. There was no hurry, no manic need to rush upstairs like a four-year-old eager to see what Santa had brought.

They knew what Santa would bring, and they were totally in sync in their restful anticipation. The rest was good. He felt a good kind of weary, like he always felt after swimming all day.

So they rested in a mellow kind of way. He had a few beers. She had a glass of wine. They shared a turkey sandwich because neither of them wanted a whole one, and he was happy to slather it with cranberry sauce because she wanted it, though he didn't usually eat it.

Later, after the kids had been put to bed and the fire had died down, they all pitched in and cleaned the kitchen. Sparks and Robbie settled in to play a video game, and Mikhail tossed over his shoulder as everyone else went upstairs, "Eat more if you like, but if you mess it up, clean it up."

Bryant had one bad moment when Jarrett said, "And remember, guys, there are some things you'd better not mess up, because they can't be cleaned up." He pretended like he was talking to Sparks and Scottie, but it was Bryant's eyes he met. "Right, Swifty?"

"You usually are," he said.

But that wasn't going to deter him. It was going to happen.

But how long did one need to wait before visiting the lady in question when her brother was under the same roof? Not to mention a judge and spy in training, otherwise known as The Saint? Bryant pondered this as he sat on his bed and stared at the clock on the DVD player.

Then there was a knock on his door. If that was Jarrett, he was going to throw him off the roof.

But it wasn't. Gabriella had come to him—in a nightgown. It wasn't a sexy nightgown, but she didn't need it. Neither did he.

She tasted like the chocolate and marshmallow of her s'more. He tasted it for a good long time because he took a good long time with her mouth. And she was fully and completely in his arms— no hand holding outside The Big Skate or under a blanket. No just touching her knee.

Finally, he broke the kiss. With his mouth millimeters from hers he said, "Secondhand s'mores."

She laughed and leaned her forehead to his mouth. "Such sexy talk."

"This room can't hold any more sexy." He lifted her face so he could see her eyes.

"Kiss me again," she said. "I could kiss you like that all night."

And he did. The kiss set the tone—slow and thorough. From there, they continued to take a good long time with each other—the undressing, the caressing, the just lying close together, belly to belly and cheek to cheek.

This time it wasn't hurried and desperate. Her hands were soft, sweet, and comforting on him and he did his best to return the favor. There weren't just moans of pleasure, but sighs of contentment, not just demands for more, but sweet words of gratification.

It had never been like this before, not just with Gabriella, but with anyone. Over the years he'd learned some things and taught some things, but this was brand new. This was a surprise when he thought there were no surprises left, the most intimate sex he'd ever had.

Aside from Swifty, he had another nickname—one invented by and circulated among the puck bunnies. Sexpert. He'd always laughed about it, but he'd never been proud of it.

This—what passed between him and Gabriella—he was proud of. Maybe it should scare him. Maybe it would another day.

But not today. Not tonight.

She snuggled against him and snored, just a little.

CHAPTER TWENTY-THREE

Gabriella woke up the next morning in her own bed—or the bed that Sharon had assigned to her. She sat up confused. Had she dreamed last night with Bryant? Surely not. Her imagination wasn't that good.

She reached for her phone to check the time. 8:43 a.m. Oh. And she had a text message from Bryant.

> Had to leave early with the boys to get back for early skate. You were sleeping really good, so I put you to bed. Olive Garden tomorrow at 11 a.m. TY.

She wasn't riding back to the city with Bryant. Disappointed rained down on her, which made no sense, because now that she thought about it, she shouldn't have expected to go back with him. She'd lived with hockey all her life. She knew there was always morning skate. They would have had to leave an hour ago at the latest. Had she just been so tired from her long work hours that she hadn't thought it through? Or had she wanted the two hours with Bryant so much that she had assumed there would be no morning skate so she could have what she wanted?

How had he carried her to bed without waking her? Come to think of it, how had he carried her to bed at all? She was nearly six feet tall. Obviously, he'd managed—and obviously she wouldn't see him tonight at The Big Skate after the game. He would probably eat with his family at the hotel before taking his parents and sister back to his house.

And what was the *TY* thanks for? For agreeing to eat a Tour of Italy? For the sympathetic ear? The sex? She didn't want to be thanked for any of that.

Overthinking. She was no stranger to it, but she'd never overthought a relationship with a man in her life. But she'd seen it in action. Amy, Hélène-Louise, Pam. They'd all done it when they were in love. Maybe it was fundamental to the process.

Only she wasn't in love. She couldn't be. Even if she had slain her demon and knew Bryant wouldn't hurt her, he hadn't slain his.

She swung her legs to the floor and stood. She was wearing the long cotton nightgown she'd worn across the hall last night, so he must have wrestled her back into it. Apparently he was better at undressing than dressing a woman, because her gown was inside out and backwards.

She set it right, combed her hair, and went downstairs to the kitchen. No need to worry about appearing in her nightgown. The oldest male in the house was five years old. The rest of them would be on the ice by now.

Sharon and Amy were sitting at the kitchen table eating pie.

"Hey, sleepyhead," Sharon said. "There's coffee and hot water for tea."

"And pie for breakfast?" Gabriella poured herself a cup of coffee. Usually, she was a tea drinker, but she needed a stronger jolt of caffeine this morning.

"Amy got up and made the guys a healthy breakfast, but I'm through cooking for the weekend."

"I don't blame you." Gabriella sat down and cut herself a slice of apple pie. "I'm cooked out myself. But Eat Cake is closed until Monday. June says no amount of money is worth opening on Black Friday after we've worked so hard."

"Your pies and cheesecakes were the best things we had. Don't tell anybody, but I let my kids have pie for breakfast, too."

"No worse than a Pop-Tart," Amy said. "Probably better."

Gabriella looked around. "Where are the kids?"

"Lucya's asleep and the boys are watching *The Lego Movie*. Don't judge me."

Gabriella laughed. "I'm only judging you on the turkey and the hospitality, and you win."

"Absolutely," Amy said. "Everything was so good. But if you're done cooking, what's Mikhail doing for a pregame meal?"

Sharon wrinkled her nose. "Oh, that. I don't really consider that cooking. I've done it so many times, I don't even think about it anymore. It's the same thing every game day. Rotisserie chicken from Trader Joe's and ziti with marinara. I used to cook the chicken myself, but Mikhail can't tell the difference. We always make gallons of marinara in the summer and freeze it in small portions for pregame meals."

"Emile doesn't eat the same thing every time. He likes marinara and Alfredo. It wouldn't work for the Alfredo, but I could freeze a big batch of marinara."

"Such good hockey wives," Gabriella said.

"Do you think Wyoming makes Webber a pregame meal?" Sharon asked.

"She's not a hockey wife," Gabriella said. "She's a hockey girlfriend." But she—Gabriella—wasn't even that. What was she?

"Wyoming's a wannabe. But she'd better know it's a full-time job," Sharon said, "especially on game day and especially after the children come."

Amy got that dreamy look on her face—no doubt thinking of babies again. "Maybe you can give me some advice."

"I've found some shortcuts, like the chicken and freezing the game day pasta sauce. Mikhail and I make it together. I always have a few containers left when the season's over, so I'll give you some, Amy. And next summer you and Emile should come over so we can all do it together. It'll be fun."

It did sound like fun, though Gabriella had no reason to make game day marinara.

Sharon must have caught the wistfulness hanging around Gabriella. "And you should come, too, Gabriella. It wouldn't be a party without you. You could make sauce and sell it to the single guys."

"Sure," she said. "Why not?"

The hockey life: Practice, stretch, practice, high protein breakfast, early skate, pregame nap, pregame high carb meal, to the rink early for sewer ball, game, post game meal, bed, and start it all over again the next day unless it was the last game of the series. She knew this life, but she'd never live it.

Unless she did. There were still problems, sure. Opening up yesterday had to be a step toward healing.

As for Emile—in the scheme of things, that wasn't much of an issue. She could deal with him.

She and Bryant had connected yesterday when he'd told her about Philie, and last night had been—well, phenomenal, and not just sex, even if he didn't know it. And she was no fool. They weren't going to stop having sex. So why not just settle back and see what would happen? You couldn't rush baking a meringue for Pavlova. It had to be low and slow. Maybe this was the same.

"Speaking of pregame, we probably should think about heading back to the city." Amy brought her back to the kitchen where there was one woman who was a hockey wife, one woman who was soon to be a hockey wife, and one who still didn't know who she was, but might feel a little possibility blooming.

"Right." Gabriella rose. "Just let me run through the shower. Fifteen minutes?"

"Perfect," Amy said.

It was hard not to wonder what Bryant did about his pregame meal. His kitchen didn't look like it had ever been cooked in.

Maybe he went out or ate those terrible shelf stable pasta meals that Emile used to eat.

Or maybe a puck bunny delivered. Gabriella couldn't say she hadn't known that going in.

But, it seemed, she *was* in—at least to see what would happen.

CHAPTER TWENTY-FOUR

"I wanted to tell you again, Swifty, great game last night." Sound team captain, Nickolai Glazov, clapped Bryant on the back as they headed to the locker room after Saturday morning early skate.

"Thanks, man. I owed the team after that Dallas game."

"We all have a bad game sometimes," Glaz said. "It is best if we do not all have them the same night."

Bryant was a hero once more. He hadn't had the game of his life again, but he'd held his own in the 3-2 win over Winnipeg last night with two assists. Maybe there was something to what Packi had said about him playing better when Gabriella was there. Though he hadn't talked to her, he'd spotted her from the bench in the WAG suite. He had thought he would see her earlier when she came for her car, but he'd missed her. When he'd gone home yesterday after eating with Sparks, Scottie, and Webber, he'd found Pam Anderson hanging curtains in the newly furnished bedrooms, but Gabriella's car was gone.

But still, it had been a good day—beginning with waking up with Gabriella. He'd taken it as a personal challenge to carry her into her own room without waking her or getting caught, and he'd won. Just like they'd won the game against Winnipeg.

And so far, so good with his family. They'd had a pleasant late dinner together at the Hyatt, and then he'd had a good visit with his parents back at his house. Turns out, he should have bought a couch or two in addition to the bedroom stuff, but he'd moved the mail off the kitchen table and they'd sat there.

And no one had mentioned Philie.

He accepted the Gatorade that appeared in his hand and sat down in his stall. "Thanks, Packi." He drank the whole bottle in two gulps.

In the next stall, Emile said, "Ah, yes. There was a time when Packi handed me a Gatorade." He was already out of his skates and was shucking his clothes.

"Uh huh." Packi grinned. "There was a time."

"I have figured something out." Emile was totally naked now. Thank God he wrapped a towel around his waist.

"Most excellent," Packi said. "I love it when my boys start to figure things out. What is it?"

"I sense that Swifty has a love interest. I even accused him of wanting spend time with my sister."

Bryant's insides froze.

"Is that right?" Packi asked benignly.

"I was wrong," Emile said. "My friend would never do that. But, Packi, you helped me out when I was trying to find my way to Amy. Only I did not know that. Now you are helping Swifty out. I am thinking he has a secret lady. *Oui,* Swifty?"

Oh, hell. *"Non,* Mr. French Kiss. I have no secrets." Plenty of lies, though, and that last statement was another one.

"We will see. I thought I had no secrets, but they were secret even from *moi."* And he ambled off to the showers.

Packi leaned in and spoke quietly. "No secrets, huh? So you haven't told him."

"Packi, I've told you. There's nothing to tell." Bryant was way past pretending he didn't know what Packi was talking about. "Gabriella is a friend—a good friend." Was that a lie? He didn't even know anymore. But no matter how he felt, there was still no future there.

"Uh huh." Packi nodded. "My wife is my friend. That's the magic. Attraction is good. Friendship on top of attraction is better. It's the liking that gets you through the tough times."

Could that be true? If so, he and Philie would have never gotten through tough times. Even in the early days when they were so wrapped up in young love, it was all chemistry. She had depended on her sisters and girlfriends for companionship, just as he had depended on his brothers and teammates.

"Do you want another Gatorade?" Packi asked.

Bryant looked down at the crushed plastic bottle in his hand. He didn't remember crushing it. "No. I'm okay. I'm about to go meet my family for an early lunch."

"How's that going?"

"Good. Really, good, Packi. They loved the ice suite. The hotel rooms are great. The drivers and cars you found have been perfect. They appreciate it and so do I. I would have never been able to organize this like you have. I don't know what I'm going to do when you figure out I don't need any extra pampering."

"Yeah? By the time I figure that out, you really won't need any help."

"Whatever."

Packi laughed. "I'll leave you to it. You don't want to be late for your family." He walked away, but turned back. "Say, did you *tell* your family you're bringing Gabriella to lunch?"

Bryant's head snapped up? *Did* he have some kind of magic power, like a few of the guys claimed? "How did you know that? Are you some kind of psychic?"

Packi laughed a shook his head. "See? That's how these things get started. A guy makes an educated guess, asks a question, and he gets a reputation for being supernatural. So, did you tell them?"

Bryant bent to unlace his skates. "Why would I? When they travel to see me play, I always bring friends when I meet them for meals. They're used to it."

"Emile? Glaz? Mikhail?"

"Sure. Jarrett, Thor, Robbie, Sparks. As I said, friends."

"Uh huh." Bryant loved Packi, but he hated how he said *uh huh,* like he knew secrets. "Leave your skates out. They took a beating last night. I'll clean them up and sharpen them."

"Thanks, Packi."

"Have a good time at Olive Garden."

"You bet."

Wait. How did he know they were going to Olive Garden?

CHAPTER TWENTY-FIVE

Dressing to meet Bryant's family would have been easier had Gabriella not had her nifty little muddle-minded realization over coffee in Sharon's kitchen yesterday—not that the realization had revealed anything except confusion.

Weren't realizations supposed to unveil mind-blowing truths so grounded in confidence that there could never be any question of the rightness of them? Or was that an epiphany? She hadn't had time to look it up since she'd been debating between a skirt and pants for her Olive Garden outing.

Last night at the game, she hadn't even tried to look at anyone else when Bryant was on the ice. He hadn't fought, though he'd taken at least one dirty hit from behind that the officials hadn't seen. And he'd been pure hockey perfection in motion.

Once, when she had been at one of Emile's college games, Gabriella had overheard one of the hockey girlfriends say to her friend, "Watching him play turns me on so much I want to sneak into the locker room between periods and have my way with him!" The girl and her friend had laughed, but Gabriella had been appalled. Over the years, she'd heard similar comments, but she'd never believed that prowess on the ice inspired sexual desire. She had certainly never understood it.

She understood it now. Yeah, buddy.

Watching a powerful, gifted athlete, who had actually had his hands on you and told you his secrets, play an extraordinary game was different from thinking in the abstract. When the game had ended last night, she'd been wrung out in every way imaginable.

She'd skipped The Big Skate and gone home to pick out her clothes—clothes appropriate for eating the Tour of Italy and meeting some people who were probably not going to be happy to meet her because they only had eyes for a dead girl.

That would be a tough battle to fight, but she'd armored for it the best way she knew how—soft leather gray knee boots over black leggings with a long grey cowl sweater and an ice blue pashmina shot with silver thread. For a little bit of the unexpected, she had added the platinum and diamond cluster earrings that Emile had given her two Christmases ago. Strictly speaking, the impressive earrings were meant for formal eveningwear, but with her height and long hair, Gabriella knew she could carry it off—especially at holiday time. Her tiny black shoulder bag was vintage Chanel—a high school graduation gift from Johanna and Paul. She always carried it when she needed a little extra luck.

• • •

"Please, God, don't let her have gotten here before me," Bryant prayed aloud as he drove around the Olive Garden parking lot looking for Gabriella's car. He didn't see it. That was good, anyway. He had meant to arrive twenty minutes ago, but he'd failed to factor in the Black Friday carryover shopping traffic, and now there was only five minutes to spare until eleven o'clock and Gabriella wasn't likely to be late. Packi was right. He should have told them she was coming.

He'd tried to make a reservation, but Olive Garden didn't take reservations and they didn't give a damn that he was Bryant Taylor. He could have used his phone to get on the wait list—which he should have done, instead of just thinking he'd get here early. He should have asked Packi to handle it. Not only would he have had a reservation, there would be already be breadsticks on the table.

No Gabriella yet, but there were the two stretch Hummers that had been hauling the family around.

"Thank you," he said to the perky little hostess as she was picking up a menu. "I'm meeting a large party."

"Around the corner, in the back," she said. So their reputation preceded them.

"Bry!" called his sister Molly. She spotted him first. They had placed long tables together to accommodate all of them—well, almost all of them. There was only one empty chair.

"We saved you a seat in the middle." That was from his younger brother David. "That way you can talk to everybody." Fat chance of that.

Regardless of what the last head count had been—and Bryant didn't even remember—counting kids, there were twenty-two of them. Like the Last Supper nearly doubled. He had to hug and kiss his way around the table. Judas kisses.

"Sit down, Bry." His mother pointed to the empty chair across from her. "We knew you'd be hungry, so we ordered. I got you chicken parmesan with double fettuccini Alfredo. They've already brought the salad and breadsticks."

He hesitated. "We're going to need another chair." *And another meal.*

"Oh?" Maggie looked across the table at the empty chair. "What's wrong with that one?"

"Nothing. I have a friend joining us."

Except for baby babbling from his former sister-in-law's twins, the table went quiet.

"Who?" baby sister Michelle asked. "Robbie?" Robbie had come out to dinner with them once when the Sound was in Minnesota playing the Wild, and Michelle had taken a shine to him.

"I'll get a chair." Luke, ever the Taylor peacemaker and perfect host, jumped up and headed to a table for four where only three people were seated.

"I don't know if there's really room …" his former mother-in-law said. "Should we get another table?"

"It's fine, Beverly," his father said. "We'll just get a little friendlier."

"Whatever," Maggie said. "Bry, if you had told us, we could have—"

"Who?" Michelle persisted. "If it's Robbie, I want him to sit here by me." She pointed to the empty chair beside her and looked at her boyfriend like she wished he hadn't come.

"Here's the chair," Luke said. "Everybody shift."

"No, Michelle," Maggie said. "Bry will sit between you and Robbie."

"It's not Robbie!"

"Then who?" Maggie asked.

"Holy Mother of God!" David said, looking across the room.

"Wow," John, Philie's brother, said. "And all the saints." John's wife, Sandy, gave him a chilling look, and that was when Bryant knew it was Gabriella.

"David, was that necessary?" Maggie asked.

Bryant turned and there she was, looking like a goddess in search of lasagna. Every eye was on her. He'd gotten used to her beauty, but he was awed anew as he looked at her through their eyes.

"Is that a country music star?" his sister Patty asked.

"No," Bryant said proudly. "She's a baker. That's my friend." And he moved quickly toward Gabriella, leaving silence in his wake.

CHAPTER TWENTY-SIX

It wasn't lost on Gabriella that when Bryant approached her, he almost touched her arm but pulled back. Okay. Rule number one. No touching. She could live with that.

"You told me your *family* was coming. Not your whole hometown."

He closed his hands into fists. Again, he didn't know what to do with his hands. "That's not even all of them. Mary Catherine's pregnant and couldn't fly. Patty's boy has a cold, so her husband's home with him. Luke's wife and kids didn't come. I forget why."

"They're looking at us. We should go over," she said.

"They're looking at us because you're a knockout. Even more than usual. Did you hear my brother take the Holy Virgin's name in vain when he saw you? Good thing his girlfriend didn't come."

"I doubt I was the inspiration for that. Maybe he just likes the breadsticks."

"Right. Come and meet everyone."

Thank God he didn't march her around the table and introduce her to them one by one. After helping her into one of the two empty chairs in the middle of the table, he said, "Everyone, this is my friend Gabriella Charbonnet."

She smiled and there were murmurs and waves.

These couldn't all be siblings and spouses. There were too many, unless there was some bigamy going on here. Maybe there were cousins, too. It was easy to pick out Bryant's parents—they were the blond couple directly across the table. Not too surprising that they were so attractive. Bryant had to get that good DNA from somewhere. But what about the other older couple? The smaller, dark-headed ones? An aunt and uncle?

The teenage girl next to Gabriella broke the silence. "Oh, for cute. I love your clothes. Are you a model?" She had Bryant's eyes.

"No. Far from it. I'm an apprentice pastry chef."

"You look like a model. Patty thought you were a country music star."

"Michelle." That was probably Patty. "She doesn't care." Patty looked like she'd been slapped. In fact, a lot of them looked like they'd been slapped.

Gabriella searched her brain for the name of the little sister. This had to be her. "You're Michelle?"

"Yes. That's the prettiest pashmina I've ever seen."

"Thank you." Gabriella was tempted to give it to her, but that would be trying too hard.

"Bry, at least introduce those of us sitting around you to your … friend." That was not a friendly tone, and the voice was straight out of Bryant's mother's mouth.

At least their world at the table had gotten smaller now. Salads and breadsticks were moving at both ends of the long table, and she would only have to contend with five or six people.

"Sure, Ma." He turned to Gabriella. "Gabriella, you've already been talking to my youngest sister, Michelle. That's her boyfriend Stephen."

Bryant, no. Your mother meant for you to start with her.

But there was nothing she could do about it. "Stephen, Michelle," she acknowledged. The boy waved and smiled.

Bryant went on, "Here on the other side of me is my brother Luke. On his other side is my friend Patrick." So there were friends in the mix. Okay.

"Patrick, Luke. Nice to meet you."

"And you," they said at almost the same time. They seemed friendly enough, but surprised, definitely surprised.

"And these are my parents, Maggie and Shane." His next words came out in a rush. "Next to them, Beverly and Alan Kelly."

The men half rose and nodded like people do when they know they should stand but there's no room.

"I'm so happy to meet all of you," Gabriella said.

"Salad, Gabriella?" the woman named Beverly held the large bowl out to her.

"Thank you." Eating would ease some of the tension in the room, but when she went to serve herself, she didn't have a bowl. She looked around. She was the only one.

"Here, take mine." Luke passed her his empty bowl. "I don't like salad."

"Since when?" Maggie Taylor asked.

"No, I couldn't—" Gabriella began.

"I'm sorry. We'll get another bowl," Bryant said. "Take mine."

She'd had none; now she had two.

Luke rose and set the bowl in front of her. "I don't like this salad, Ma. Italian dressing. I don't like it." Then he met Gabriella's eyes. "I'll get you a knife and fork."

Angels above and demons below. These people had not known she was coming. That's why she'd had no bowl or flatware. And now that she noticed, the chairs on this side of the table were more crowded than the other. They'd probably crammed in a chair at the last minute. But why hadn't Bryant taken care of it? Or had he forgotten he'd invited her—no, not invited. *Implored.* Great.

"So you're a baker?" Bryant's father smiled and took a bite of his salad.

"I am," she said. "I can't sing or play the piano, but I can make a pie crust."

"Interesting," Maggie said. "I use those in the refrigerator section at the grocery store, don't you, Beverly?"

"If I don't make a graham cracker crust."

"Those are good," Gabriella said agreeably.

"Of course, Beverly and I have such large families that we have to make so many pies for Thanksgiving that we wouldn't have time to make anything *but* pies if we made our own crusts. I made nine this year. It would have been more if we'd not been leaving to come here the day after."

"Gabriella probably made a hundred pies," Bryant said. "Would you say that's about right?"

"Not sure," Gabriella said. "It's surprising how many people buy their desserts from a bakery at holiday time."

"I just couldn't do that," Maggie said. "My children like my pies."

"Home baked is best," Gabriella agreed.

"Are you kidding?" Bryant said. "That chocolate pie you brought to Thanksgiving was the best pie I've ever had in my life." *Oh, God. Kill me now.* Gabriella could practically feel Maggie Taylor's hackles rising.

"Bry likes Rice Krispie Scotcheroo bars. I brought him some," Maggie said defensively.

What the hell was that? "Sounds delicious. I don't know how to make those."

"So, you and Bry had Thanksgiving together," Maggie said.

"Of course we did," Bryant said. "We went to Sharon and Mikhail's lake house, just like last year. I told you."

Okay. Maybe this was good. They probably thought she was a puck bunny. Once they found out she was Emile's sister, maybe things would ease up.

"Bryant and I have been friends for five years. I'm Emile Giroux's sister."

Maggie grimaced. Clearly she did not like Emile. How could that be? Everyone liked Emile.

"Emile. That's who the engagement party was for, wasn't it? The one that kept you from coming home like you'd planned."

"He couldn't very well miss the party, Ma," Luke said. "He's best man." Gabriella recognized Luke now—not that she'd met him before, except in the mirror. She'd give him the secret pleaser handshake later.

"You're best man?" Maggie asked.

"I didn't mention it? I thought I did." Bryant shoved a breadstick in his mouth, probably so he wouldn't have to say anything else.

"When's the wedding?" Bryant's father asked.

"December 22." Gabriella answered because Bryant's mouth was full.

"December 22?" Maggie said. *This* December 22?"

Bryant nodded. "They didn't want to wait."

"Bryant, you said you'd be home December 22."

"Did I?" Bryant seemed unconcerned. "That must have been before I knew about the wedding. So I'll be home on the twenty-third." He smiled at Gabriella. "After the wedding."

"I guess it can't be helped," Maggie said. "But we see you so little."

"You're seeing me now," Bryant said. "So let's talk about something other than how little you see me."

Excellent idea. Time to turn the table, like they did in Regency romances, and talk to someone she hadn't talked to.

"So, Beverly, Maggie mentioned that you have a large family. How many children do you and Alan have?" For whatever reason, the den that had been humming at the table ceased.

Beverly exchanged looks with Maggie. "Well ... I have five children ... now."

Now. She'd said *now.* A bad feeling crept not only through Gabriella, but the whole room too.

"Patrick there, is our younger son," Beverly went on. "That's Sarah and Teresa holding Sarah's twins, kitty-corner from Patrick. Our older son, John, and his wife Sandy are next to Sarah." Gabriella glanced to the end of the table. The younger women smiled tight little smiles. John looked at the table. "Our oldest daughter, Monica, couldn't come." She took a sip of her water. "And our youngest daughter died."

Then it all snapped into place—these extra people, the dark-headed ones, weren't cousins. They were in-laws.

Gabriella looked at Bryant, "So they are …"

"Philie's parents."

"We're Bryant's parents-in-law," Alan Kelly said.

Yes. They were. And they always would be. And there was no place for her in that picture. The little light that had bloomed in her at the lake went dark.

"Bryant, son," Shane Taylor said, "I thought you hadn't told anyone here that you're married."

Married. Present tense.

Bryant glanced at Gabriella. "I haven't told anyone else. But I told Gabriella."

But he never would have if she hadn't overheard him.

Maggie looked up from her salad bowl. "I, for one, am relieved." She gestured to the table. "Losing Mary Philomena was hard on all of us. Of course, it was worst for Bry. They'd been sweethearts from such a young age. It's good that the people who know Bry know about his life—our life."

And that's what it was always going to be—his life, their life. She was just something to get him over a bump in the road.

"Are you coming home with Bry for Christmas?" Michelle asked.

"Michelle!" Maggie admonished—and there were audible gasps up and down the table.

"No," Gabriella said. "No. Of course not. Why would you think that?"

Michelle shrugged. "Aren't you his girlfriend?"

"No," Gabriella said flatly. "I'm not his girlfriend."

Relief swept over the room like a cool breeze on the hottest July day. A den of noise broke out—laughter and words, though she wasn't sure who was speaking which words.

"So sorry. We thought …"

"Did you hear her? They're just friends."

"To be fair, Bry never said …"

They were acting like Philie was alive and they'd just found out that Bryant wasn't cheating on her after all.

"Did you get breadsticks, hon?" Gabriella was pretty sure that was Patty stretching across three people to offer her the breadbasket.

To her left, Bryant whispered, "I am so sorry."

To her right Michelle said right out loud, "I wish you were his girlfriend. I was hoping you'd marry him."

Yeah, Michelle. I might have been starting to hope that myself. But no more. This was an unhealthy situation that was never going to get better. And she knew unhealthy. She'd lived it and she wouldn't live it again. Not that anybody had asked her to. Certainly not Bryant.

"Oh?" Gabriella said to Michelle, maybe the only person at the table who didn't view her as the enemy—and at this moment, she would include Bryant in that, because he was the one who was never going to put a stop to this toxic hamster wheel that just kept turning and turning.

Michelle smiled a big sunny smile. "Those are the best earrings I've ever seen. I thought if you were my new sister, you'd let me borrow them."

Gabriella fingered the diamonds and platinum and manufactured a laugh that she didn't feel. "You know what, Michelle? My big NHL star brother gave these to me. Maybe yours will do the same for you."

"Did you hear that, Bry?" Michelle said. "Gabriella said you'd buy me some diamond earrings like hers."

"Michelle! Gabriella did not say that. And I've told you not to ask your brother for things." Maggie smiled at Gabriella and winked.

Yeah, buddy. They were friends now that it was clear she wasn't Bryant's girlfriend and had no intention of trampling on the memory of Mary Philomena or tempting Bryant to retire from hockey anywhere except in the smothering bosom of this family. Maybe they would exchange cell numbers and Maggie could enlist Gabriella to convince Bryant to build a marble stature of Philie in the St. Sebastian town square where they could all gather daily to gnash their teeth.

"Here's the food," Shane said.

Plate after plate swimming in red sauce appeared and chaos ensued. Who had the ravioli, who had the manicotti, and Molly couldn't remember what she'd ordered. She'd wavered between the eggplant Parmesan and the shrimp scampi, but couldn't remember what she settled on.

"And what did you have, ma'am?" the waiter asked.

"Uh ..." Gabriella looked at Bryant. "Tour of Italy?"

Bryant's face froze and he raised his hands to his face. "Holy hell!" He gave her a look of remorse. "They ordered before I got here and they didn't know you were coming." He turned to the waiter. "Give her mine. Chicken parm and a double order of Alfredo."

"You can't do that, Bry. You need to carb-up and then go nap before puck drop," Maggie said. She turned to the waiter. "Bring her a plate. We'll all share."

"Ma," Luke said. "Just let her order what she wants."

"We'd be finished eating before hers came. Gabriella, do you like chicken Marsala?"

"Gabriella, I'm so sorry," Bryant said. "I was going to come early, but the traffic ..."

"Ma'am," the waiter said, "I can bring you some soup right out. That takes no time. And some breadsticks and marinara."

Holy hell, indeed.

Michelle pulled at her sleeve. "I got Tour of Italy. It's a lot. I'll share. You said you wanted Tour of Italy."

She didn't even know what Tour of Italy was.

What the hell was she doing here? He'd said he'd needed a friend, but to what end? He hadn't told them she was coming. Her presence had made things worse—and not just for him and his family. She'd been wrong when she'd chosen to believe that Bryant would never hurt her. Sure, he'd never hit her, but fists were not the only things that hurt.

"You know what?" Gabriella picked up her little Chanel bag—and briefly wondered just how bad things would have gotten if she hadn't brought her good luck charm. "I'm not hungry. I'm just going to go and let you all visit."

"Gabriella, no!" And suddenly Bryant knew what to do with his hands. He put them on her arm.

She gave him her best smile. "Really, Bryant, it's fine. It was great to meet everyone, but you need this time with your family. I'll see you later." She flashed her smile up and down the table, meeting some eyes, avoiding others. "It was a pleasure."

"I'll see you out." Bryant stood up.

"Don't be ridiculous." She laughed a little. "Your food will get cold." She could be imposing when she wanted to, and she forced him back into his chair with her eyes.

"But you'll be at the game tonight?" Bryant asked.

"Of course."

"And at The Big Skate afterward? We'll all be there."

"Wouldn't miss it." She knew this hockey life, knew all the rules. *Never upset a player on game day, even if you have to lie.*

She was almost gone, but turned back at the last second. "Since you admired it." And she removed her pashmina and looped it around Michelle's neck.

"Really?" The girl stroked the scarf.

"Enjoy it." And this time she really was gone.

CHAPTER TWENTY-SEVEN

Bryant had a bad feeling about watching Gabriella walk away. It was something he usually took pleasure in, but this walking away felt different. Final. And who could blame her? What a disaster.

"Turn around and eat your food, Bry," Maggie said like he was four years old and balking at broccoli hot dish.

But he didn't have time to care about that. He was still looking at the door Gabriella had just exited.

I'm not his girlfriend. That's what she'd said. Why had it hit him so hard when he already knew it—when they'd both practically signed a contract to that effect? He turned back to the table.

Michelle was twisting and turning the pashmina Gabriella had given her around her neck. It probably still smelled like Gabriella, but he'd never know. He couldn't very well sniff his little sister's neck.

"I can't get this like Gabriella had it," Michelle said. "I'm going to find her at the game tonight and get her to show me."

"No, Michelle," Molly said. "You don't need to do that. I'll help you when we get back to the hotel."

"You don't know how. I've never even seen you wear a pashmina."

"We'll look it up on YouTube," Molly said.

"But I—"

"Enough, Michelle," Maggie said. "Don't bother Gabriella. She'll probably have a date to the game."

No, she will not! But it was possible. After all, she wasn't his girlfriend, wouldn't be marrying him and lending Michelle earrings.

His chest grew tight.

"I'm sorry about not having food for Gabriella, son," Shane said. "If I'd known, we'd have ordered her something."

"My fault, Dad. You guys didn't know." Yeah, he'd screwed that up—the whole thing, really. His family should have been warned. Gabriella should have been warned Philie's family would be here.

Maggie set her wine glass down. "It was a bit of a shock, Bry— to see you bringing a woman we've never heard of here today. It was awkward, for sure. If you'd told us she was just a friend, it would have saved all that."

Bryant rubbed the place between his eyes. "Right, Ma."

"It doesn't matter," Patty said. "We'll probably never see her again. But, Bry, think next time." Molly nodded.

"I hope we see her again," Michelle said. "I liked her. I'm going to sit with her tonight at— Bry, where did you say we're going after the game?"

"The Big Skate."

"There. I'm sitting with her."

"No you're not," Molly said. "Now, Michelle, be quiet. You don't know anything about all this."

Hell. Beverly was wiping her eyes. Sarah shoved her baby into Sandy's arms and went to put an arm around her mother, slaying Bryant with her eyes with every step.

"Leave it go," Maggie said. "It's over." *Over.* That's what he was afraid of. "We'll talk about it tomorrow, as far as that goes. Bry has a game tonight."

The table went completely silent, except for the clink of flatware against plates.

"Excuse me." Patrick stood up.

Great. Now his oldest friend was going to either leave in disgust or lower the boom on him. Probably both.

"I have some things to say," Patrick said. Great. Let the ass-chewing commence. He could take it. Gabriella was gone. If he could take that, he could take anything.

There was no clinking now. Every eye was on Patrick. Philie's sisters looked like they couldn't wait. Come to think of it, so did his own sisters—except Michelle.

"Go on, Patrick," Shane said.

He met Bryant's eyes briefly, but Bryant couldn't read him.

"Mary Philomena is alive and well in all of our hearts." There were nods and smiles all around the table. Not a few glasses were raised. "But Philie is dead."

What? The nods stopped, the smiles ceased, and the glasses thudded on the table.

"She was my little sister and I loved her, but this has to stop."

Maggie slipped an arm around Beverly. "I don't take your meaning, Patrick. *What* has to stop?"

Patrick shook his head and gestured to the whole room. "This. What happened here today. Look, if I'm tired of this, it's got to be killing Bry. No." He put up a hand. "Sarah, don't start. I'm having my say here. I don't think many of you remember much about Philie. She was the baby—spoiled rotten. Our whole family has to take a share of that blame, but so does the whole town. After she started dating Bryant, she became insufferable. She never paid for another manicure or haircut. Everywhere she went, there was always free movies, free pop, and free burgers with her name on them. Anything for the hero's girl. She would have probably gotten free clothes if she hadn't worn Bry's jersey 24/7."

Bryant had not known that, but he wasn't surprised. He'd been pretty catered to himself.

Beverly burst into tears in earnest.

"Son, that's enough!" Alan took his wife's hand.

"No, Dad. It isn't nearly enough. I remember these things about Philie, but I loved her anyway. She had a good heart and, while she would have always been high maintenance, she would have grown out of being an entitled princess. But, guys, she made Bryant miserable."

"She did not!" Maggie exploded. "Bry loved Philie!"

That was the first time in five years that Bryant had heard his mother call Philie by her correct name.

"He did," Patrick said. "He loved her as much as a boy can love a girl."

Had he? All this time, he'd thought he hadn't. It had been a long time since he'd been able to picture her face—but there it was. Dark eyes, saucy little smile, dark hair curling around her pretty, little, pixie face. He'd been so taken with her—skating on the pond, kisses on her front porch, her in the stands in his jersey. But Patrick had said *boy*. The boy he'd been had loved her. If she'd lived, maybe the man would have learned to love her again.

And if all that were true, maybe he did deserve to love again—to love like a man loved a woman.

The way that he loved Gabriella.

"But just because Bryant loved her doesn't mean Philie was easy to live with," Patrick said.

True, and no wonder. She'd been young, homesick, guilt-ridden, and living with the knowledge that his feelings had changed.

"Bryant, I'm surprised at you," Maggie said, "that you would tell Mary Philomena's own brother that she made you miserable!"

"Ma, I never—"

"He didn't," Patrick said. "He wouldn't. I'm sorry to say all this. Maggie, I grew up eating as many meals at your table as at my own house. I love you. You have been a second mother to me. But Bryant needs some peace. We have to stop ripping this wound open.

"But after what happened here today, I have to speak my piece. Bryant invited a perfectly nice woman here—a woman who is clearly in love with him—and you treated her like Bryant was cheating on Philie with her."

Gabriella was in love with him? No. But Packi had said that, too. Maybe he *was* that lucky.

"You're being a drama king, Patrick," Molly said. "That woman is not in love with him. You heard her. They're friends."

"I hope she is!" Michelle said.

Me, too, baby sister, me, too.

"What was she going to say, Molly? Of course she's in love with him. Why else would she have subjected herself to this—to us—for as long as she did? And unless I miss my guess, Bryant's in love with her, too."

Damn straight. His heart beat faster.

"We thought we'd watch Bryant and Philie have children and come home …" Beverly said.

"I know, Mom," Patrick said. "And I thought Bryant and I would go off to the NHL together and become big stars. But I think we all knew by the time I was fourteen that I was never even going to make juniors. And I know something else that I'm not sure anyone else in this room knows. Bryant doesn't have to be who he was when he was seventeen or have to come back to St. Sebastian to be my friend."

Bryant didn't know what to say. But wasn't that the problem? Wasn't that what Gabriella had tried to tell him? He was grateful to Patrick but he had to find the words himself.

He stood up and hugged Patrick, but he knew he didn't need to thank him.

"I have to go," he said. "But I have a couple of things to say first. I have to move on. I love you all. Philie was my first love, and that's always going to be true. But I love Gabriella now and I'm going to try to win her. But whether I succeed or fail, this never-ending funeral is over for me. I don't think it's good for anyone, but you all have to decide what's right for you. Mourn Philie and the baby as you must and trust me to do the same in my own private way. But it will be private. Also, I would like to remind you all that she wasn't a saint named Mary Philomena. She was a girl named Philie. I don't think it's too much for me to ask you to call her that. You always did before.

"I don't know where I will live once I retire. I don't have to live in St. Sebastian to be part of you. The kind of relationship we have is going to depend on if you can accept what I've said." Was that harsh? Maybe, but there it was.

"Yes!" Michelle said.

He stroked her cheek and turned to go. "I'll see you all after the game."

"Bry!" Maggie called. "What about your carb-up meal? You have a game to get ready for."

"I've got a life to get ready for, Ma. There's no meal for that."

CHAPTER TWENTY-EIGHT

Gabriella almost didn't go to the game. But in the end, she decided she couldn't let Bryant affect her life. If Bryant had never walked into Eat Cake and demanded ice cream, if he'd never rescued her from the sidelines and taken her to the dance floor at the engagement party, if he'd never taken her upstairs after that dance, she'd be going to the game to see Emile play.

So that's what she did. She put on her silver leggings, her purple suede knee boots, and her brother's jersey, and went to the WAG suite and took her seat in the second row.

Where she belonged.

It was a rough game—a rough night. The Sound couldn't do anything right and the Jets couldn't do anything wrong. It happened. This wasn't football where an undefeated season could be a realistic goal. In hockey, there were too many games. There would be losses and it looked like this would be one of them. That was hockey.

She had a bad moment when Bryant got slammed up against the boards so hard that she expected a fight to break out, but it didn't— at least not then. Bryant didn't rise to the bait, though Thor did take it up later and get thrown out of the game. Again, that was hockey.

Somewhere along the way, she'd learned that she didn't have to look away during a fight. Really, these days they wore so much protective gear that the likelihood of a real injury was rare. With that in mind, she even found that she could take some pleasure in seeing Thor get the better of the guy.

Take that, you Jet. That's what you get for messing with Swifty. He's got people watching his back.

Only she wouldn't be one of them anymore. But some good had come out of her non-relationship with Bryant. She no longer felt that all hockey players had to pay for the man her father had been.

She still wasn't open to dating hockey players, but not because she was afraid. She wasn't going to date anyone—not for a long time. Her heart was too bruised for that.

The game ended 3-2, Winnipeg, and the atmosphere in the suite was subdued.

"Big Skate?" Amy asked as they were gathering their things.

"I don't think so," Gabriella said. "It's been a really long weekend."

"Do you want to spend the night with us?"

"No, thanks. I think I'll just head back to Beauford. I want to sleep in my own bed."

"I envy you a little," Amy said. "The taking a pass on The Big Skate tonight. But Swifty's family is in town and Emile's met them before—at least some of them. He wants to say hello."

"Ah, the expectations of a hockey wife!" Gabriella did her best imitation of cheerful. "Being a hockey sister is much better. Less pressure."

"Too late for that," Amy said. "I don't think my brother would be much good at hockey. He can't skate."

• • •

"I told him," Packi said.

"And he's all right with it?" Bryant had half expected Coach to deny his request to speak to the team after Coach's own speech—especially after the loss.

"He is. He knew it was important."

"How did he know that?"

"I told him so," Packi said. "You're doing the right thing."

He hoped so. Yesterday after leaving his family, he'd driven straight to Emile's condo with the intention of coming clean with him, but had decided it wasn't the right time. Just because his game day had been discombobulated didn't mean he had the right to discombobulate Emile's. It would keep until after the game. But there was something else he needed to do: tell his teammates about Philie. He'd blamed his family for preventing him from moving on, but he had to take a share of the blame because he'd carried this inside him, pretending it had never happened. He had no idea how it would go over, but for all the times he'd done what he wanted instead of what he should have done, he was going to do the right thing.

"I guess it's long overdue."

"No." Packi shook his head. "It's only just due."

Bryant barely listened to what Coach Colton said. He'd heard it all before. Loss was bad. Loss was not the path to another championship for that trophy that must not be named lest Nickolai Glazov have a complete meltdown. But it's over. Learn from it and put it behind you. No off day Monday. Ten o'clock skate. Don't be late.

"And one of your teammates wants to say a few words to you," Coach Colton said. "Swifty."

There was more than one surprised face when Bryant rose. It only occurred to him in that moment that maybe he should have told his close friends before this public announcement. Well, it was too late now. If they were upset with him, there was nothing he could do about it. But he had to stop running his life like that. He needed to think more, think in advance when there was something he could do about it.

"I have something to tell you guys. You're my brothers on the ice and I've kept something from you. I failed someone in the worst way possible. I never lied, but I never told you the truth either. It's time. When I was nineteen, I was married ..." He talked on, told it all—well, almost all. He didn't tell that Philie had deliberately conceived. He would never tell that to anyone. No matter what life would offer him in the future, keeping her secret was the only thing left that he could do for her.

"And that's it. It's a long time past, but I wanted you to know."

And his teammates—led by Emile and Jarrett—lined up to offer him comfort—comfort that he needed and was willing to receive.

When everyone had dispersed, Packi handed him a Gatorade. "Most excellent."

"I have a few more things I need to do." He'd dealt with his family, though who knew what their reaction would be, but there was nothing he could do about it.

As much as he wanted to go to Gabriella, he had to set things right with Emile first. If he was going to have any chance with Gabriella, that had to go well. But it would. He'd go there first thing in the morning. Breaking the Bro Code wasn't really an issue anymore. Sleeping with a bro's sister was one thing, but loving her was another. He would just explain to Emile that he loved Gabriella and wanted to marry her. He would never, ever hurt her. Who could argue with that? If Bryant got his way, they'd be more than brothers on the ice. Emile would probably be happy.

Packi nodded. "Uh huh."

CHAPTER TWENTY-NINE

Gabriella was almost home when she noticed the flood of lights coming from Pam's shop, Halfway Home. Could Pam be there this late? It wasn't in Gabriella's nature to bare her soul, but suddenly there was nothing she wanted more than a hug and a sympathetic ear. There was no doubt that Pam would supply both.

She pulled in front of the shop, took out her cell phone, and sent Pam a text.

> Are you at Halfway Home?
> Pam: Yes. Where are you?
> Out front. Can I come in?
> Pam: Right out.

Pam opened the door just as Gabriella climbed out of her car. "You're here late," Gabriella said.

"Black Friday was wild and today wasn't much better. I came back after dinner to get a few things done."

Gabriella hesitated. "I'm interrupting you." She should leave.

"No. I just finished. I was about to head home."

"Then I won't keep you." She wasn't sure she wanted to talk anymore anyway.

"Gabriella!" Pam cried. "Come inside. Right now. You're going to tell me what's wrong."

Gabriella was so emotionally weary that it was easy to do what Pam said.

"Let's go to my office. I'll make tea." Pam led her through the beautiful little shop that sparkled with Christmas decorations. The glittering ornaments, wreaths, and garlands only made Gabriella sadder. How could there be so much sparkle in a world where she felt so flat?

Pam had even decorated her office—a crystal snowpeople family on her desk and a small tree with mercury glass ornaments in the corner. Gabriella sank down on the soft, overstuffed loveseat in front of Pam's desk. If Pam would only give her a pillow and blanket, she could stay here forever.

"I'm sorry it's not wine." Pam handed Gabriella a mug of tea and took a seat beside her.

Gabriella sipped the tea. Perfect. Lemon and a little honey. "I might worry about you if you kept wine at your place of business."

Pam smiled. "I could have used some the last couple of days."

"I'm sorry you've had bad days."

Pam shook her head. "Not bad days. Busy, hectic days. I think you've had a bad day, though."

Gabriella shook her head. "You might say that."

"Tell me what happened."

"I don't know where to start."

"Then say the first thing that comes into your head and we'll go from there."

"I seem to have fallen in love."

"Ah!" Pam smiled, showing her dimples. "And that's a bad thing?"

"It will never work. We can't be together."

"Are you sure? Sometimes it only seems that way."

"Not this time."

"Is he married? Gay? From outer space?"

Gabriella laughed. Pam could always make her laugh. "No, but he might as well be."

"Sanity is important. Is he sane?"

"As sane as any of us. Saner than he ought to be considering what he's been through."

"Who is the lucky guy?"

"My brother's teammate and best friend, Bryant Taylor. I don't know that I'd call him lucky."

Pam nodded. "I've seen him on television—those beer commercials. And they interview him sometimes after Sound games."

"Yes. He's very good." There was pride in her voice when she said it, like he was hers. How pitiful was that?

"What's the problem?"

"What's not the problem? I've never told you this, but my father was abusive."

"I know." Pam sipped her tea. "He beat Emile, broke your arm, and rots in prison today because he killed your mother."

Shock washed over Gabriella. "How …?"

"Emile told Hélène-Louise. Hélène-Louise told me. We've never brought it up because we figured you would say so if you wanted to talk about it."

Of course Emile would have told Hélène-Louise—probably told her in French since she was the only person he knew who was as fluent as he was. Gabriella would have known that if she'd thought about it.

"What has that got to do with you and Bryant?" Pam asked.

"Oddly, nothing—at least not anymore—though we did get off to a rough start because of it. There was a time when I would not have gotten involved with a hockey player, because I was afraid he would turn out like my father. But I've worked though that. Bryant isn't like my father."

"Then it's good that you aren't carrying that around anymore. If that was the only problem …"

"It's not. I'm just getting warmed up."

"All right." Pam sat back and waited.

"Emile wouldn't like it. And that's an understatement. The only thing he has ever asked of me is that I not get involved with a hockey player—particularly a member of his team."

Before Gabriella got the next words out of her mouth, Pam was shaking her head. "I almost ruined things with Sammy because my parents expected me to marry a doctor or an attorney or somebody a lot more highbrow than Jackson Beauford's personal assistant. Emile has no right to ask that of you."

"Emile has done everything for me. And getting involved with Bryant could make for bad dynamics on the team if things didn't work out."

"*Could. If.* Do you mean to tell me Emile would want you to throw away a chance for love and happiness over *could* and *if?*" She shook her head. "I don't believe it. Emile loves you. I simply do not believe he's that selfish. And if he does feel that way, shame on him. He's getting married. He has who he wants. Why shouldn't you?"

"*Why* shouldn't I, indeed? That isn't up to Emile or me. Bryant doesn't want me. At least not enough." It hurt to say it, but it was true.

Sadness blotted out the sun in Pam's eyes. She had no answers for that. "Are you sure?"

"Sure enough. He's been through a lot. It would take from now until Christmas to tell the whole story, but I'll give you an abbreviated version. Bryant married his high school sweetheart. Philie. She was pregnant. She and the baby died while he was on the road with the Red Wings his rookie season."

Pam gasped. "That's horrible."

"You bet." Angels above and demons below, now she was talking like him. "Not only has this frozen him emotionally, but his family is also intent on preserving Philie's memory. Believe me when I say they are not open to another woman in his life. He says he doesn't like wallowing in the grief, but he won't put a stop to it. There just isn't any hope."

"I know you, Gabriella. You don't dive into something for no reason. Bryant must have done something to make you fall in love with him, must have shown some indication that he cares for you."

Gabriella pushed her hair off her face. "There have been some things. Sure." She wasn't thinking so much of their time in bed as that odd phone call when he'd talked about his name, rescuing her from the corner and taking her to the dance floor at the engagement party, and holding her hand outside The Big Skate. "A few things."

"Then Emile and Bryant's family need to stay out of it."

"There's really nothing to stay out of. I told him I wasn't looking for a man, that I was looking for a friend. And that's what I got." Gabriella rose.

"Maybe you should tell him differently."

"It wouldn't matter." She couldn't go through the Olive Garden hour for the rest of her life. "But thanks for listening."

"We can talk all night." Pam stood up. "I can go home with you. We can watch movies, drink wine, and eat ice cream."

Gabriella smiled at the thought of ice cream. Bryant demanding ice cream was what started it all. "No, we can't. You should go home to Sammy."

Pam brightened at the thought but tried to hide it by casting her eyes down. "I'm here for you."

"I know you are. Thank you."

Pam moved to embrace her. "Gabriella, don't count him out yet. Or yourself."

"All right." But really where else was there to be except out?

• • •

Bryant parked his car and headed down the street. The Big Skate was a lot more fun after a win; that was for sure. But despite the loss, he felt lighter after his confession to his teammates. He would have preferred to skip The Big Skate and get on with the business of straightening out his life, but he'd promised his family the full Sound experience, and the team hangout was part of that.

Of course for all he knew, they might have gone back to St. Sebastian after the Olive Garden debacle. But no. When he opened the door, there they were—taking up at least five tables pushed together.

Shane stood up. "Son! Over here." And the noise level went up. That was promising. He relaxed and walked toward them.

"Tough loss, but it happens. You'll get 'em next time!"

"But you looked good."

"Do you want a beer? We've got a pitcher."

When he approached the table, his mother stood up and hugged him. "Bry, I'm really sorry about what happened at lunch. We saved Gabriella a seat." He wasn't fooling himself. That didn't mean Maggie had accepted one word of what he'd said. She was known to give away a battle to win a war.

"Here. Sit down," Luke said. Sure enough there were two empty chairs side by side in the center of the table. "Gabriella isn't here yet. When is she coming?"

Good question. She was usually there by the time he arrived. But Amy wasn't here either. Maybe they had waited for Emile. Unusual, but not unheard of.

As soon as he sat, the table got quiet. That never happened.

Shane cleared his throat. "Son, we wanted to talk to you before Gabriella gets here." Apparently, his dad had been appointed to deliver a speech. "We talked about the things you and Patrick said. Things are going to change."

"That's right," Maggie said. "We want you to be happy. We will always remember and love Philie, but it's time for us all to move on. If Gabriella makes you happy, then she makes us happy."

Damn. He was speechless. After a five-year war, it was hard to believe it was over. And maybe it wasn't, but this was a start.

"We want you to know we feel the same," Philie's dad spoke.

"Yes," her mother agreed. "You are like a son to us. We have already lost one child. We don't want to lose another."

"I—" he began but he never got any further.

"Maggie! Shane! Lovely little Michelle!" came a voice behind him—a voice with a French accent.

In that moment, Bryant knew with that voice was going to come a big old wagon full of hell. He glanced around. Amy was hanging on to Emile's arm, all smiles, but Gabriella was nowhere to be seen. That was something.

"Emile!" Maggie had changed her tune about Emile, for sure. She embraced him. "You are a bad boy! Planning your wedding on the day Bryant was supposed to come home!"

"Oh, but you must come to the wedding. You should all come so you can celebrate with Amy and me and be with Swifty!"

"We just might," Maggie said.

Now Emile was introducing Amy all around and Shane was introducing everyone who hadn't met Emile before.

Luke was rounding up more chairs and somewhere along the way Emile had gotten his hands on one of Sarah's twins. What were those babies doing out this time of night anyway?

"Emile," Michelle said.

"Yes, *chérie*?"

"Where is Gabriella?"

Emile looked confused, as did Amy. Emile eyes flitted to Bryant and back to Michelle. "You know my sister?"

Yep. The hell wagon was rolling.

"Yes!" Michelle said. "I love Gabriella. She gave me this." She stroked the scarf around her neck.

"Did she? That was kind of her. Tell me, *chérie*, on what occasion did she give it to you?"

"No occasion. Not my birthday or anything. Just at lunch today when she came out with us to Olive Garden. When is she coming? I want her show me how to tie it."

"Gabriella went home after the game," Amy said. "She was tired."

"No!" Michelle said. "I wanted to see her. Bry, go call her. Tell her to come. She can spend the night at your house. I'll share my bed."

Holy hell. Emile's face was the color of chalk. He looked like a vampire—a French vampire who was about to let loose his hell wagon.

"Emile," Shane said, "We had some miscommunication about lunch today, and I hope we didn't offend Gabriella. She is a great young lady. I know there's nothing official, but I want you to know if things work out the way we hope with Bryant and your sister, we couldn't be more pleased."

Amy's lips parted and she closed her eyes. She knew a hell wagon when she saw it coming, too. Only it wasn't going to be her hell. Or maybe it was. Maybe it would be everybody's hell.

"Bryant and Gabriella." Emile nodded and looked around. "Yes." He was putting things together, probably thinking about how Bryant had denied it. "Well."

"Emile—" Bryant began.

"Michelle," Emile said. "Please?" He handed her the baby.

Bryant braced himself, but not in time. The next thing he knew, he was flat on his back and his nose was bleeding.

Somewhere along the way, The Saint had appeared. "I told you he was going to kill you."

"What! You knew it, too!" Emile screamed.

And Jarrett tumbled on top of Bryant.

Knowing his family, Bryant would have expected chaos to ensue with Maggie beating Emile with a menu, his sisters screaming, Luke trying to make peace, and David taking a swing at somebody just to get in on the action.

But there was total silence.

"So, son," Shane spoke. "I'm guessing you hadn't told Emile you were interested in his sister. That's bad business."

Emile exploded with a string of French words that didn't sound one bit polite.

"Do I smell a fight?" Bryant looked up to see Thor standing over them.

"What are you doing here?" Bryant said. "You never come here."

"Clearly that's not true. I'm here." He looked around. "Swifty, Saint. Get up from the floor, please. Now."

"*Oui!*" Emile exploded. He looked like he was ready for another round.

"Emile, stop it!" Amy said. "At least find out what's going on."

"Yes," Thor said. "Or don't find out. I don't care. But I want this settled. I am getting the feeling that the problem is with Emile and Bryant. Jarrett was just incidental."

"More or less," Amy said.

"The two of you go settle this. This will *not* affect this team. Do you understand me? Losses on the ice and trouble off the ice equals Pickens Davenport wanting rid of the Sound even more than he already does. I, for one, do not want to be sold to Massachusetts, and what I want matters more than whatever infantile thing is going on between the two of you."

"Hey!" Bryant and Emile said at the same time.

"Good. You agree on something. You agreed to say *hey.* Go agree on something else."

Bryant glanced at his family.

"I think we're just going to go, Bry." Maggie dabbed at his nose with a napkin. "We'll see you back at the house."

They all filed out with Jarrett and Thor behind them.

Amy put her hands in the air. "Don't. Just don't."

"I wasn't doing anything," Emile said.

"You were going to. Should we go back to the condo?" Amy asked.

"*Non,*" Emile said. "He is not welcome in my home."

"It's just as well we stay in public." Amy ushered them to a booth in the corner. "Though that didn't stop you before."

"This is not my usual booth," Emile grumbled.

"Thanks to you, I'm not in my usual mood. Sit." She pointed. "Across from each other."

As if they would sit beside each other in a booth on their best day. Bryant chose not to voice that thought.

Amy slid into the seat beside Emile. "What is wrong with you? Hitting your best friend? In public, no less."

"Clearly he has been sleeping with my sister."

"Not true." It might be true, but it wasn't clear. "The only thing that's clear is that we went to Olive Garden. And she didn't even eat."

"With your family! Nobody takes a woman to Olive Garden with his family if he's not sleeping with her."

"Never let it be said that you let logic get in the way when you have a point to make. That's the stupidest thing I've ever heard in my life."

"So you deny that you've been having sex with my sister?"

There was no easy answer for that. "I deny that it's any of your business."

Emile lunged and would have crawled across the table, but Amy restrained him. "Stop it, Emile. Right now."

"Did you hear him? He as good as admitted that he had sex with Gabriella."

Amy looked miserable.

"Where?" Emile demanded. "Probably right under my nose."

I don't know, Emile. What do you consider under your nose? During your engagement party? Down the hall from you at Thanksgiving? If that's the case, yes. Right under your nose.

"You are not answering me. *Where* did you disrespect my sister?"

"Nowhere," Bryant said.

"Are you saying you didn't sleep with her?"

Okay. Time to stop cowering and act like a man. *You're the only one who can get control of this situation.* That's what Gabriella had said. She'd been talking about his family, but it applied.

"I'm not saying I didn't sleep with her, or that I did. I'm saying I've never disrespected Gabriella."

"But I was right. You have been spending time with her behind my back."

"Yes. That I have been doing. Every chance I got. For that I'm sorry—not the spending time with her, but the keeping it from you."

"I asked her to never get involved with a hockey player. She agreed, never even wanted to."

"I'm not sure she is involved with me. For what it's worth, I love her."

"That's not the point," Emile said. "She's not supposed to be with a hockey player! I wanted something better for her."

"Yeah, well. She deserves better. But I'm still going to have her if I can."

"You will not!" Emile exploded.

"Look, I mishandled this. I own that. But who the hell do you think you are? You will not stop me!"

"Stop it!" Amy pounded a fist on the table. "Bryant, does Gabriella love you?"

Good question. He rubbed his eyes. "I don't know. Sometimes it seems like it. But I've handled things poorly."

"No surprise there!"

"I wouldn't throw that stone if I were you, Emile," Amy said. "And I have some questions for you. Why is a hockey player good enough for me, but not your sister? Especially when the hockey player in question is your best friend and Gabriella is a grown woman?"

"Because I know myself! I know I would never hurt you! And Gabriella is my little sister! I must protect her! I failed her before. I cannot do it again!"

Their little world went completely still—devoid of energy. Emile deflated like a balloon that had been left out in the sun. The truth hung in the air like broken toys in a tree after a tornado.

There was anguish in Emile's eyes—the anguish of the abusive childhood he'd spoken of so matter-of-factly, insisting that it was over and he carried no psychological baggage. Emile's reasons for wanting Gabriella to stay away from hockey players had nothing to do with team dynamics. It was because his stepfather had been an abusive hockey player and he was afraid there were more out there.

"I should have told you," Bryant said. "I should have told you weeks ago. I was going to yesterday. I went so far as to drive to your place, but I decided to wait until the game was over. I understand how you feel. You heard what I said in the locker room earlier. I couldn't protect Philie and my baby. You couldn't protect Gabriella. We were boys. We did the best we could." Until that moment, Bryant had never believed that, but he did now. "But we're men now. We'll do better."

Except to shake, Bryant could not remember ever in his adult life taking another man's hands in his, but he reached across the table and did it then. Emile looked surprised, but he didn't pull away.

"Emile, after all my blunders, I don't know if Gabriella will have me. But if she will give me a chance, I promise you I will never hurt her. I will live my life to help you protect her. I don't just love her. I want to marry her." He gave his best friend's hands a squeeze. Bryant knew there was something else he needed to say—something that the scared, abused boy who was still a part of the man Emile was needed to hear. "And as God and all the saints as my witnesses, I swear I will never let anyone hurt you—ever again. I will protect you or die trying." On a different day, Emile might have said he didn't need anyone to protect him, but this wasn't a different day.

Bryant would never be sure if a few tears collected in Emile's eyes, but he knew for certain he saw relief there.

Amy stood and broke the silence. "All right, then. I think it's safe to leave you two alone now. I'm going home."

And they talked most of the rest of the night—though they didn't continue to hold hands.

CHAPTER THIRTY

Gabriella smeared marmalade on her third piece of toast. In Regency romances, the brokenhearted couldn't eat, could barely manage to swallow a sip of tea.

Well, she wasn't that woman. The way she saw it, being brokenhearted took a lot of energy and she needed sustenance to maintain this level of pain—which she intended to maintain for a long while. She didn't want to forget it.

So she'd already had half a pot of tea, plus all that toast—not wimpy toast either. She'd arrived home last night wound up and made two big, fat, sourdough loaves, from which she'd sliced big, fat slices, and smeared them with Irish butter and artisan Meyer lemon-ginger marmalade from Beauford's own Jam Jar. As she bit into the third slice, she was already thinking about some eggs and sausage.

And the doorbell rang. She considered not going down. It was clearly posted—even on the back door—that Eat Cake is closed on Sunday.

It rang again. Clearly, she would get no peace until she went down. After all that bread and jam—plus the eggs and sausages she intended to have—a trip down the stairs wouldn't do her any harm.

In a Regency romance, it would be *him*, but this wasn't a Regency romance. That had already been proven well enough by her appetite and the fact that she wasn't sitting in Emile's servants' quarters in threadbare hand-me-downs. Also, no ball, though she had taken care of the tea and toast well enough.

She peered out of the peephole. Angels above and demons below. This was a Regency romance after all. Except he wasn't wearing a top hat and cravat. Not a cane in sight. He looked good in his Lululemon sweatpants and Sound hoodie, but that didn't sway her. But what was wrong with his face? It was a mess—black eye and swollen nose. If that had happened on the ice last night, she'd missed it. But not her problem. He'd heal.

She stuck her head—and only her head—out the door. "Go away. Get out of here."

"What?" He looked not only surprised, but also amazed.

"What do you mean *what*? Has no female ever denied you entrance before?"

"Not that many."

"Add me to the short list. No top hat, no entrance."

He frowned and shook his head. "Gabriella, what in the hell are you talking about? What top hat?"

"Never mind. I wouldn't let you in even if you had a top hat and a tussy mussy. And I'm not having sex with you."

He looked at her in a way that every woman wants a man to look at her. He'd done that before. She closed her eyes so she wouldn't have to see it. "I'm not here for sex. I'm here to talk to you."

Down the block, the bells of the First Methodist Church of Beauford rang on—eleven o'clock. He wasn't supposed to be here. "Aren't you supposed to be at the cathedral lighting candles?"

"No. I'm supposed to be *here*. I'm done lighting candles. And I told my family just that."

Now *that* was a surprise. "And they let you go?"

"They couldn't have stopped me, but to be fair, they didn't try."

Maybe she shouldn't have, but she opened the door a little wider—probably because curiosity will make you do stupid things. "Then I guess you'd better come in and tell me about it."

Once upstairs, she sat on the sofa. When he went to sit beside her, she pointed to the Stickley Morris chair. "Over there. What happened to your face?"

"I'll get to that, but I'd like to tell you about what happened with my family first."

"Did one of them hit you?"

He shrugged. "They probably should have for not telling them that you were coming to lunch yesterday. You should probably hit me, too, for the same reason."

"Don't forget about depriving me of the Tour of Italy."

"Believe me, I never will, Gabriella—not for the longest day I live." He looked pretty miserable, but she refused to feel sorry for him.

"So tell me."

"You were right. I had to put an end to it. I told them that they should mourn Philie as they chose, but I am done with the never-ending funeral, that I have to move on. I said that whether I ever returned to St. Sebastian to live or not, we were family and that I loved them." He opened his eyes wider and leaned forward. "And I told them I love you. There was more, but that was the important part."

The toast and the tea and the marmalade rolled in her stomach. It was good. It was bad. It made her hope. It made her want to run.

"But you're emotionally unavailable. Seven good women and a puppy dog told you so."

He moved from the chair to the sofa and took her hand. She didn't stop him. "Turns out seven good women and a puppy dog didn't know as much as they thought they did." He closed his eyes for a moment. "Do you remember when I told you I was emotionally unavailable because I didn't love Philie?"

"Yes."

"Turns out I had that all tangled up, like I had a lot of things tangled up." He took a deep breath. "It was something Patrick said that made me remember that I did love her—as well as I could at that age. She was my first love. Things weren't good when we got married, still weren't good when she died. But I think we might have turned it around. I would have done my best."

"I never thought any different," Gabriella said. "Of course you would have. That's who you are."

"Maybe it would have been enough. Maybe not. But I had to come to terms with that before I could give myself permission to acknowledge that I have fallen in love with you. Plus, there were some things my little sister said. When Michelle asked if you were my girlfriend and you said no, it was like a knife in my gut. I thought that was exactly what I wanted—until she said she was hoping you'd marry me. I knew then that's what I hoped, too. So please, Gabriella, put me out of my misery. Do I have a chance?"

It was a lot to take in, and she couldn't just pick out the parts she liked and ignore the ones she didn't "I won't be the thing that divides you from your family."

"You wouldn't be. I swear. They actually listened and accepted what I said. I think we'll all be better for it. They saved you a seat at The Big Skate." He smiled a little half smile.

But his family wasn't the only problem. There was also hers. "Emile would go completely off the rails."

"Oh, that." Bryant closed his eyes. "He would. He did. And I'm glad you weren't at The Big Skate to see it." He gestured to his face. "I had it coming."

"Emile *hit* you?" For a moment, she felt lightheaded. "Tell me."

"When Emile and Amy got there, they came to say hello to my family. Michelle asked Emile where you were and told him you gave her that scarf."

"Pashmina." Why she bothered to correct him, she didn't know.

"Yeah, that."

"I shouldn't have given it to her. My motives weren't pure. I wanted her to like me—maybe more than you."

"No problem there. But that wasn't the half of it. My dad told Emile how great you are and how they all hoped things would work out for you and me."

"And Emile hit you? Except for Amy's ex, he has never hit anybody."

"Now I'm in the ranks with Cameron Snow. And so is Jarrett. Emile hit him for knowing about it."

"What? How?"

Bryant raised his hands. "Please, Gabriella. I'll tell you everything, though it might take a year. I've been up all night with your brother. Can't we just talk about the important parts now?"

"A year? You think we're going to have a year?" So many unanswered questions, but she felt happy at the thought of the year. An hour ago, she thought she'd never see him again except across a room or on the ice.

"If I have my way, we'll have the rest of our lives. Forever."

Her heart raced. *Forever* was the best word ever invented. She wanted to write it on a cake. "But what about Emile?"

"He's fine, happy even. Turns out, his reasons for not wanting you with a hockey player were never what he said. On some level, he didn't trust that you wouldn't end up with a hockey player like your father—someone who would hurt you."

Chills went over her. "I never knew," she whispered. She felt frozen. The ranges of emotions were wearing her out.

Bryant moved closer and put an arm around her. "Are you all right?"

"You see, that was my reason for never dating hockey players, too. I was afraid."

He placed a hand on her cheek. "But now?"

"I know you aren't like my father. I know you would never hurt me—or a child."

"Our child," he said and her stomach turned over. "And Emile knows that now, too."

The feelings in her heart flowed over and bubbled out of her mouth. "I love you, Bryant."

From time to time, she'd thought he looked like an angel, but never more than now with the glow of happiness lighting his face. "So we can go shopping for a ring?"

She laughed. "Yes. But I warn you: I won't marry you for a year. You and your family need some time to heal. And we might want to think about getting some furniture for your house." Her furniture was perfect, but there wasn't nearly enough.

"*Our* house. Do you really think it will take a year to buy some couches? We could go to Pottery Barn. That would be quick."

"No Pottery Barn. I also need some time to plan the wedding. Michelle and I aren't wearing off the rack."

He frowned. "I don't know what that means."

"You don't need to."

"Maybe I need to buy Michelle those diamond earrings. I owe her big."

And then he kissed her so thoroughly that she didn't even have the presence of mind to think where she would put her library table in what would be their house.

ACKNOWLEDGMENTS

Many thanks to Jess Verdi for helping us dig a little deeper.

And to those precious boys Justin, Joe, Ian, Brandon, and Kevin, who always have the answers for our hockey questions.

ABOUT THE AUTHOR

Alicia Hunter Pace is the pseudonym for the writing team, Jean Hovey and Stephanie Jones. They are *USA Today* best-selling authors who live in North Alabama and share a love of old houses, football, and writing stories with a happily ever after.

Find Alicia Hunter Pace at:
Their website *www.aliciahunterpace.com*
On Facebook at *www.facebook.com/pages/
Alicia-Hunter-Pace/176839952372867*
On Twitter @AliciaHPace

Subscribe to their newsletter at:
http://aliciahunterpace.us3.listmanage.com/subscribe?u=8dee88
167294a57b8b340f8e7&id=2054b7cbe8

MORE PRAISE FOR ALICIA HUNTER PACE

Check out *USA Today* bestselling author Alicia Hunter Pace's entire collection:

NASHVILLE SOUND series:

Face Off: Emile

CROSSROADS series:

Misbehaving in Merritt

Misunderstood in Merritt

Mistletoed in Merritt

"I absolutely love Alicia Hunter Pace's books. They have such a quirky sweetness, and the characters always ring true and make me cry!" —Linda Howard

BEAUFORD BEND series:

Forgiving Jackson

Nickolai's Noel

Reforming Gabe

Redeeming Rafe

Heath's Hope

"…much more than boy meets girl. Crisp dialogue …[and] supportive secondary characters add to the solid story line." —Library Journal

"…[an] engaging story of healing and discovery." —Heroes and Heartbreakers

"Whether you like sports-themed romance, small town settings, family and tradition, or compelling characters, there's something for just about everyone…" —The Romance Reviews

"Pace's writing is so real that you experience it. There was one argument in the novel when I could actually hear the characters yelling at one another." —4 stars, Pure Jonel

"A story that will both lighten your heart and pull on it at the same time, this one is well worth your time." —Eat, Sleep, Read Reviews

"For a short story to warm you on a cold night, take a trip to Beauford Bend. Plus, there's a cool bonus at the end of this book. Don't miss it!" —LAS Reviewer

LOVE GONE SOUTH series:

Sweet Gone South

Scrimmage Gone South

Simple Gone South

Secrets Gone South

"For a sweet and fun romance that will make you laugh and enjoy from beginning to end, *Scrimmage Gone South* by Alicia Hunter Pace is a great choice." —Harlequin Junkie

"…a heartwarming, sweet and entertaining read that will keep you laughing and sometimes even have you shed a tear or two." —Harlequin Junkie

"What a story! Pace has nailed writing emotions into her stories … She definitely had me jumping for joy and bawling like a baby more than once … This was a thoroughly enjoyable read that I couldn't put down." —Pure Jonel

Printed in the United States
By Bookmasters